BETWEEN FRIENDS

BETWEEN FRIENDS

KRISTY KIERNAN

BERKLEY BOOKS, NEW YORK

THE BERKLEY PUBLISHING GROUP
Published by the Penguin Group
Penguin Group (USA) Inc.
375 Hudson Street, New York, New York 10014, USA
Penguin Group (Canada), 90 Eglinton Avenue East, Suite 700, Toronto, Ontario M4P 2Y3, Canada
(a division of Pearson Penguin Canada Inc.)
Penguin Books Ltd., 80 Strand, London WC2R 0RL, England
Penguin Group Ireland, 25 St. Stephen's Green, Dublin 2, Ireland (a division of Penguin Books Ltd.)
Penguin Group (Australia), 250 Camberwell Road, Camberwell, Victoria 3124, Australia
(a division of Pearson Australia Group Pty. Ltd.)
Penguin Books India Pvt. Ltd., 11 Community Centre, Panchsheel Park, New Delhi—110 017, India
Penguin Group (NZ), 67 Apollo Drive, Rosedale, North Shore 0632, New Zealand
(a division of Pearson New Zealand Ltd.)
Penguin Books (South Africa) (Pty.) Ltd., 24 Sturdee Avenue, Rosebank, Johannesburg 2196,
South Africa

Penguin Books Ltd., Registered Offices: 80 Strand, London WC2R 0RL, England

This book is an original publication of The Berkley Publishing Group.

ISBN 978-1-61664-311-9

PRINTED IN THE UNITED STATES OF AMERICA

Dedicated to the memory of

My granddaddy, Robert E. Smith
1920–2008

My grandmother, Mildred Marguerat Claiborne
1921–2009

And the best dog ever, Niko
1997–2008

ACKNOWLEDGMENTS

As you can tell from the dedications, life during the writing of *Between Friends* was dark. But the following people made things easier and provided light, and I am in their debt:

My agent, Anne Hawkins.

My editor, Jackie Cantor.

My publicist, Kathryn Tumen.

And the entire Berkley team: publisher Leslie Gelbman, editorial director Susan Allison; managing editor Jessica McDonnell, editorial assistant Niti Bagchi, copyeditor Amy J. Schneider, and the art, text design, marketing, and publicity departments all contributed to making this book the best it could be.

For their support, professionally and personally, thank you to Tasha Alexander, Montese Miller Crandall, Amy MacKinnon, J. D. Rhoades, and Janna Underhill. Your friendship is an honor.

Thank you to the following for their selfless contributions: photo goddess Amy Nichols; Toastie blogger, kidney patient, and animal lover David Seidman; angels of the North Naples Dialysis Center: Jeanetta Tepper, Pam Hall, and Emmanuela Baptiste; and Associate Professor John C. Orr of the University of Portland.

My appreciation to both the Kiernan and Claiborne families, and additional thanks to Elizabeth and Russ for their many kindnesses over the years, as well as to Natalie Cox Watts, who cracks me up and produced the most adorable, brilliant child ever: Ian.

My favorite book club, The Divas of Naples, is a source of inspiration and grand examples of the kind of woman I want to grow up to be.

Finally, my heartfelt gratitude to my husband, Richard Kiernan, for his loving support, sense of humor, and unwavering belief in me and in our life together.

1

ALI

Hope is selfish and hungry, even when you believe you have given it exactly what it wants. And what it wants, always, is a miracle. Most people only get one, if they're lucky.

I was lucky; I got Letty.

Thirty-two matted and framed stories on us—newspaper clippings, magazine articles, even a *People* magazine cover—spanned the wall just inside our bedroom door, tracing the path Benny and I, and Cora, took to create our family.

The Miracle Wall started its life in the living room. When Letty was a little girl, we sat in front of it on her birthday, and I would tell her the story of her conception. By the time she was in second grade she could explain in vitro fertilization as well as I.

When we had visitors, she would pull them by the hand, pointing to the *People* cover, herself as a baby tucked in between Cora and me, our heads tilted together, grinning as if we'd both just won the lottery, with the bright pink caption, "Two Women, One Miracle," and under that, "How Modern Medicine Is Making Mothers."

Letty lost interest in the Miracle Wall almost three years ago, just before she turned twelve. In fact, she became so dramatically embarrassed by it that I moved it into our bedroom. I'd been staring at it steadily ever since, slowly feeding the ravenous hope, letting it grow.

And now I was ready for a second miracle.

The day I finally came to my decision was the same day Todd Jasper's house blew up. Benny was a detective with the financial crimes unit, but the Jasper house had been in his old neighborhood, and he didn't come home for almost forty-eight hours. And when he did, he carried such rage within him over the loss of a teenager he didn't even know, that I couldn't possibly bring up what I had been thinking about.

But now, two months later, two months of Benny's unpredictable anger alternating with silence, I could wait no longer. I'd passed forty, and time was not on our side. I even thought it might snap him out of his funk, would help him find his way back to the sweet, if occasionally moody, man I married.

I'd chosen my day, gazed at the wall for strength, prepared my speech, and then Benny walked in . . . in uniform.

For a minute all I could do was stare at him.

"Benny?"

"Yeah."

He looked down the length of his body as if he were as surprised as I to see it encased in uniform rather than a suit.

"What have you done?"

"I didn't—I didn't think it would come through this fast. I—"

"You what?" I interrupted, all the anger he'd vibrated with for the past two months suddenly flashing through me, as though it had just been looking for a solid place to land. "You didn't think? You didn't *think*?"

And he shut down. I could see it happen. He pressed his lips together and strode across the bedroom and into the closet, slamming his hand against the doorjamb as he passed it. I jumped as the impact made the wall shudder.

"Are you planning on talking to me?" My voice carried, higher and more desperate than I expected.

He ignored me and unlocked his gun safe, stored his equipment, and changed his clothes, hanging the uniform carefully.

"Benny?"

"I don't want to talk about it."

"Well, you're going to have to," I insisted. "What happened?"

Benny was a good cop, a great cop. The idea that he'd been demoted wouldn't settle in me. Demotions didn't come from out of the blue. There were lengthy procedures, accusations of impropriety or ineptitude.

He walked past me, and I reached out, but he stepped just out of range and my arm was left hanging in midair, connecting with nothing but the empty space between us.

"Benny, what happened?" I demanded of his retreating back.

He stopped for a moment but didn't turn around. "It was my choice, all right? I *asked* to go back. I just didn't think it would happen so fast. I've gotta go feed the birds."

And just like that, with hardly a word, Benny was back to being a patrol cop.

Who *did* the man talk to? That was what I really wanted to know. In the beginning there were a lot of cop friends, a lot of cop families. Death, divorce, firings, promotions, demotions—they all took their toll.

Benny had slowly reduced his circle of confidantes over the years until, as far as I knew, there were none left. Apparently, not even me. The frustrating part was that he'd never wanted to be a detective to begin with. He'd wanted to be a street cop from eighth grade on. And I was fine with that. I married him being fine with that. I'd never been a cop groupie until Benny became a cop.

I was a Benny groupie.

He got promotions, and he got awards, and when he decided he'd like to become a detective, we *talked* about it. And I supported him, though I admit I missed the uniform.

And now it was back.

But where the hell was Benny?

Because I didn't recognize the man who had just been in our bedroom, refusing to speak to me. And his timing couldn't have been worse.

For years I'd been working this out, watching our daughter grow into an independent, occasionally sullen young woman, and becoming increasingly aware of time moving forward. And always thinking of them.

The embryos.

My totsicles, waiting for me.

I was ready. I was ready to talk about it, and he'd blown my timing out of the water.

Though I supposed if he could spring something on me out of the blue, I shouldn't have felt such a need to broach things delicately. One good surprise deserved another. And it was too late to stop it. I was full up with it, too rehearsed to halt it.

As he made his way through the living room, heading to the backyard to tend to his birds, I took a deep breath and let it rest in my lungs a moment, allowing my voice one last chance to change its mind. It didn't.

"I want another baby."

The gritty rumble of the sliding glass door stopped for a moment, and then resumed, slowly, firmly easing closed.

I saw a flash of red swoop down from one of the magnolia trees. The cardinals knew Benny was home. He would be out there for at least an hour, filling the feeders, spraying out the baths, studiously ignoring the birds so they'd trust him.

It didn't matter; I'd said it. I grimly poured a glass of wine. I'd need to quit drinking, of course, and needed to start eating better, too. Oh, oh now that I'd said it, the lists I'd been making subconsciously came and flung themselves at me, one task loading itself on top of the last like pages chattering out of my printer.

There was a lot to do. And it was all up to me. I couldn't just grab an ovulation kit at the store and jump my husband the way other women could. I'd spent a long time being jealous about that. Seething with it. Those women who spurt viable eggs each month, with no thought, no contribution necessary from them. Children, little girls, twelve and thirteen years old, floating fat, life-filled eggs out of their fallopian tubes, slutty little eggs wafting around, existing only to be slipped into.

"I want another baby," I whispered in singsong to myself, slipping a finger around the rim of my wineglass. It didn't sing. It was glass, not crystal, but the tiny vibration of it traveled into me, a

quickening, imitating the thrill of new life that I remembered from
being pregnant with Letty.

And then, in addition to the lists of healthy new habits, here
came the practicalities of it, the solid facts of in vitro that I'd not
allowed myself to think about until I got past the purity of *I want
another baby.*

I needed to talk to Cora. And Dr. Collins at the fertility clinic.
I didn't even know if the embryos were still good after ten years,
but my recent reading seemed to indicate that there was definitely
hope.

I knew the doctor would suggest that we harvest new eggs.
There was no way Cora would be willing to go through it all again;
the shots, the hormones and the crazy mood swings, the harvesting itself. She did it for us twice, but we were both on the slick side
of forty now, in wholly different stages of our lives.

The giving end of IVF was a young woman's game, the younger
the better. But I wanted a biological sibling for Letty. The same
genetic pool. Cora and Benny weren't the best of friends, but there
was no question that they'd made a beautiful, healthy daughter.

And the embryos were all sitting there, waiting patiently for
me to rescue them from their chilly tubes. I'd paid the fees, three
years in advance, a regular reminder—like Letty's birthday—that
I could sustain life, bring it into the world and shape it. When paperwork came in about the embryos and my choices, I'd never even
given it a second thought. I'd chosen "Continue to Preserve" and
written the check, and for the first couple of times Benny had been
right beside me, excited about doing it again.

Cora and I hadn't talked about it for years, but it was only con-
siderate to talk to her first. Of course I had no idea where she was.

I didn't follow the winds; I had no idea if she was in California for the Santa Anas, in Russia for the boras, or in South Africa for whatever those were called. I could wait. A month rarely went by that we didn't talk on the phone, though it seemed as though even that was slipping lately.

It was possible that I'd see her that summer. Meteorologists had predicted a busy hurricane season, and if we were threatened, she'd show, hauling along other researchers. They'd turn Cora's mother's house into a dorm, with people sleeping on sofas and up all hours of the night, rushing to the storm-beaten beach with their equipment like kids running toward the circus.

I glanced at the clock. Letty was late, due home twenty minutes ago. No more cheerleading this year, but she'd started babysitting for a toddler two blocks away. I'd give her ten more minutes, and then call her cell.

Benny had finished his ministrations for the birds and was now sitting staring out at the yard, patiently watching for the arrival of his favorite brown thrasher family looking for their overripe pears. I would usually take my glass of wine and join him, let him point out the ones I never noticed when they arrived, the female cardinals and painted buntings, both drab in comparison to their mates. But not yet, it wasn't time yet. I could tell from the set of his shoulders, high and tense. No words were going to get past.

All I could do was wait and fantasize about my baby.

LETTY

"My mom is probably already home," she said to Seth. "Just let me off here."

She pointed to a house that had been empty for almost two years. It was only a block away from her house, but it was like a whole different neighborhood. Her mom said it was foreclosed and would go to auction soon, but nobody had bothered to clean it up or anything. Her dad always said he was going to take the lawn mower down and do it himself because he was sick of looking at it, but he never did.

Seth didn't argue. He knew her dad was a cop. Everyone in town knew everything about her. Her mother, with her big mouth and dead eggs and stupid Miracle Wall, made sure of that.

He pulled into the driveway and under the carport, the shade sliding over them, and peered at the house.

"Nobody lives here?" he asked.

She shook her head, nervous about the time. Her mom was going to call her cell—and there it was. She jumped to answer, suddenly embarrassed about the ringtone. God, the Jonas Brothers? Ugh. She should have found some rap, something harder, older.

"Hey, Mom."

"Hi, sweetie. Are you on your way?"

"Yeah, Mrs. Hailey was a few minutes late. I'm walking home now."

"Okay, see you soon."

"Okay, bye." She slid the phone closed.

"She trippin'?"

Letty shrugged. "No, I'm just later than I said I'd be."

Okay, she knew. But she loved it when he talked like that. She knew it was stupid, to love how someone talked, especially because she knew her parents would hate it. And she knew that was supposedly why she loved it, but it wasn't.

She didn't want them to disapprove of him; she already knew they would.

He wasn't trying to sound tough, he just was. He was so tough, and he was so hot, and she swore to God if he wanted to do it, she thought she would. There were times, late at night, that if he showed up in her room she wouldn't even wait for him to make a move.

She'd always thought she'd wait until she was at least fifteen, but she hadn't counted on Seth, that was for sure. He hadn't really done anything, gone too far or pushed her. She thought that, if anything, maybe she was pushing too far. Besides, she'd be fifteen in just a couple of weeks.

He pulled her toward him and she let him, sliding her rear over the center console. It wasn't at all comfortable—the emergency brake bit hard into her hip—but she never noticed after a few minutes. She had a bruise from it last week, like a brand, and she pressed it at night, liking the dull pain of it.

"Here," he murmured, reaching around her waist, pulling her up so her head almost brushed the roof. She had no idea what he was doing. But then he pulled her hip across him, and she got it, and pivoted, swinging her leg up over his lap and settling down on top of him, so they were face to face, her rear against the steering wheel.

It wasn't like anything could really happen. She wasn't wearing a skirt, she was wearing jeans, and so was he, but when he pulled her up close to him, oh.

Oh . . . wow.

CORA

The wind was from the west, less than six miles an hour, in Puerto Aysen, Chile. It was a good night to fly, and I was ready to go. Drew and Dr. Cho waited for me in Seattle, but the final destination on my ticket was Ft. Myers, Florida. By the time I arrived in Naples, Drew would just be arriving at work, hours before he would have to leave to pick me up from the airport. My itinerary change wouldn't be of any practical inconvenience for him.

The emotional inconvenience would be more difficult to overcome, and though I dreaded the inevitable confrontation, it didn't make me consider changing my mind. The wind shifted direction slightly, and I breathed deeply, careful to not move as it lifted the edge of my skirt, toyed with the ends of my hair. I considered turning slowly, allowing the wind to slip across my shoulders, tease my ankles, but I knew there were students watching from behind the tall windows of the center.

I knew that they made fun of me—my long hippie hair, the music of multiple bracelets, the gauzy skirts that lifted and floated around me with each breeze.

They called me Dr. Stevie Nicks.

I shouldn't have known about the nickname, but I did. And maybe I shouldn't have been amused by it or liked it, but I was, and I did.

They didn't understand that these bits, these extensions of me, my air-buoyed clothing, the hair I rarely trimmed so the ends would get wispy and thin, were scientific instruments. I felt the changes in the air through each hair lifted—how much, how long, how high—through each sleeve tugged, each hemline that tickled my calves.

I had stopped being self-conscious about my perceived eccentricities years ago. I vacillated between believing them myself, inhabiting them joyfully and consciously, considering ways to expand them, and being irritated by others' concentration on them when they'd developed, sometimes to my horror, without prior thought.

Breaking into Carole King's "I Feel the Earth Move" during a lecture at Cal State had been spontaneous, while ripping my shirt down the front in the wind tunnel in New Mexico had been planned days ahead of time as a joke.

The first went over incredibly well, and I often got requests to reprise the performance. The second . . . well, that wasn't considered eccentric or amusing so much as extraordinarily unprofessional, and I'd spent months rebuilding my credibility.

Singing and funny clothing? Apparently acceptable. Brief nudity in a wind tunnel? Not the way to advance a career. I've learned lessons. There were always more to come.

So I was a joke, to some. To others I was nearly mystical. Those were the ones I avoided. Because while I could live up to and eventually overcome a joke, I couldn't ever live up to that mythical being the others want me to be: goddess of air, of wind, a pure element, a sacrament. They were looking for something to believe in and thought I was available for duty.

The breeze picked up, and then I did turn, slowly, a solo waltz on the balcony, and as I did I saw Suyai, a student, one of those who lay in wait for me, like a child spying on fairies.

I didn't acknowledge her presence, and she pressed against the glass, her eyes intent, the scarf she had wound about her neck flashing with silver thread. I had little strength for a proper twirl, and ended with my hands clasping the railing again, the breeze a memory slipping past me.

Suyai owed me nothing. And I'd asked nothing of her but a ride to the airport. There were others who owed me. But what currency were my notes written in? Some owed me money, some owed me appreciation, some owed me, at the very least, time, maybe a Christmas card. But nobody owed me what I most needed.

Except, perhaps, Ali. Because Ali owed me everything. Or she always said she did. And she was the one person I couldn't ask. So why Naples? Hurricane season didn't start for months. And maybe, for me, hurricane season was a thing of the past.

I needed to see Ali, certainly, always, but the person my thoughts kept coming back to was Letty. Was I not there when she was conceived, there when she was born?

I was. I was there; I saw her wailing and infuriated, hauled from her mother who lay pale and exhausted on the table but clutching my hand with the inherent strength of motherhood already.

And no matter where the wind took me, I went back to south-west Florida. I didn't just keep the house for a base during hurricane season, a place to house the other researchers, my students. I'd kept it for Letty; for my friend, Ali; for the only connections that were family to me.

So I'd seen Letty plenty, not every year, but sometimes more than once in a year. And, as if that angry birth had been brought about by my presence, I most often saw her mad. I saw her wailing and infuriated on her second birthday, flinging cake at the dog. Wailing and infuriated at six when her mother wouldn't allow her out on the catamaran with me. Indeed, most of what I knew of Letty was her fury.

Ali was never furious.

I'd like to think she got all that anger from Benny, but that would just be convenient. Benny wasn't an angry man, just a solid, slightly boring one. He wasn't boring to Ali, though; I knew that. No matter how the idea of marriage and settling down bored me, the two of them were as strong an example of a conventional life as I'd ever seen. They were, always had been, kind to each other. They could have been poster children for an enduring marriage.

So that left me as progenitor of that rage. How much more did Letty get from me? What had she inherited besides a weakness for anger? That was what really drove me to Naples.

In my three-in-the-morning-can't-sleep moments, my most selfish, greedy-of-life moments, I thought of what Ali owed me. She got what she needed.

A child.

But when those selfish moments are over, I know I won't ask anything of her.

I can't.

Because what I've given her is quite likely broken.

And the winds that took me away, that drew me to the ends of the earth, were the same winds I was relying on to take me home to meet my daughter. It was wind again that would force me where I need to be. Wind: resistance to bear and hold me aloft, and tail to shove me home.

*　*　*

The flight had been smooth so far, though the pilot warned we might run into turbulence ahead and kept the seat belt light on. Chances were good that I was the only passenger on the flight hoping for turbulence. I wanted to analyze it, to decipher what was going on in the atmosphere, what we were plowing into, what was plowing into us. But I also wanted to fantasize about what I would do were I in the cockpit, how my knowledge would alter my decisions, and what might happen if I were wrong.

I never got my commercial jet license. I had no interest in being a pilot as a career anymore. I was doing exactly what I wanted with my life.

I'd simply wanted the feel of air beneath my hands, wanted to know if it was controllable. I'd stuck my arm out the windows of cars, I'd learned how to sail, I'd studied birds, but it wasn't until I flew that I understood.

Once you learn the rhythm of current, you recognize it when you see it . . . and then you see it everywhere. You feel it in the beat of your heart, the pulse of blood in your wrists, the throbbing ache of an injury.

The tides, the air, our breath, our blood. We were all connected by these things. The dust storms off Africa become the hurricanes of the southern states, which become the nor'easters of the northern climes, which go on to become the other winds of the world. Not that Africa is the generator, Patient Zero, of the world's wind. All the winds are recycled from other places, and there is no one birthplace, though I was going to miss searching for it, nonetheless.

After this trip home, it was quite likely that my travel window would be firmly shut, locked tight, and storm shuttered. No wind getting in.

"What can I get you to drink?" the steward asked, opening a tiny bottle of scotch and glugging it into a plastic glass for the man next to me. I stared at the burnished gold, smelled the sharpness of the alcohol as it passed inches from my face.

"Water, please," I said.

Contrary to popular belief, people with kidney disease can drink without immediately keeling over. I knew several who did. But I'm not stupid. Even if Dr. Cho hadn't had the big talk with me before leaving Seattle, I knew I was on the dialysis countdown. After the first six months of my diagnosis, when I went through some standard denial, I realized things were progressing much faster for me than for the other people in my support group.

I wasn't the only one who noticed.

We all went through a careful inventory by the members already present when we arrived at the meeting. After it was clear that I was deteriorating more rapidly than everyone else, I tried to be the first one there so at least I could be seated. But I couldn't hide my bloated, tired face from their shrewd gaze, their narrowed eyes. And I saw the relief there, the relief that at least they looked better than me.

So I changed everything overnight. I can do that; I've always been able to. Stop drinking? Bam, no problem. Low-protein diet? Zing, done. You make the decision and you do it, it's that simple.

And I stopped going to the meetings.

The steward set the water on my tray and held out a bag of pretzels. I shook my head. Too much sodium. He moved on to the people behind me and we hit a pocket, dropping the plane momentarily. It wasn't much as far as turbulence went, but the man next to me inhaled quickly through his teeth. It wasn't quite a gasp, but it was sharper than it should have been, and he brushed my arm with his elbow as he tossed his scotch down.

The man next to me was afraid to die.

I was, too.

2

A L I

Benny didn't come to bed until after midnight. I wasn't quite asleep, but I wasn't quite awake either, and when he settled in, all I thought was that things were as they should be, even though we'd not spoken about his job or the baby. At least some of the tension in the house had been defused. We both knew what was on the table, even if we didn't know why.

I had to open the store early for Simon, a music teacher who was bringing in a student and her mother, and in the morning I kissed Benny good-bye tenderly, happy with the feel of his whiskers against my lips. We'd talk that night, about everything.

I had time to take the scenic drive to the store, turning off 41 and down to Crayton, slipping past the massive ficus that had managed to survive hurricanes. I loved these trees, their aerial roots patiently floating like jellyfish tentacles, waiting to meet the ground and secure themselves. They filled me with a great sense of calm, digging themselves in so adamantly.

After Hurricane Charley came through in 2004, I cried more for the downed trees on Crayton than I did for our own damaged roof and mangled pool cage. Letty and I spent that one in the master bedroom closet, while Benny roamed the house, cursing the wind and the dark and the screaming of screws and bolts ripping out of concrete and stucco.

Enough time had passed that I was hard-pressed to remember which yards had had the trees and which hadn't, and there were enough left that it was still the most relaxing drive in Naples. I passed by Cora's house and slowed, as I always did.

She had a company that stopped in once a month to check the shutters, take care of the pool, and ensure everything was okay, but Benny drove by regularly to check too—though I think sometimes he just enjoyed the fact that she wasn't in town—and I always cast a critical eye over the property, looking for anything that might need attention.

The inspections were voluntary and even a bit surreptitious. They were my own private way of keeping my childhood close. Our little town had changed so much, but there were still pockets that maintained the dignity of restraint, dwindling every day, true, but still there if you knew where to look.

Cora's place was a holdout, a squat old Florida house with concrete tiles on the roof from the 1960s. New, Mediterranean-style homes rose up on either side of it like monoliths. I knew Cora had been offered plenty of money to sell years ago when the real estate boom was in full swing, but she told me that she'd never considered it.

Everything looked buttoned up tight, the edge of the lawn straight, no palm fronds battering the roof. All was as it should be.

There were two cars in the lot when I arrived at the music shop, and though I wasn't late, I was apologizing to Simon before I'd shut my door.

"Don't worry about it, Ali," he said, grinning at me as his student slowly got out of the other car.

I flushed. I should never have noticed how handsome Simon was, but it couldn't be helped. And it certainly hadn't escaped my notice that he flirted with me, despite not having flirted myself since I was about twenty.

The student's mother remained in the driver's seat with the door closed. I could see the outline of her with a cell phone to her ear behind the dark tint.

"Ali, this is Laura, my star pupil," Simon said, pulling the girl out from behind him. She looked up at me only briefly from behind a veil of dark hair, her eyes meeting mine for a fraction of a second.

"Hi, Laura. I have some beautiful cellos for you to look at. Shall we go in?" I asked, casting a glance at her mother again. She continued talking on her phone, though, to be fair, all of us were still technically early.

"Sure, we can look around," Simon said, not bothering to see where the mother was. Laura said nothing.

I left them in the front while I turned the lights on, and by the time I returned Simon was already looking at the cellos I'd pulled out for them the night before. I didn't keep many in stock—they're about as convenient to store as a tuba—but I had one in particular I thought would be perfect for her skill level.

This was my favorite part of the business. My parents opened the store when I was just an infant, and I learned to walk by grasping the low metal shelving that held musical scores. I dabbled in guitar when I was in middle school, and I still tooled around on it when things were slow, but other than that I didn't know how to play an instrument.

I didn't need to make my own music; my skill was in helping others make theirs. I'd gotten to the point that I could tell what instrument a customer played, or wanted to play, instantly.

Laura had surprised me, though. I'd have pegged her for flute, maybe French horn.

But when she sat and Simon placed the Eastman before her, everything seemed to elongate, and she stretched tall, and became a cellist right in front of my eyes. She began tuning, and even I, without a gift for perfect pitch, could hear that she had it. Once her preparations were done, she was still, her eyes closed. Simon winked at me and silently mouthed, "Wait."

As soon as she opened her eyes, she tucked her head and the prelude of Bach's Cello Suite No. 1 filled the store. It wasn't perfect, but it was perfectly haunting, and I closed my eyes and filled my lungs with air that suddenly seemed clear and dry and cool. She stopped abruptly, and I opened my eyes to see Simon adjusting her bow.

"Hang on," I said, taking advantage of the break. I grabbed the Doetsch 701 I'd had for two years. I rarely brought it out. I was the main supplier of instruments for our local youth orchestras and schools, but despite the fact that Naples was a wealthy town, most students never achieved the level that would prompt their parents to spring for an instrument like the Doetsch.

Laura went through her preparations with it, glancing at me appreciatively when she heard its silken tone, and then started the prelude again. Simon and I looked at each other triumphantly. This was the instrument for the girl, no question.

As she played he spoke to me in low tones, merely confirming the price but making me feel as if we were in a shadowy bar whispering over a candlelit table. I'd never seen him speak to another woman, but I assumed this was simply part of his personality, that he was barely aware of it.

Simon and I were so lost in enjoying the music that we didn't hear the car door slam, but Laura must have been paying attention, because just before the bells on the door chimed she stopped playing, and her mother entered the shop.

"So," she said, barely glancing my way. "We find something?"

"Your daughter plays beautifully," I said.

"Thank you," she replied, but there was no warmth or pride in her voice. "Where are we at?"

"Within your budget," Simon replied.

"Okay, let's wrap this up then," she said, nodding at Laura. She dug in her purse and pulled out a credit card just as her cell phone rang again. She handed the card to me and made a circling gesture, indicating the whole store. I looked questioningly at Simon as she turned away and walked back out the door.

"Strings, case, everything," he said, while Laura began tuning the Doetsch again. I followed him around the store as he picked up all the accessories and rang up the order. Simon took the receipt outside for the woman to sign. She rolled the window down and signed it on her steering wheel, as if he'd just pumped her gas, and never took the phone from her ear.

The purchase was probably less than the mother spent on shoes in a week, but it covered my expenses for the month. It was the most thrilling part of having your own business, hitting what my father liked to call the "gravy mark." Once you hit it, everything after that was gravy.

As they left, Laura turned back at the door and said, "Thank you," in a clear, distinct voice, filled with the genuine warmth her mother lacked. I told her to come back anytime, and she smiled as the door shut behind her. I stared after her, comparing her to Letty. I should have asked where she went to school, though I'd be willing to bet that Laura went to a private school.

I'd tried to interest Letty in music, even forced her to take piano lessons for a few years, but nothing ever took. She learned to walk at the mall, pushing her own stroller. I placed my hand low on my belly imagining another baby growing inside me, smiling at the thought of being pregnant again.

Letty checked in with me when she got home from school, and I promised to bring her home Thai food for dinner, feeling generous about my bright, pretty daughter, thinking that she'd make a wonderful older sister.

I left early, skipping my drive down Crayton, anxious to get the food and get home. Tonight I wouldn't be put off by Benny. Hitting the gravy mark felt auspicious, and I was looking forward to sitting with Benny in the backyard and talking about our new lives.

LETTY

She hardly remembered how they got to her room. Well, that wasn't really true. She'd brought Seth there, feeling really excited, walking backward and pulling him with her, but when she was close enough to breathe him in, she barely remembered her own name. They had more than an hour and it seemed like forever, but also not enough time to really get in any trouble.

He pulled away before she got him through the door, making her face redden, as if she were acting desperate.

"My mom's not going to be home for a while," she protested.

"It's not your mom I'm worried about, baby."

"My dad?"

"You think? Damn, I don't feel like gettin' popped. I'm gonna find a place for us."

"What do you mean?" she asked, feeling uneasy for the first

time. She felt okay in his car and in her house, but she wasn't sure she should go to *a place for us*.

"I can't keep staying at Paul's, his mom's getting tired of me."

"How long have you been there?"

He shrugged. "Week or so."

She thought back over the past month and the different friends he'd said he was staying with. "Do you go home at all anymore? Doesn't your father get mad that you're not there?"

He laughed and kissed her and didn't answer.

"We could check out that house," he said.

"What house?"

"That empty one you showed me. Come on, you didn't take me there by accident."

She blushed again, and he turned around and left her in the hallway.

"Wait, Seth . . ."

He was looking out the front window, cracking the plantation shutters, then snapping them back up.

"So when's he supposed to be home?" Seth asked.

She shrugged. "I don't know, after my mom."

"Where's he keep his guns and stuff?" he asked, setting off toward the master bedroom.

She hurried after him. Her dad had a safe he kept his guns in. She'd never known the combination, so she wasn't worried about Seth getting it open, but still, she didn't want him bothering anything. She knew her parents would know. Her dad had been a cop since before she was born. He knew everything.

Almost everything.

He didn't know about Seth, but only because he hadn't thought to ask.

Seth was already in the closet, looking at the safe.

"It's locked, it always is," she told him, listening for the sound of her mom's car even though she wasn't due home. He didn't turn around, just ran his hands around the outside of the safe, like he was looking for a hidden catch or something.

"Come on," she said, tugging at him. He turned in her arms, and finally, *finally*, bent to kiss her. She started moving out of the closet, tugging him with her. Just when he took over, pushing her toward the door rather than her pulling him toward it, he stopped, and she opened her eyes to see what had caught his attention.

"What's this?" he asked, nodding his head toward the wall filled with all the stupid articles, all framed like they were works of art.

She sighed. It always had to be talked about. She gave the canned story she'd been giving practically since she could talk. She could say *sperm* and *egg* and *uterus* more easily than most adults.

"No shit?" he asked.

She didn't reply.

He moved down the line, scanning them and then coming back to the *People* cover. He stared at it for a minute and then looked at her critically, squinting.

"Yeah, you look like her, I see it."

"I do not," she protested. She didn't look like Cora. Did she? She hadn't looked at the picture in a really long time, but she wasn't going to stand there and inspect it. She didn't want to talk about it anymore, and she backed up toward the bed.

"Are you going to look at me up there, or right here?" she asked, putting her hands on her hips.

And then he wasn't looking at the clippings anymore. He walked over, really slow, like he had all the time in the world. It was hard to breathe sometimes when she looked at him. He got right up in front of her and pushed her onto the edge of the bed, making her sit, so she was looking at the middle of his T-shirt, his belt buckle just a few inches below her chin, and her heart sped up.

Just as he started to smile the house shook slightly, and then the rumble of the garage door opening changed her freak-out to total panic. Seth looked wildly around.

"Oh shit," he said. "Is that your dad?"

She pointed to the master bath. "There's a door to the pool—"

She didn't even finish and he was on his way. She cringed, waiting for the screen door to slam, but Seth wasn't stupid, and she saw a shadow slip past the window before she even got out of the bedroom. She was in the kitchen when her mom came through the garage door and into the laundry room with Thai takeout in her hands and a big smile on her face.

"Hi, punkin," she said.

Her knees felt weak. She wasn't going to *punkin* her if she suspected anything.

"Thought I'd knock off a little early, spend some time with you."

She would have loved that a year, six months ago. Spending time with her meant they went shopping, they got manicures and pedicures. But really, she didn't want to spend time with her mom anymore. She wanted to spend time with Seth.

She took the Thai and put it in the refrigerator for later, answering questions about her day, amazed her voice wasn't shaking. That was a good sign.

Maybe she wasn't as scared as she thought.

CORA

I never thought I missed southwest Florida until I got there. Within twenty minutes of leaving, I'd forgotten it, looking forward to my destination. But there was always a moment on my return in which I felt such relief that I felt a watery weakness in my knees.

The timing of the moment itself varied. If I had a window seat, it was when we were low enough that I caught sight of the coast-line. It made no difference if it was the west coast, skidding along the length of Florida like a slide, or the east coast, cutting across the tip like a knife through a finger. I'd see the canals, the un-mistakable, impenetrable thickets of palmettos and live oaks, and would be grateful that I was sitting down.

If I had an aisle seat, it wasn't until they opened the cabin door and the humidity rushed in, filling my lungs with the salty softness of Florida air, and I would have to hold on to the seat in front of me to stand.

I loved Seattle, and I loved Africa, and India, and Holland, but it was the air of southwest Florida that my body embraced, its cells open fully only for it, as if holding their walls rigid until the right latitude and longitude were crossed and then becoming the loose, semipermeable things they were meant to be.

It caught me by surprise every time, and this time was no different. I was exhausted by the trip. It was always an exhausting trip—the leg from Santiago to Miami alone was nine hours—but this time I was especially tired. The steward asked me if I was feeling all right halfway through the flight, after my seventh trip to the bathroom.

I wasn't sure what he'd have done if I'd said I wasn't. That, in fact, I thought my kidneys might be failing *right then*, and did he happen to have one to spare?

But then we touched down in Ft. Myers, and despite my exhaustion, that air hit me and I *breathed*, as if for the first time in years.

I'd left the taxi window down all the way down to Naples. The driver didn't say anything, but I could tell he was irritated, that he was sweating in the heat and couldn't wait to drop me off. Which was fine, though I regretted it slightly when he left me in the driveway with all my bags, and I realized I was going to have to wrestle with the storm-shuttered door by myself.

I sat on the stoop and dumped half of my belongings out, looking for the little key. I finally found it in my makeup bag, and once I was in the house, dim as twilight though it was early afternoon, I folded myself into the tweedy sectional sofa and called Drew.

"Cora the Explora," he answered, my name obviously coming up on his Caller ID. "Where are you?" he asked, his voice full of smile and love and concern.

"I had a little change of plans," I said, trying to keep my own tone light, trying to keep my exhaustion out of it.

But he was instantly on guard. It wasn't going to go well.

"What change of plans?"

"I'm in Naples," I said.

"Florida?" he asked. Not as ridiculous a question as it might first seem. In my past, yes, I might have actually changed plans and flown to Italy.

"Yes," I said, forgetting about the deep breath of humid air, forgetting about the beach a few blocks away that I was aching to get to, forgetting about Ali and the things I had to tell her, the things I had to worry her with. And Letty, I forgot about Letty, just for a moment. I closed my eyes and heard him breathe on the opposite side of the United States and wondered if I'd made the right decision after all.

"And?" he asked.

That hurt, the brevity of that single word. What Drew and I had always had was words. We spoke more than the same language; we spoke all of the same languages. Upon first meeting each other, neither of us could shut up, and yet we never spoke over each other. We both had profound things to say; we sounded brilliant together. It was not until later, when we'd expressed interest in each other through mutual friends, that we'd discovered that neither of us were particularly talkative people by nature.

But now he was taking that away from me, and I deserved the punishment, but it hurt nonetheless. Drew was rarely cruel. Even when I'd moved out months ago, unable to take the panic that had infiltrated our relationship because of my disease, he had been kind. It hadn't been the first time we'd broken up, but we both knew it was the last time, and we were gentle with each other over it. Had we lost our conversation, the basis of our friendship, I would have been heartbroken.

But he had, instead, simply moved into the slot I had always reserved for Ali, empty then only because I had not been ready to tell her everything I had to tell her, still trying to understand it myself. Drew had been, for the past six months, my Ali replacement.

"I had to, Drew," I said softly. "I have to talk to Ali. I can't let something happen without talking to her, warning her."

"There's nothing to warn her about."

"You don't know that. I don't know that. Dr. Cho doesn't know that. I owe it to her. And I owe it to Letty, too. And I want . . ." I stopped, nervous about the fact that I was about to say it out loud.

"You want what, Cor? Everything's set up here. Everything is ready to go for you. Your classes are set, your access operation is set. Dr. Cho went to a lot of trouble—"

"I want to know her," I said, the admission catching in my throat. "This is my only chance."

"No," he said, raising his voice, determined to fix me. "No, it's not your only chance. Dammit, Cora—" He stopped and I could hear him quickly typing on his keyboard. "There's a flight tomorrow from Ft. Myers, connects in Atlanta, that would put you here midafternoon. I'm going to book it, and I want you on it," he said, his fingers tapping.

"No."

"This isn't negotiable, Cora. I will be there tomorrow at three. I want to see you get off that plane."

"I won't be there, Drew. Please don't make this harder for me than it already is," I pleaded. I've never pleaded with a man before in my life. With any other man I would have been disgusted. My first mother pleaded with men. It had disgusted me throughout my childhood, and she stopped pleading when I was eight, when she pleaded with the latest boyfriend who was beating her to stop.

Her pleas were the last thing I heard from her. After that I was in and out of foster care, until Barbara took me in at eleven and gave me a life. Barbara was a successful real-estate agent who made her own money, never married, but who wanted a child. I never saw her plead with a man—I never saw her plead with anyone—and I modeled myself on her.

But I didn't have the strength, not with Drew. And oddly, I did not feel disgusted with myself. My pleas felt like relief, a breeze cooling my face, and it succeeded in stilling his tapping fingers.

"Cora," he said, and now here was another surprise—his tone had turned pleading, too. "Please come home. You have to be exhausted. You're going to make yourself sick."

I had to laugh at that.

"I already am sick," I said. "I'm doing everything I'm supposed to, everything I can. And I have to do this, too. Drew, don't you understand? Not doing this will make me sick; not doing this is what would make me weaker than anything else."

I could hear him take a deep breath and knew I had won a temporary reprieve. "I don't agree with this decision," he said.

"Acknowledged."

"I don't suppose you'd care to give me a date that you'll be home?"

I caught myself just before I said *I am home.*

"Not yet," I said. "But soon."

"I'll call Dr. Cho right now and have her set you up with someone. You have to go in right away, okay?"

"The second she finds someone, I'll be there," I promised. "I want to be well, Drew. I won't sacrifice my health."

"I'm afraid you already have," he said.

There was nothing I could say to that.

"I miss you," he said, breaking the silence.

"I miss you, too. I'm sorry," I said.

"I'll be here."

"Thank you," I whispered.

I hit the off button on the phone and sat with it in my hand for several minutes, considering calling Ali. I was so tired. I would wait for a day. Give myself a chance to rest, to let my body recover, however slightly it might, from the punishing travel schedule I'd put it through over the last four months, getting to all of the winds I could.

It would be the first time I'd ever arrived home without making Ali my first call. I often didn't even wait until I'd made it out of the airport. I put the phone down and gave in to my exhaustion. I didn't bother getting up. I just kicked my shoes off, put my swollen legs up on the couch, and nestled my head on a pile of throw pillows. It wasn't long before I fell into a deep sleep.

I woke four hours later with a raging headache and a cop car in my driveway.

3

A L I

"Cora's back," Benny announced, his hands already on the buckle of his belt, already falling into the routine of a street cop he'd given up years ago. The careful storing of the equipment, his gun. I hadn't seen it in so long that for a moment I just admired him.

And then his words sank in.

"What? But I just drove by this morning," I protested. When Cora was coming into town, she called ahead to the company that took care of the house and they opened it up for her. I was never surprised to drive by and see the shutters up, because the next call she made was always to me.

"Talked to her," he said as I followed him into the bedroom. "She said she didn't have time to call, it was a last-minute thing."

"Last-minute? Since when has Cora been anywhere that was last-minute from Naples?"

"Al, I'm just telling you what she said to me."

I wrestled irritation that she'd not called me and joy at her being back for only another moment before joy won out, and I hurried to the kitchen and picked up the phone.

"Hang on," he called. "She said she'd call you tomorrow."

I hesitated, on the verge of irritated again. Benny and Cora's childish tug-of-war with me was so old that I rarely noticed it anymore, but with everything I needed to talk to her about, I wanted to see her as soon as I could.

But then I realized the directive had come from her, not Benny, and slowly put the phone down.

Benny appeared in the doorway. "She said she was tired, and man, Al, she looked it. Looked rode hard and put away wet, to tell the truth. She said she came from Chile." He shook his head and resumed unbuttoning his collar, turning back into the bedroom. "Don't know how she does it."

I stared at the phone. Sometimes she called from the airport so I could meet her at the house, help her get her bags in, collapse on the patio, and open a bottle of wine to hear about her travels, while the sun went down and the humid air slowly relaxed us both.

Chile was, where? I searched my geographically challenged mind for a moment, and finally grasped the info I was looking for. South America. Not like she was all the way around the world. She'd come in from Australia and seen me the same day.

Okay, okay, if she didn't want me to call right away, I wouldn't. I wasn't sure what that meant, but I wanted her in a good mood, rested, happy. So we could talk about the baby.

She'd never asked about the remaining embryos. I think she felt like Benny: There was a problem, we took some shots, along came Letty, problem solved. Tried again a few years later, didn't work out, okay, done. Despite their simmering animosity, Benny and Cora were actually very alike.

But for me, having a baby wasn't a problem to be solved; it was an organic need. And the embryos were just sitting there, waiting for something to be done with them.

It just took me a while to know that I still wanted another one.

Getting Letty had taken so long, been such a heartrending process, the miscarriages, the failures. All of them precious. All of them grieved more than anyone else could possibly understand.

At first I just wanted to revel in Letty, and Benny did, too. Then two years went by, and Benny started asking about doing the next round. But I wasn't ready. Not yet. Not while Letty was still such work. I thought, maybe, when she was three, maybe then I would feel as though I had this mothering thing nailed down more firmly and could handle the next one.

And, to be honest, I was scared to death of doing it all again. I was afraid of the mood swings when I had a young child to take care of, afraid of the crushing grief when a transfer, inevitably, didn't take, or when one did, one that I would inevitably miscarry. I thought about a success, I did, but the odds seemed so stacked against me.

So we waited four years, and then I, reluctantly, agreed to try again. Cora agreed to more harvesting of her eggs . . . and then I did only one fresh cycle, transferring three, and we froze the rest of the embryos. None of the transferred embryos implanted. I simply couldn't take it again, and I promised Benny that we'd try again in a year.

Six months later my father had a heart attack and my parents decided to retire in Arizona, to play golf in the arid air of what was a foreign country to me. They would sell the store, or simply give it to me. If I'd had a couple more years, the decision would have been easy, but I didn't. And it was a good excuse to put it off for a while.

Eventually Benny stopped asking.

There were nine embryos left. Who knew how many of those were still viable? I could have gone and done it without speaking to either of them about it. In fact, that would have been the easiest thing, even if the preparations for it would have been difficult to hide. I wouldn't have to contend with objections from either of them, and if nothing came of it they'd never even have to know.

But what if something did come from it? Just the thought of holding an infant in my arms again made me shiver. Once it was done, there wasn't anything they could say. What was the alternative? Destroy them? Let it go, stop paying the bill, and try to forget about them?

If the ones I'd lost had been so precious, why weren't these?

It was up to me. Once upon a time, the embryos had been ours, collectively. I'd felt we all had a stake in them, all had a say. And that went for the imagined baby, too. And then the child, the young adult, the adult. I think I had an idea that we would raise him, or her as it turned out, communally, always discussing issues, problems, joys, achievements, milestones.

But once we'd done it, once we'd gone through the procedures and I was pregnant, the embryo firmly implanted in my womb (I'd stopped thinking about it as a uterus the second I got the positive pregnancy test), I had become, privately at least, incredibly protective of the fact that this was my baby. Thoughts I'd never considered having before crowded my mind. What if, when the baby was born, Cora wanted to play a larger role? When the baby was two? Four? Nine? Twelve?

Truth was, Cora's lifestyle suited me just fine. She blew in on the wind, and then blew out again. Our agreement, that it was my baby, always, stood as long as she wasn't around very often.

I loved having her back in town.

But there was no question that when she left I felt a momentous relief. I never kept Letty away from her in any conscious way, but I had noticed that in the last few years I'd made more excuses about why I didn't bring Letty on our excursions around town. She had school commitments, after-school commitments, babysitting.

So now, Cora had arrived back in town without letting me know she was coming—a first. And when she was discovered, she'd begged off for another day. I couldn't help it; I was worried. And I wasn't even sure about what.

I handed Benny a beer when he got out of the shower and then sat on the counter, my rear sliding into the sink, while he dried off. He took a drink and eyed me carefully before placing the beer down and toweling his hair dry.

"What's on your mind?" he asked.

"How did you know she was home?" I asked.

"I drove by, saw the storm shutter on the front door was open, and stopped to check."

I frowned. "None of the other shutters were up?"

"Nope. I asked if she wanted me to open them for her, but she said she wanted to get some rest. So I left."

"How long were you there?"

"I don't know, maybe twenty minutes?"

"Well, what else did she say?"

"God, Ali, I don't know. I obviously surprised her. She asked me in, I sat down on the sofa, asked her if she wanted me to open the shutters, she said no, and said she'd call you tomorrow. That's it. What is the problem?"

I shrugged and followed him into the bedroom, watching as he pulled on shorts and a T-shirt. "I don't know. It's just odd that she's not calling me until tomorrow. She's never done that."

"No? Well, like I said, she looked like hell. I guess she's just really tired. Did I say she came in from Chile?" he asked, making his way out to the backyard. I followed.

"Yeah, you said."

I watched as he cleaned out the birdbaths and refilled the feeders. A cardinal was already in one of the magnolias, peeping at him. When Benny came back into the cage, he started skimming the surface of the pool while the birds flitted down to feed. Taking care of the pool was supposed to be one of Letty's chores, but Benny had gotten tired of keeping after her about it and had quietly taken it over again.

"So," I started, "did you want to tell me about your new job?"

He squinted at me across the pool, the sun still bright enough to flash off the ripples he caused with the skimmer.

"I know," he said, resignation heavy in his voice. I'd take resignation over the quick anger any day, and any irritation I might have been harboring fled. "Sorry."

"It's all right," I said. "Just . . . what happened? Why didn't you even talk to me about it?"

"It was something I've been thinking about for a long time. Maybe, I guess, since the kid, the Jasper kid. You remember?"

"Of course, I remember," I said. It didn't seem to need more. Chances were, had Benny still been a street cop when the call came in about Todd Jasper, he'd have been in the vicinity. Not for sure, no, but chances were good; it had been his favorite area to cruise, the area he'd grown up in, where he could do the most good.

Todd Jasper had been a bright kid, by all accounts a good kid, rarely in trouble. But he'd been living a double life, or at least hiding a frightening one. His parents had operated the largest meth lab in the county from their house.

Todd was fourteen when his kitchen exploded. He'd tried to save his mother from the chemical fire and was killed when a second explosion obliterated the back half of the house.

The Jasper house had been one block away from the house Benny had grown up in.

He sank the skimmer to the bottom of the pool and rested his forearms on it as he looked at me.

"I didn't want to be a cop to fill out paperwork," he said. "I wanted to help people. I could have helped that kid, Ali. He didn't have to die."

"Benny, it wasn't your fault."

He sighed and turned to look at the birds jostling each other for a spot on the feeders before he shook his head and turned back to the pool. He plunged the skimmer to the bottom violently, avoiding my eyes, his lips pressed together tightly, slamming the skimmer back down into the water with every few words.

"I *know* that it's not my *fault*. But if I hadn't lost *sight* of why I became a cop to *begin* with, I'd still be on the *street*. I'd be on *that* street, Ali. That was *my* street."

His vehemence took me aback. He'd been moody ever since it

happened, quick to anger, followed by long periods of silence. I had noticed that, of course. But for the first time in months I really looked at my husband. His shorts hung loosely on his frame, and his face was haggard with worry.

After twenty-seven years of knowing Benny, I'd seen him moody plenty, and he'd put up with my moods over the same amount of time. But over the past several months the silences had become longer, and he'd been spending much more time in the backyard, and on the patio, dealing with the birds, the chores. We had the fattest cardinals and blue jays I'd ever seen, and entire squirrel families now chattered in the trees when Benny came out with his bucket of cracked corn and seed.

I hadn't been paying enough attention; that much was clear. I'd been busy with my own obsession over the Miracle Wall. And though he hadn't exactly noticed that, either, I hadn't given him the wake-up call he'd just given me.

I was paying attention now, desperate to make up for lost time.

I nodded. "Okay, I understand. I really do. I just wish you'd been able to talk to me about it. So, what's your plan now?"

He seemed to relax a little, swirling the skimmer through the water gently.

"I was thinking that maybe I'd get involved with the Explorers program again. Talk to the kids at schools, make an effort with them right at the age that I could really make a difference."

"Benny, I think that sounds great. Kids love you, they've always responded to you. You should definitely do that," I encouraged. As frustrated as I'd been with him, now I was delighted to hear that he was interested in becoming more involved with kids.

He shook his head and went back to cleaning the pool, pulling the skimmer back up and finding minuscule contaminants only he could see. "I'm going to look into it soon. Not just yet. I want to get back to some kind of schedule with what I'm doing now, you know? Be a presence out there. Get to know people again. Even things out. But it's what I'm thinking about for the future."

I smiled at him. This was more the Benny I'd known, more the way our marriage had always been. The past two months were in no way representative of the bulk of our relationship. We were sweet to each other, and we'd talked about the future. I took a deep breath, relief working its way through me.

"But you know, Al, what you said last night?" he continued.

My hand halted midway to my wineglass. I hadn't expected him to bring it up. I'd assumed I would. I'd assumed that I would be very understanding about this whole job thing, would move forward, embrace this change and be supportive. And then I would bring up the baby thing and he would be very understanding, embracing, and supportive back.

"Yeah?"

"I am not up for that. Not now."

"Hmm," I said, swallowing a sip of wine, turning this over, figuring the best way to deal with it. I wasn't ready to breach the tentative truce we'd seemed to be working on.

"Ali," he said sharply, and with that the stranger was back in the house.

I looked up at him across the pool, this man I didn't recognize.

"I'm serious. I mean, that was a total shock. I had no idea you were even considering going through it all again. I don't want another kid now. I don't want another kid, period. Hell, Letty's already fifteen in a couple weeks. What possesses you to want a baby now? Ten years ago there wasn't anything I wanted more. I practically begged you, and you wouldn't do it."

"So that means the subject is just closed?" I asked. "You get to make decisions, big, life-changing decisions, without my input at all, but I'm not allowed to even talk about this?"

"I don't need to talk about it to know that I don't want to do it. How long have you been thinking about this, anyway?"

I stood up. I wouldn't get any further with him in this mood.

"A hell of a lot longer than you thought about Todd Jasper," I said. As I expected, he didn't answer, and as I slammed the sliding glass door closed I could see him staring after me, the skimmer pole held before him like a shield.

LETTY

The Thai was killer. The *pad see eu* was hot enough to make her sweat under her eyes, but it was hard to enjoy it. Something was obviously going on. Her parents weren't really talking to each other, and her mom wasn't talking to her at all. Her dad was, though. He was asking all kinds of questions.

At least he wasn't acting all angry like he had been lately. It didn't really feel like he was interrogating her, like he knew they'd been in their room, but he was definitely getting at something.

"So, big birthday coming up," he said.

"Um-hmm," she said, taking a big gulp of cold milk.

"Fifteen," he said. "Wow. Time to get your permit, I guess."

"Yeah," she said cautiously.

"You sure are growing up," he said, shaking his head as if he couldn't believe it, and looking pointedly at her mom, who totally ignored him.

You have no idea, she thought, stifling a laugh.

When the phone rang at eight like she and Seth planned, she jumped to get it.

"Oh, hey, Em," she said, then acted like she was listening to Emily, her best friend since kindergarten, while she leaned against the counter. Seth kept his voice low so her parents wouldn't hear anything in case the phone was turned up loud.

"I don't know," she said. "Hang on, I'll ask." She pulled the phone away from her ear and held her hand over the mouthpiece. "Hey, Mom, can I stay over at Em's tomorrow? It's Friday, it's not a school night."

Her mom didn't even look at her as she pulled pineapple chunks out of her *masaman* curry.

"Okay," she said, "but I don't want to see you trying to catch up on homework on Sunday night. I want it done before you go over."

"Can I just do it there so I can go on the bus with her?"

She acted like she was thinking, but then her dad said, "Oh, let her go, Ali. She'll do it there."

Go, Dad, she thought. Maybe going back to being a patrolman had made him lose his detective skills or something. She hadn't stayed over at Emily's in months. Em was still hanging out with all the kids they'd gone to elementary and middle school with.

Her mom waved her fork at her. "All right, but I'm serious, I want it done."

She put the phone against her ear again. "Hey, Emily?"

"Yes?" Seth answered, his voice all high like he was talking like Emily. It didn't sound like her at all, but she laughed anyway.

"It's cool," she said, already wondering what she was going to pack.

CORA

"So how are you feeling?" Dr. MacKinnon asked, pressing into my ribs, feeling his way across my kidneys. You'd think a man would be less gentle than a woman, but Dr. Cho had dug her fingers into me so far that I expected to see holes in my back when she was finished.

By comparison Dr. MacKinnon was practically a masseur.

"Tired," I replied. "But travel will do that to you."

"So will kidney disease. How's the pain?"

There hadn't actually been much pain. And I wondered if there should be. And I wondered, as I often had before: *If I'm not in pain, how bad can it really be?* But I only had to remember the ultrasound images to know how bad it was. And to know how close to pain I was getting.

"One to ten," MacKinnon prompted me.

"Two," I said with a shrug. What I should have said was, *Two on a good day, five on a bad day, today I am a three, it is a good*

day and what do you make of that, how will it change anything?
Eventually it might be a ten. Some people have it better, some have
it worse.

"Headaches?"

"Yes, last night especially. But nothing excruciating, just travel
pains."

"Mmm-hmm," he said, pulling my shirt back down over the
back of my jeans and coming around to the front of the table to sit
on a little rolling stool. "Dr. Cho is an excellent nephrologist."

"And she said the same of you," I replied.

"That's very flattering, but at this point what we're both wondering is why you're here. It's time to get your access installed and
prepare to begin dialysis. Dr. Cho—"

"I've told her the same thing. I have my reasons, they're important, and I'll go back to Seattle when I'm ready."

"Your kidneys are saying they're ready now," he said softly.

"My kidneys never have and never will dictate what I decide to
do with my life," I said. "Until, of course, they do."

He gave a short laugh. "Dr. Cho said I'd like you."

I shook my head. "Dr. MacKinnon, I'm not plucky, or feisty,
or whatever it is we're calling brave heroines these days. I'm not
being strong for my loved ones. I'm here because I'm too much of
a coward to not be."

He took that in, and I could tell he was revisiting his decision to
like me. That was okay. I would be here only for as long as it took
for me to become an adult and tell Ali that I might have given her
a child who might die before she did.

"Well, whatever it is you're here for, I suggest you get to it and
go home. Unless you plan on starting your dialysis here. We have

a center across the street that I'm affiliated with and it's a superb facility, but I'd rather see you at home, with your support system already in place."

Home. I didn't know what that was. Where was home? I was all right without defining home, but apparently nobody else was.

Was it where my daughter was? The daughter I had no claim on. She was always an abstract as *mine*. Yes, there was genetic material there, but she was certainly not mine. She was theirs, Ali and Benny's.

I'd never understood Ali's attraction, beyond the physical, to Benny. He was so . . . solid. He was so solid as to seem immobile. And immobile was barely breathing, wasn't it? I wanted movement for Ali. I wanted her to dance on currents, trembling leaves and undulating rivers and swirling waters.

But she had been so firmly hooked by the whole thing. Marriage, babies. The cruel betrayal of her reproductive organs was devastating. She had been ready, truly ready, at twenty. Who's ready for a baby at twenty? But Ali really was.

The rest of us had wanted to wait until we'd graduated college, until we'd had careers firmly established, until we were *ready*, as if some inner switch would flip and we'd just wake up and know one day. Her struggle had been frightening for everyone. If Ali could be infertile—and at such a young age—then what might we eventually be facing?

We got degrees, we had careers, those who wanted to married, and then as our friends from high school got pregnant, they slowly dropped away. I imagined they'd say they were dropped, that Ali had become too jealous and heartbroken to maintain the friendship, but I knew better.

The fact was, Ali's beautiful, naked longing was too much for them to witness. She cradled their infants, cuddled their babies, played with their toddlers in a loving way they seemed unable to sustain. They dealt with the dirty diapers, the teething, the tantrums, the loss of time, of romance, of sleep.

I think they couldn't stand to watch her delighted around their children in a way they couldn't muster anymore. I think she made them feel inadequate, as though they didn't appreciate what they had. Perhaps I was wrong; perhaps I was uncharitable. But as far as I was concerned, the only one I needed to be charitable toward was Ali.

When I visited, while Barbara was still alive, Ali would come to our house and stay the night the way she had when we were girls. Only this time we were allowed to stay out on the beach for as late into the night as we wanted.

We'd duck through the sea grape hedge, finding our old paths, bursting through to the wide white sand. We'd walk for hours, the moon a ghost high in the sky, the sun throwing its last desperate rose-gold fingers over the horizon, as reluctant to surrender the beach as we were.

And she would tell me about how all she'd ever wanted was for someone to call her *Mommy*. How she needed to hear that word from the mouth of a child, how it thrummed in the core of her body. And how she was certain that she had heard it called to her, across the house, from the nursery she'd optimistically painted yellow and green, in the hazy moments before sleep took her.

The idea of someone calling me *Mommy* filled me with dread. It didn't just feel wrong in my head, it felt wrong in my heart, and it made me shudder at the comedic horror show I was certain I would create if I tried to raise a child. We were close enough that I confided this to her, and if anyone ever wanted to know why I loved her so much it was this: She laughed.

She did not recoil in horror, look at me in pity, question my womanhood, or grow hurt that I didn't want, or understand, something that she so desperately did. She simply stared at me for a moment and then burst into laughter. She accepted my truth in as open a way as she ever had. The same way she had when we'd first met on that beach, when I told her that I might be adopted by the rich woman up the road, that my mother had been an alcoholic killed by her own boyfriend.

She had always had the most perfect, appropriate responses to my secrets.

I came home for a visit on my twenty-seventh birthday, and as we leisurely walked down the same beach that had seen us race down it as children, she told me that she wouldn't be having her own children. That she'd gotten bad eggs in the big supermarket of life, and they wouldn't ever create a child, not with Benny, not with anyone.

But there was hope, she'd said. IVF, in vitro fertilization, a procedure still new enough that it wasn't on every news anchor's teleprompter yet. She'd done her homework on the specifics, and it sounded viable to me.

"So do it," I'd encouraged, and she laughed.

"I don't know," she'd said. "It's so expensive, and it's so uncertain, you know? I don't produce viable eggs, so you have to use donor eggs, of course, and who knows what you get there, right?"

"God, here," I said, turning toward her and thrusting my hands at her from my hips. "Take mine! I'll never use them."

And we both laughed, the soft, salt-heavy wind twining strands of hair across our faces. And then I stopped laughing.

"Hey," I said. "Why not?"

"What?"

"I'm serious. Why not? Why couldn't you use my eggs? I'd be willing to bet they're the most ripe, fertilizable things in the world just because I don't want them. Why couldn't I be the donor?"

She looked almost confused. I think that, until then, the idea had been a fantasy, and here I was, offering it to her on a platter as if it were just that simple. It must have seemed incredibly frivolous to her, for me to be so free with the one thing she felt so abjectly inadequate in producing herself. As if I were offering her hard candies from a never-ending bowl.

"I couldn't ask you to do that," she said slowly, obviously thinking about how she might, indeed, do just that.

I never had a second's hesitation. If there'd been a speculum and petri dish on the beach, I'd have done it right then. Of course, I learned that it wasn't quite so simple.

I moved back home for a year, injecting myself with hormones, enduring procedures only slightly less personal than giving birth myself in order to make my ovaries overproduce and sync my and Ali's cycles. There were failures to implant, and two miscarriages, and I grieved with her, and with Benny, as if they had been my own. I helped plant the magnolia trees in their backyard in honor of those tiny babies.

And I felt horribly guilty, too. When the embryo didn't implant or she miscarried, I couldn't help but wonder if the flaw lay within my eggs. Though of course, I wasn't the only genetic material in there. Technically, they were mine and Benny's. That little irony, considering the fact that neither of us could be less attracted to each other, never escaped me, and perhaps that was part of why they never made it; perhaps even at our cellular level we didn't play well together.

I would often catch her looking at Benny and me in turn, with a Madonna smile on her face, and I knew she was putting an ideal child together in her mind out of our individual parts.

"God, I hope the kid gets your teeth," she said fervently once, and remembering Benny in middle school with his mouth full of metal, we'd laughed. That had been early on. The humor turned black after the second miscarriage. After the fifth try we called a halt to it.

But it was the magic cycle, because then there was Letty, Letitia, named for Benny's grandmother. I'd been graced with the honor of choosing her middle name, and while I'd considered Barbara, I finally settled on Makani, Hawaiian for "the wind." Of course she grew up to hate both of them.

But what joy she brought my friend. What gratitude and satisfaction and fulfillment. The craziness of the press coverage—generated by the PR firm her doctor had hired to jump-start his infertility clinic—only added to her excitement.

"Every woman who gives birth should have her picture on the cover of *People*," she said to me with a grin. It was if she had truly accomplished the impossible, and Letty, tiny, perfect Letty was the proof of it.

Four years later we did it again. Only after the first unsuccessful cycle, Ali froze the rest of the embryos, and I don't think she ever tried again.

The doctor who'd done the procedures opened IVF clinics around the nation, and I'm sure he is partly responsible for the egg donation ads I see on the backs of bathroom doors in ladies' rooms everywhere now. It was all very impressive, and now thousands of women sell their eggs to infertile couples.

But it's illegal to sell an organ to someone who will otherwise die.

Legal to create life and store it indefinitely in a freezer, illegal to save one that's already here, warm, contributing to society, taking care of jobs and families.

I tried to not think of the ethics of it all, but it grew more difficult every day.

"So how long am I looking at before dialysis?" I asked Dr. MacKinnon.

He shrugged. "Based on Dr. Cho's information, a couple of weeks, maybe a couple of months at the outside. We're going to want to go ahead and get your vascular access."

I nodded. I knew all about it.

"A fistula isn't really an option for you with these narrow veins—"

"I know," I interrupted. "We'll have to do an arteriovenous graft."

He smiled slightly. "Yeah. We'll get you set up for it this week, and if we have to go to dialysis sooner, we can use a catheter. You're going to do fine."

"I know," I said, sliding off the table.

Dr. MacKinnon stood and put his hand on my shoulder.

"I'll meet you out there," he said, "and we'll make an appointment for the graft and to set up a dialysis center orientation. You should at least start to get familiar with the process, even if you'll be doing it in Seattle."

I nodded, his hand still heavy on my shoulder. Did he think I would run?

As I pulled away from him and stepped into the hall, it took all I had to not do exactly that.

4

ALI

By the time I left for work in the morning, my anger had mellowed to a calm, determined patience. I reconciled myself to the fact that the baby discussion was going to go more slowly than I had anticipated. With Cora in town, I changed tactics. I would talk to her first.

Benny and I kissed good-bye after breakfast as if everything were fine. I managed to keep from driving by Cora's and pounding on her door, and I spent the morning practicing deep breathing exercises whenever I thought of either of them.

I ate lunch at the counter, pricing boxes of guitar strings in between bites of salad and mulling over Cora's undercover arrival. I clipped the phone to the pocket of my jeans and hooked the earpiece over my ear so I was ready for her call and wouldn't have to dash across the store.

By midafternoon she still hadn't called. I started going back over the last times we'd talked or e-mailed, looking for a reason, any reason, she might be angry with me. Had she e-mailed last? Or had I?

By four I was in the full throes of paranoia, and at ten minutes to closing I had made my plan to go straight to her house and ask her what her problem was and feeling quite righteous about the whole thing, when something slammed into the door hard enough to make my entire front window shake and my heart leap.

It was Cora, plastered against the glass like a bird, her face comically screwed up in surprise, her eyes crossed, a bottle of wine in one hand. I burst into laughter, completely forgetting everything but the joy I felt at seeing my friend. She stepped back and laughed, and then I saw what Benny had neglected to mention in his "looks like hell" assessment, as if she had merely looked a little tired.

She didn't just look tired. She had dark circles under her eyes, and she'd . . . expanded. She hadn't exactly gotten fat; it looked too soft, somehow. She looked bloated. Not period bloated, not I-drank-way-too-much-wine-and-ate-too-many-pretzels-last-night bloated, but *wrong* bloated. That was it, she just looked wrong.

But she was still there, in the mouth, that crazy grin, those eyes, and now that she was here I didn't care if she'd eaten a salt lick and drunk a bottle of gin rather than calling me. I pulled the door open and held it for her, and she didn't bother setting down the wine before she wrapped her arms around me.

"Hey," I said into her long hair, hugging her back, rocking with her, and laughing. I started to pull away, but she held on, and after a moment I realized her shoulders were hitching slightly.

"Whoa, hey," I said, pushing her back more forcefully. She dipped her head down, avoiding my gaze. "Cora, honey, what's wrong? Are you okay?"

She laughed and held the wine out to me. I set it on the counter while she wiped her face and pulled her hair back. She gave me a tremulous smile and said, "Oh, Ali, I'm so sorry. I'm just jet-lagged and—"

"Okay," I assured her, taking over, doing for her what she'd done for me countless times. "Go on and get out of here. Go home, put that wine in the fridge, and relax on the couch. I'm going to close up now, run home and grab some things, pick up some take-out, and I'll be at your place in less than an hour." I brushed her too-long bangs out of her eyes and made her look at me. "Hey, it's okay. You're home. We'll have a sleepover and by tomorrow you'll feel so much better. All right?"

She sniffed, but her smile was steadier now. "All right. You sure?"

"Sure about what?" I asked.

"You don't have plans or anything?"

"Plans? You kidding? Have you seen my life lately? Besides, if the queen were coming to dinner I'd cancel. Now go on, let me get closed up."

She hugged me again, tightly, then took the wine and left, hitting the horn on the little Toyota she'd had since we were in high school, and I watched her drive away, completely mystified. At least my concerns about her being mad at me were gone. I had no idea what was going on, but I was going to find out.

I rushed through my closing routine and got home before Benny. I gathered everything I thought I'd need, and plenty I probably didn't, like magazines and books and deep conditioner and facial masks. I was almost excited that she was in such a state. Cora had always held me up, always had the solutions, been the one I turned to.

I'd been the one looking like hell, trying to not cry—and most often failing—more times than she had. Now I could be strong for her. As I packed a duffel bag I went over all the things that could have gone wrong. Maybe she'd been fired.

Maybe she and Drew had broken up. Again. They'd been in and out of it for years, but she'd never been so upset that she'd come back home.

I didn't think anyone could have died. She had no idea who her father was, her mother had been killed when Cora was just eight, and Barbara had died almost ten years ago. Technically, Cora didn't have any family left at all.

I settled on Drew. That had to be it.

Benny came home while I was tossing my bags in the car, and I followed him back into the house.

"Leaving me?" he asked lightly as he began putting his work away, teasing, his way of easing back into our relationship after an argument.

"Only for a night," I said, playing along, but on guard.

Benny and Cora might not have been crazy about each other, but he was grateful to her for our daughter, grateful to her for being the shock absorber of my crazier emotions, my darker moods during those years.

There had been times throughout my relationship with Benny— started and ended frivolously at fifteen, begun again in all seriousness at seventeen—when I thought the combination of Benny and Cora would make the world's perfect husband.

And when she came back into town, no matter how long it had been, how long Benny had had me to himself, there was still a bit of resentment at my being a ghost of a presence in the house while she was here. It wasn't that he minded my being gone, it was Cora; specifically, her free spirit, her adamant personality.

I imagined it had started as adolescent jealousy over my time, but neither of them had fully grown out of it. He didn't trust her independence, and she didn't trust his conformity. I needed both, and I usually had the best of both worlds. I swung between them like a hammock, gently at times, tangled at others.

But right then, when it came right down to it, I thought my absence was likely a welcome break. When he teased me about leaving him rather than falling silent, I could tell he was looking forward to an evening at home alone, hanging out with the birds and a beer. I decided to tread lightly, making conversation before dashing off.

"So how was it?"

"How was what?" he responded, slipping his shoes off.

"Your day, Benny, how was your day? Do you like being back out there? Anything happen? Catch any bad guys?"

He smiled at that, but he looked tired. I'd grown used to his face aging above a button-down and tie. Seeing it above a uniform again was a little startling, and for the first time I stopped thinking about the fact that he hadn't consulted me about the job change and wondered if he wasn't taking on more than he could handle at this point in our lives.

"No bad guys today," he said. "Lots of speeders, red-light runners, the usual. I caught a couple of kids trespassing at the Jasper place. It's still a mess there. Talked to them for a while. Good kids, just curious."

"Okay, good. You happy you're doing this?"

"Ali," he said, "stop worrying. I'll get back into the swing of things. Give me some time, okay?"

"Okay," I agreed.

"Going to hang with Cora, I take it?"

"That all right with you?"

He shrugged. "Would it matter if it wasn't?"

I closed my eyes briefly. "Of course it would. Do you need me here?"

He didn't answer that. "How long did you manage to hold off before calling her?"

"I didn't, actually. She showed up at the store. But you were right, she does look awful. I think she and her boyfriend must have broken up."

"That's too bad," he said, but he wasn't really listening. He pulled on his after-work clothes, ready to get out to the yard. "Anything in the fridge for dinner?"

"Not really, unless you want a sandwich. I left a couple of delivery menus on the counter for you."

He nodded. "Letty check in yet?"

"No, but she's over at Emily's tonight, remember? Your night stretches out before you, totally unencumbered by women, my dear."

He reached his arms above his head, grasping the door trim, and stretched his back with a happy groan. "Sounds lovely," he admitted. I playfully punched him in his exposed stomach, and he dropped his arms around me and kissed the top of my head. "Have a good time," he said, giving in. "Call if you need me."

"Love you," I called to him as I left, unable to keep from smiling at the echo of his "You too" just before the sliding glass door closed.

CORA

I rested my head against the steering wheel when I got back in the car, exhausted by my unexpected breakdown. I'd done my bird-against-the-window routine for her before with great success, and I'd just wanted to see Ali with all that laughter and joy on her face.

But the second her arms were around me, all I wanted to do was break down and sob.

I'd occasionally wondered over the years if there had been any-thing wrong, ethically, with what we'd done. But then I would see Ali with Letty, or be the recipient of Ali's mothering instincts myself, as I was today, and I wrestled no more. Of course I had done the right thing. Ali was supposed to be a mother, there was no question.

But now I wrestled with something that was not so abstract. What, exactly, had I given her? A loving gesture from a best friend, or heartbreak? And feeling her arms around me made me wonder if I had fooled about with something that I shouldn't have. Perhaps the reason I'd never felt any maternal itch was because I wasn't supposed to have children. Perhaps my flawed genes were being flushed out of the great Darwinian pool.

I wanted to go back to when those thoughts were abstract. Once I started getting specific, other specifics began creeping in. How did Letty feel about me? How did I feel about her? How would she feel if I died? How would she feel if she had the same gene? It wasn't a given. She had a fifty-fifty chance.

I did have the option of simply saying nothing, going back to Seattle, getting the hemodialysis, hoping for a kidney, and if things didn't pan out, or the dialysis didn't work well for me, well, then eventually I'd die and wouldn't have to worry about it any longer anyway.

I never said it was a good option.

I did some deep-breathing exercises on the drive home, determined to hold myself together and have a good night with Ali. I panicked slightly when I saw the state of the house. I hadn't had the energy—or the time, thanks to Dr. Cho's zippy referral—to open the storm shutters, and I certainly hadn't bothered to neatly remove my clothes from my bags. Things were strewn about, and I was ashamed of myself, ashamed to imagine what Barbara would think of how I was treating the home she'd so generously provided for me.

I hurried around gathering my clothes together and shoving them in my dresser drawers, drawers I hadn't looked in for years. I continued to stay in my old room, not out of some misguided respect for Barbara's room—she'd have expected me to move into it—but because I liked my old room in the back corner of the house, its French doors leading out to the patio and pool, doors I used to sneak out of in high school to meet Ali and our friends down at the beach.

When she rang the bell, the interior was as good as it was going to get, though it was still dark without the shutters open. I forced a smile on my face, and when I opened the door, it softened into something more natural. Ali had arrived laden down with enough stuff to stay a week.

"What all did you bring?" I asked, throwing bags onto the sofa while she went back out to her car for more. I laughed when she brought in a stack of DVDs and books. I nearly expected her to whip a puppy out of her pocket.

We both fell back onto the couch and just looked at each other for a moment.

"It's good to see you," Ali said.

"Oh, honey, you too, you have no idea."

"How long are you staying?"

I surveyed the array of supplies she'd brought spread before us. "Apparently not as long as you are."

"Well, I wanted to plan for every contingency," she said. "I've got heartache movies, funny movies, funny heartache movies, books on changing careers, books on midlife crises, books on cultivating coleus . . ."

"Cultivating coleus?"

"I don't know. It looked pretty," she said, holding up a book with photos of brightly colored plants with white veins running through them. "I had no idea what sort of mood you might be in, so I just grabbed everything within reach," she said with her old Ali grin.

I shook my head and took the book from her. "You're a nut," I said, "but I do love you."

"Okay," she said briskly, standing and surveying the living room. "Let's get the shutters up."

I collapsed back against the couch. "Really? Isn't it nice and soothing in here?"

"Yes, it's quite soothing. For mental patients. And if I can help it, you're not going to become one just yet. On your feet, lady."

I stood with a groan. "All right, but if I collapse, I'm holding you personally responsible."

"The fresh air will do you good," she said. And, as usual, she was right. It took well over an hour, and by the time we'd worked our way around the house cranking the rolling shutters up into their cases, I'd worked up a fine sheen of sweat. It exhausted me, but it felt good, too.

Granted, Ali was doing most of the work, physically and emotionally. She'd kept up a constant stream of chatter, and I hung on every word. She told me about Letty, how she was getting used to high school, how her grades had slipped a little, but that was to be expected with the tougher classes.

Letty was going to be fifteen in a couple of weeks. My God. Fifteen.

"She says she doesn't want a party, can you believe that? She says she's too old for a party. The girl who had to have pony rides at seven, a bounce house at eight, all those ridiculous theme parties we threw every year with all those screaming girls?"

I did remember. I'd been there for a few of them and had always thought they were the most absurd waste of money. I thought they were spoiling her, but I kept my opinion to myself, of course. They kept her limbs intact and air pumping through her lungs, and what more could you ask, really?

"So, will you be here for her birthday?" Ali asked, and if I wasn't mistaken, there was a slight edge to her voice that I couldn't readily explain.

"I might," I said. "What's the plan if there's no party?"

"Well, dinner out, I guess, and we'll go ahead and start looking for a car—"

"What? I thought she was fifteen?"

"She is," she said, sounding surprised. "But we thought it would be good to have her learn to drive on the car she'd actually be driving. Besides, we're just starting to look; it's not like it's going to be sitting in the driveway with a big red bow on it. We'll get it during the year and make it low-key; you know, we don't want it to look like we're spoiling her."

I gaped at her.

"What?" she demanded, hands on her hips. "That's not that unusual, you know. You don't have kids; you don't know how it is now."

"Oh, come on," I protested. "You and I both had to work for our cars. What's Letty doing?"

"Letty is being a kid—"

"Kids don't have cars," I pointed out. "Young adults have cars, and young adults work, and pay for their insurance and their gas—"

"Cora!" Ali interrupted me. "Look, yes, we did all that, but things are different now. You have no idea how much work these kids do at school, how crazy and busy their lives are. And I don't want Letty to have to work yet. We can afford to get her a car, a good, safe car so we don't have to worry about her breaking down on the side of the road."

I started laughing. "Remember when your Fiat lost half its gears and we had to drive home from the beach in first gear the whole way?"

I thought she'd laugh over the shared memory, but she frowned.

"That's exactly what I'm talking about," she said. "Do you know how dangerous that was? What were we even doing out that late at night? Anything could have happened, and we'd have been able to go all of twelve miles an hour to get to safety. I don't want Letty in any situation like that."

"Well, we managed to live through it," I said, turning back to the shutter on the front window, the final one. Ali was still standing in the driveway looking at me with her arms crossed over her chest. "And I don't think we turned out too badly. Do you?"

I didn't know why I was pushing this. I didn't want to fight with Ali.

"It was a different time," she said, narrowing her eyes at me. "And I have no idea what my parents were thinking, letting me stay out so late, letting us do some of the stuff we did."

"Wow, I think that's pretty harsh."

I was truly surprised. Ali's parents had been great, ideal parents as far as I had been concerned, and after my mother, foster homes, and then Barbara, I had certainly considered myself something of an expert on what constituted a good family.

"They let you do things because you'd proven yourself reliable and responsible," I said. "You worked at the store from the time you were ten; you saved your money; you made good grades; you made good choices, I'd like to think, in friends."

She snorted at that. "Well, I guess I did at that. Sorry. Benny's been a bear lately, and I'm feeling a little frazzled this week."

"Me too," I said, trying to give her an understanding smile, but puzzled by the pained look on her face.

"What's going on?" I asked, and she laughed and shook her head.

"I'm supposed to be asking you that," she said, then gave the house an appraising look. "Come on, let's get cleaned up and start downing some wine. I'm feeling like we've done enough work, how about you?"

"I thought you'd never ask."

I got in the shower, and Ali passed various potions and unctions in to me, directing me as to what part of my body they were to be used on. At one point I smelled like a pine-infused mango with lemon zest, but still, it was lovely to feel taken care of.

"Here," she said, talking over the patter of the shower and handing in a white device. When I took it from her, I realized it was vibrating and nearly dropped it in surprise. There was cream on one end.

"What the hell am I supposed to do with this?" I called from behind the curtain.

Ali pulled a bit of the shower curtain back and looked at me disapprovingly, but she was unable to keep from laughing, too.

"It's for your *face*, Cora. My God, where have you been for the past five years? It's microdermabrasion. Just rub it around on your face."

She let the shower curtain drop, and I applied it to my face, still giggling.

"And try to not get any in your eyes or your mouth," she called to me, making us both laugh again.

When I finally got out of the shower, microdermabraded, deeply conditioned, and loofahed until I tingled, I had to laugh at Ali's disheartened face.

"What? You thought I'd look better, didn't you?" I asked with a grin.

"You look great," she said, but I'd seen her face. I believe *dismay* was the predominant emotion, though it was lightly tinged with concern.

"We should get massages this week," she said brightly, and I could see her mentally cataloging the procedures I'd need to have done in order to look myself again. She was probably thinking about lymph node–draining rubdowns, toxin-releasing wraps, and all manner of luxuries that weren't going to do a thing.

I wanted to reassure her that it was merely an incurable disease I had, just to make her feel better about her ministrations' lack of power to transform me.

"You want to go up with me tomorrow?" I asked, surprising myself.

Her eyes widened. "I have to open the store," she hedged.

This was an old tug-of-war between us. "You know, people actually ask me to take them flying. I'm trusted, sought out, beloved for my safety record."

"How 'bout I belove you for staying on the ground?"

I turned my head upside down and rubbed my hair dry, and Ali pointed to the low stool we used to sit on to apply makeup. I sat and rubbed lotion on my arms—the one beauty regimen I'd embraced in recent years, trying to combat my dry, itchy PKD skin—while Ali started running a comb through my hair.

If I didn't look in the mirror, we could have been fourteen again. She gently worked out tangles and then began tugging my hair into a French braid.

"Come on, Al. Go for a ride with me?"

She avoided my eyes in the mirror. "Maybe."

"What are you afraid of?"

"Crashing in a ball of fire."

"That's all?"

"Crashing in the Everglades."

"Uh-huh. Anything else?"

"Crashing on I-75."

"I'm sensing a theme here."

"The crashing part?"

"Yes, that seems to come up a lot."

"As will my lunch if I get in one of those little planes."

"I'd be ever so careful. Come on, please? It's perfect flying weather."

"How do you know you can even get a plane?"

"I'll call Keith. Season's over, he'll have one open."

"Maybe."

"What about Letty? Think she'd like to go up?"

"Oh, I'm sure she'd love to. You kidding?"

"Well, why don't you see if she'd like to go, and I'll pick her up at the store tomorrow afternoon. You can meet us at the field after you close."

"She's staying with Emily tonight," she said. "They usually go to the beach on Saturday."

"We should go down in our bikinis and mortify them."

"Please. The only place I wear a bikini these days is at my own pool. At night. When there's no moon."

"Remind me to call the pool company to come out next week so we can swim while I'm here. It doesn't look like it's been done this month, and I don't feel like cleaning it. I never get the chemicals right anyway."

Her hands paused in my hair for a moment. "You'll be here for that long?"

"Maybe," I said.

"I'll call for you tomorrow. Okay," she said, snapping a band in place at the end of my braid. "My turn. You get started with a glass of wine, and I'll be out in a few minutes."

I smoothed my hands against the sides and top of my head, feeling the satisfying bumpy line of the braid. "You've still got it," I said.

"You too, hot mama," she said, and we smiled at each other in the mirror, both painfully aware that she was lying.

5

A L I

I didn't bother using any of the beauty products I'd given to Cora on myself. Not that I didn't need them, but I wanted to get some wine in her and loosen her tongue as quickly as possible. There was obviously something major going on.

The last time she'd been here for more than two weeks was when Barbara died. I'd stayed with her most of that time, going home only to pick up more clothes. She'd tried to get me to fly with her then, too, and I'd finally gone just to make her happy, but I was nauseated and kept my eyes closed the whole time.

I trusted her skill. Cora had always done exactly what she set out to do, and then she did it better than anyone else. She was an excellent pilot, I was certain. But I'd have been terrified with Lindbergh himself. I did not trust it, I did not want to, and I did not have to.

Letty would love it. I paused for a moment with my fingers tight against my scalp, suds dripping down my face, and then began to massage again, slowly. Yes, it was true. Letty was a lot like Cora. Okay, there it was.

And Cora was right. We'd been little hellions, and we'd partied, and we'd taken outrageous risks, and we were very lucky nothing awful happened to us as teenagers, but we'd been pretty good kids, too. I still looked back and wondered that my parents had been so permissive, but we'd come through it all right.

So Letty, really, was a combination of all of us. Me, Cora, and Benny, and that wasn't a bad pedigree if you asked me. And maybe there would be another one. I felt a warmth deep in my belly, already anxious to talk to Cora about it. But her first. There was obviously something wrong, and I needed to get to the bottom of it.

This was the first time that we hadn't fallen into full-disclosure mode as soon as we'd seen each other, but of course she was the one who'd started things off so oddly. I rinsed off and wrapped myself in a towel, braiding my own hair over my shoulder.

As promised, Cora was waiting for me on the patio with a glass of wine and some of the cheese and fruit I'd brought, blueberries gathered in her hand. I collapsed into the chair across from her.

"You know, getting those shutters done was a lot easier when we were sixteen," I said.

"Wasn't everything?"

"I suppose," I agreed, taking a sip of wine. "So. Are you going to tell me about it?"

"What?" she asked, raising her eyebrows at me.

"Oh, come on. First of all, you've never not told me you were coming home before. I wouldn't even have known if Benny hadn't driven by." Now that I'd said it out loud, it stung again. "Were you planning on telling me, or did you want to be alone?"

"Ali, of course I was going to tell you. I just changed my plans at the last minute and was so tired when I got in . . . I was in Chile."

"So I heard. Why were you in Chile, and why did you change your plans? Did you and Drew break up again?"

"We did, actually. But that's not why I changed my plans. I was in Chile teaching a seminar on wind energy, and I just suddenly wanted to be in Florida more than I wanted to go back to Seattle. I'm sorry if it hurt your feelings that I didn't call immediately."

"When did you break up? What happened?" I asked. "Why didn't you call?"

She sighed. "It was the same old stuff. We're just better off as friends. We both know that. I'm sorry I didn't call."

"But . . . ," I started, trailing off when I realized that what I wanted to say would be embarrassingly immature. We weren't fifteen anymore. We didn't have to call each other the second something in our lives happened anymore. But it still hurt.

She put her wineglass down and leaned forward, grasping my wrist in her hand. "Hey, really, I'm sorry. I've been sick, and I was just tired."

She'd been sick. I quickly ran through whatever I knew about South American illnesses she could have contracted, and just as quickly realized that I didn't know much about South America. Malaria came to mind. Sleeping sickness. What else? Rabies. Yes, I knew it was ridiculous, but I thought rabies. I've never really known what all she did on these trips besides try to talk people into putting up windmills, but I'd always envisioned her as a combination of Indiana Jones and Amelia Earhart, flying into remote backcountries, dodging bats, hair flying in the wind.

"What kind of sick?" I asked.

"Just sick, you know."

"Are you better? Do you need to go see the doctor?"

"Actually, yes. I saw him today. That's why I wasn't waiting on your doorstep first thing this morning. And I'll be going back in a few days. So, see? I'm taking care of myself. It's not catching, I'm just run-down."

I looked at her searchingly for another minute, and then believed her.

"Well," I said, "then take a break. I won't bother you anymore about it. I'll just ply you with wine and food and friendship, and you'll be back to yourself in no time."

To my surprise she looked genuinely relieved.

"Thanks," she said. "I can't have much wine with the pills I'm taking, but I'll sip anyway, and I'm obviously trying to cut way back on my salt."

She grinned ruefully, and I thought, *Well, that's that. She's doing everything she needs to do. Gone to see the doctor, taking a break, cutting back on alcohol and salt.*

Cora was fine. Which made my little issue less of a complication. "So, I'm really glad you're here," I said, taking a swallow of wine. "There's something I've been wanting to talk about."

"You sound serious," she said, closing her eyes, sighing heavily, and lifting her feet onto the chair beside her.

I looked out over the pool, thinking of Benny attacking the clean water with the skimmer, and took a deep breath. Cora was sick, exhausted, and heartbroken. The only one ready to talk about a baby right now was me. Patience had served me well before. It would again.

The sun was just starting to set, the light finally softening to a warm ivory, with just the beginning hints of pink and lavender. The shadow of a crane slipped over the patio, and areca palm fronds bounced gently against the screen.

I relaxed back against my chair and put my feet up, too.

"Nothing that can't wait a couple of days. Welcome home," I said, holding out my glass, which would need refilling in another swallow. Cora's had barely been touched, and we tilted them together and smiled at each other.

"It's good to be back," she acknowledged. "Want to head down for the sunset?"

"Let's do it." We transferred our wine to plastic cups and strolled the few blocks to the beach. We sat in the sand, still hot enough that it burned through my shorts and soft enough that it cradled me like a mother.

We fell asleep that night as we had when we were teenagers, deeply, after talking for over an hour across the darkened room, the air-conditioning unit in the window humming white noise, each of us in a twin bed in Cora's childhood room.

Just after three I woke to my cell phone's irritating rising notes and leaped out of bed to silence it before it could reach peak volume and wake Cora. It was Benny, on his way over to get me.

Letty, our little miracle, had been picked up by the police.

CORA

When the phone rang, I assumed Letty, of course, and my heart raced, already filled with regret for the things I hadn't known about her. I couldn't say, for sure, that I thought she was dead, but my remorse at having never known her, never known my daughter, was suffocating.

Ali immediately went out to the hallway, softly closing the door behind her, unaware that I had woken. I threw the covers off and opened the door, startling her. She shook her head and held a finger up to me.

"But she's okay? She's all right? Okay, okay, no. Yes, come get me, of course. I'll be out front. Just—calm down, Benny, yelling at me isn't going to help anything."

She flipped the phone closed and held her hand to her forehead as if feeling for a fever.

"What?" I demanded.

"Letty," she said. "Unbelievable. Letty's been picked up by the police at a house party out in Golden Gate."

"Is she okay?"

She hurried into the bedroom and began changing into her jeans and a tank top. "He said the cop said she was fine. Scared, of course. Dammit, what was she thinking?" She suddenly stopped tying her laces and looked up at me. "I should call Emily's, shouldn't I? I hate to wake them, but I hate to think of Jean panicking if she sees they're gone before we get back."

"I guess so. Would you want to be called?"

She started dialing, then held the phone against her ear while she bent over to finish tying her shoes. I pulled on jeans and a T-shirt.

"Jean? It's Ali, no, yes everything is okay, but I guess the girls went to a party tonight—"

She stopped speaking for a moment, then, "Well, I guess they sneaked out a window or—I—what?"

Another brief pause.

"Jean, Letty told me she was spending the night at your house."

I mouthed *What?* at her, but she just shook her head.

"I see. I'm so sorry to have woken everyone, Jean. We'll take care of things."

She slowly flipped the phone closed and stared at me. "She lied."

"What happened?"

"The phone rang at dinner yesterday, and Letty answered, had this whole conversation with someone, and asked permission to spend the night at Emily's tonight."

I got it. "Oh. I gather she was never there?"

She shook her head slowly. "No. Jean says Emily and her friend Jainie, who did go over to spend the night, are sleeping in Emily's bedroom. Jean never heard about Letty going over at all. I can't believe she did this."

"Well . . ."

"Well what?"

"I'm just saying, we did that."

"We did what?"

"We said we were spending the night at each other's house and then hung out, all night, on Ft. Myers beach. You don't remember that?"

"Yeah, well, Letty's not us," she said, grabbing her overnight bag and her purse and stalking past me. I hurried after her.

"Of course not," I said. "I'm sorry—"

She turned around so quickly that we nearly collided, and I stumbled to regain my footing.

"You have no idea how hard it is, especially these days," she said. "She's only fourteen, Cora."

I wisely didn't point out that she would be fifteen soon enough, and that fifteen was exactly when we'd started sneaking out. Frankly, I was surprised that the ruse had taken her in. She'd done it; why was she so amazed that Letty had? In fact, why hadn't she been expecting it?

"Of course," I said. "I'm sorry. I'm still half-asleep, you know. I'm not used to being woken up at three thirty."

I was trying to make light of it, but she wasn't in the mood.

She looked like she was about to say something, but then she turned away from me and nearly sprinted for the front door. I was on her heels and grabbed my purse from the kitchen counter as she stepped into the dark, humid morning. Her timing was perfect; I could see the headlights of Benny's truck swinging into the driveway, and she turned to close the door as she left, seeming surprised to find me standing there with her, holding my keys.

"What are you doing?" she asked.

"I— Coming with you? Do you want me to come with you?"

"Oh my God, no. Go, go back to bed. She's not your responsibility. I'll call you tomorrow."

She gave me a quick kiss on the cheek, and then I was left standing in the driveway, one hand clutching my keys, the other raised in a wave as Benny pulled out and accelerated down the street, heading out to save, and punish, their daughter.

6

ALI

On the long drive out to northeast Golden Gate I'd made Benny repeat everything, every word spoken, every tone the officer had used with him. It was woefully little, but Benny's face was grim. He'd broken up plenty of high school house parties over the years.

Benny told me what had been said, but other than that he stayed silent, anger radiating off him like heat, and I wondered if he was thinking back to our high school years, too. Benny had always been a straight arrow. We'd run into each other at parties occasionally, but Benny was always the designated driver, always offered to be. I'd calmed down considerably by the time we began dating again at seventeen.

"And you want to do this again?" he suddenly said, his voice hard.

"What?" I asked, the embryos out of my mind for the first time in well over a year.

"This is just the beginning, you know," he said. "If she's sneaking around now, at fourteen, you have any idea what she'll do at fifteen, sixteen. God help us, Ali, and you want to add a baby onto it right when we have to start being real parents."

"Real parents? What are you talking about? Since when haven't I been a real parent? I've always been the parent."

"And I haven't?" he yelled back at me. "You've had the store, you take off for days at a time whenever Cora's in town—"

I gasped. "Once a year, *maybe*, my best friend, the only reason we even have that child, comes back in town. I might spend two nights away from you all year. I don't think that's too much to ask."

"My mother never spent a single night away from her family."

"Your mother was an old woman by the time she was forty, Benny. She spent her entire life breaking her back in the fields and then working just as hard at home. Was that what you wanted in your wife, what you wanted from me? Because if so, you really should have mentioned it earlier."

"Shut up, Ali," he said, "just shut up."

He'd never told me to shut up. Ever. I was so stunned by his outburst that I just sat there, staring out at the pines rushing by the windows as we moved farther into the darkness of Golden Gate, the road narrowing, the black stretches between streetlights growing longer.

How had I not been the mother to his child that he'd wanted?

No, my entire existence hadn't revolved around every breath she'd taken once she'd turned eight, nine, ten. What else was I supposed to do? Children grow up, they become independent. I'd certainly been more involved than many other parents.

The more I looked for a reason, the more I couldn't find one, and the angrier I became at Benny, nearly forgetting that I was angry at Letty and that we were out driving around in the middle of the night arguing because of her. Finally I couldn't stay silent any longer.

"You know, that was completely uncalled for," I said, the words stark in the quiet.

Benny just sighed.

"What was I supposed to do, Benny? Let my parents sell the store?"

"You could have," he said.

"You can't be serious."

"You could have. You didn't want to."

"Why are we talking about this now?" I asked, desperate to get to the core of how this was all my fault.

"Because our daughter is out of control, and you didn't know it. And now you want another."

"Oh, it was strictly my job to keep track of her? You're the one who said she could stay at Emily's tonight."

"You're her mother," he said, as if pointing out the obvious.

"And you're her father. Why are you suddenly absolved of any responsibility?"

"My entire life is responsibility, Ali. I have the responsibility for our bills, for the maintenance on the house, all on top of being responsible for the safety of the people in this county. I thought you at least had Letty covered."

"Oh, wow, that *is* a lot of responsibility. What the hell is it you think I've been doing all these years? Getting my hair done? I've worked just as hard as you, I've made just as much money, and sometimes more. And I take care of everything inside the house, everything. I had no idea your life was so hard, Benny. How *do* you stand it?"

He leaned his head against his window, and he sighed again, and I looked over at him and saw a tear sliding down the side of his nose, and he said, so quietly as to be nearly a whisper: "I don't know."

I didn't know where to look. I stared at him for another moment, then looked down at my feet, up at the sun visor, at the handle on my door. My eyes couldn't stop moving, but my lips couldn't start. I couldn't begin to form a coherent sentence in my mind, much less allow it out of my mouth.

Neither of us spoke again on the drive to the party. Benny got through the snarl of cars at the head of the street by showing his badge, and when we pulled in behind a row of patrol cars, he said, "Stay here," and got out.

I looked around at the sad scene and wondered what would happen to the parents. If they were present, they'd probably been arrested. If they were out of town, I quailed at the phone call they would be getting and at the condition of their house when they returned.

Benny's command to stay in the truck meant little. After the things he'd said, I wasn't particularly inclined to listen to him. In fact, I wanted to make sure that he, and I, knew that I was still my own person. My daughter was somewhere in this mess of flashing red and blue, and I was going to find her.

Benny strode purposely toward the house, but I stayed outside, trying to not miss anything. And then I heard the panicked cry of "Mom!" Surely I was the only one there who could rightfully answer to that, and within a moment I'd found her, locked in the back of a police car.

She looked awfully, heartbreakingly young. And for a breathless moment, I believed Benny's accusations: I was, indeed, a terrible mother.

LETTY

She knew she was so dead.

She was so stupid, and so dead.

So.

Dead.

Seth got away, but they had his car, so she figured they'd probably be able to trace that. A bunch of kids got away, the ones smart enough to run on foot. Some tried to take off across the empty lots in their cars. That was a big mistake. Where did they think they were going to come out? The cops just blocked off the street and caught every single one of them.

She should have run, too. She just couldn't. She couldn't run from the cops. She froze instead. Besides, she had all her stuff in there, her school ID and everything in her purse. And then it would just be worse.

She'd told the cops who came into the bedroom that her dad

was a cop. She thought, stupidly, that they'd just let her go. Instead they asked her name and got on the radio.

The neighbors had all come out to their driveways to watch the fun, and a little boy, like, eight, wearing camouflage pajamas, stood beside the cop car and stared in at her. She tried to ignore him, but he wouldn't go away, and she finally smacked the window with her hand and made him jump. But he still didn't go away.

A helicopter showed up, an actual helicopter, like it was a murder scene or something. Oh, she was so dead. Why wasn't she at Emily's? Jean had promised Emily a new bedroom for her birthday, and there were paint chips taped to the walls, and pieces of fabric hanging over the curtain rod, and masking tape on the floor where a queen bed would replace the bunk beds.

She closed her eyes and could practically see Emily and Jainie sleeping in the beds.

The back of the car stank. She wasn't supposed to be there. She had no idea what would happen when her dad got there. Maybe he'd tell them to arrest her, just to teach her a lesson. The way he'd been acting lately, it wouldn't surprise her. But she was even more scared of what he'd find when he went to get her things.

See . . . there was stuff in the bedroom where her things were. Especially, well, especially there were condoms. There were a couple in their wrappers on the floor beside the bed.

And there was one that was . . . unwrapped. It was on the floor, too. They didn't use it. They tried, but it didn't work. She didn't know, something didn't work, she didn't know why, but it wasn't . . . going anywhere. They'd tried it without one and that worked, and he promised he'd pull out and he did.

It was all very weird. It didn't feel like she thought it would.

She knew it was going to hurt, but she didn't realize it was a hurt like that. It wasn't, like, a good hurt, the way she thought it was supposed to be.

They say it's better the second time, but she just didn't see how that got mixed up with feeling good. It was really just, sort of, nothing. Just pushing at her. And she wished she'd gone to Emily's. And she prayed, just prayed and prayed that nobody would see the condoms.

She watched out the opposite window of where the neighbor kid stood and saw her dad's truck pull up. *Oh God, oh God, let this not be happening*, she thought. There was just no turning back from this.

But he got out, looked around; it was definitely her father, and it was definitely happening. He didn't see her in the backseat, and she watched him wander around, talk to a couple of cops, show his badge. He took off in the direction of the house, she guessed to find the cop that had called her in.

And then, because her life always just got worse and worse, she saw the passenger door of the truck open and her mom got out. And at first it was even worse than seeing her dad, but then all she wanted was to see her. She slapped her hand against the back window and yelled, "Mom, Mom! Mom! I'm here! Mom!"

Her mom swiveled her head around and finally saw her. She came running and pressed her hands against the window.

"It's okay, baby, it's okay, I'm here. It's going to be all right," she yelled in at her.

She didn't have to yell, Letty could hear her okay, but it sounded good, and she laid her forehead against the window while her mom turned around with her hands still pressed against it, like she'd found Letty at a sale and wasn't going to take her hands off until the salesman got there.

And here he came, the cop who'd stuck her in here. Her dad wasn't with him, but her mom talked at him, and he finally opened the door.

And then her dad was there. He had the overnight bag and purse in one hand, and he stopped when he saw her. He didn't say anything, he just stared. She'd never seen his face like that before. Then he came over and opened the door to the truck, shoving her things in the back.

"Get in," he said. Her mom didn't say anything to him. She just nodded.

"Come on," she said to Letty. "Hop up."

That was when Letty really started crying.

"Get in the truck," her dad said, only he said it through his teeth, and she scrambled up. Her mom got in and closed the door, and they watched without speaking as her dad and the cop who'd put her in his car talked.

Dad looked back once, and Letty flinched. She reached out for her mom's hand, and for a second she didn't think she was going to take it.

"Oh, honey, what were you thinking?" she asked.

"I'm sorry," Letty whispered. And she really, really was.

CORA

Keith, my flight instructor when I was a teenager, did have a plane available for the afternoon, and he said he'd have it fueled up and ready to go for me as long as I promised to meet him for lunch next week so we could catch up. That was a promise easily made.

Ali didn't call as she'd said she would, but I imagined it had been a tough night. When I arrived at the store, I was surprised to see Letty first, sullenly straightening music scores. She barely looked up at me when I initially opened the door, but then she did a double take, and such relief washed across her face that I thought things must have been even worse than I thought.

"Aunt Cora," she cried and ran to me, launching herself at me in a way she hadn't since she was eight. She was also heavier than she was at eight, and I stumbled backward when I caught her.

"Hey there, Letitia Makani, how's it going?"

I ran my hand over the top of her head, amazed at how straight girls could get their hair these days. With a start, I realized she had my hair, fine and silky under my palm, and wondered how on earth she managed no frizz in southwest Florida.

She groaned and pulled back. I let her go reluctantly.

"You know?" she asked.

I nodded. "I know enough." I looked for Ali, but there was only a couple looking at guitars in the store. "Where's your mom?"

"She went to pick up lunch," she said.

"Well, I haven't talked to her today yet, so tell me what happened. Was it really bad?"

She nodded and bit her lip, and I felt a surge of sympathy when I saw her eyes fill with tears.

"Come on," I said, keeping my voice low, mindful of the customers. I steered her toward the counter and grabbed a tissue from the box there.

She sat on one stool, and I sat on the other and we watched the man fit a guitar to the woman he was with, adjusting the neck up toward her shoulder, stepping back to see how she looked. Letty blew her nose and took a deep breath. I'd sat on this stool hundreds of times, Ali on the one Letty now occupied, talking in hushed tones about one teen angst or another.

It was familiar and sweet, and I felt oddly proud and excited to be sitting here now, with this child going through the same things. It should have been all about her and how upset she was, but it was about me too, being someone she could turn to.

The man put the guitar back, and they left the store. Letty called out "Good-bye, thanks" as they left, and then turned to me, her face miserable.

"I'm grounded, of course, for life. And Dad went all through my room and went through my drawers, and he took my phone and my purse, and notes, and . . . other stuff." Her face flushed bright red, something I'd never been able to control either. I wondered what else they'd found.

"Okay, wait," I said. "Start at the beginning. You told your parents you were staying with Emily, but you obviously didn't even go over there, so who took you to this party?"

She looked away. "This guy."

"Oh," I said, understanding. "What's his name?"

As I watched her struggle with wanting to tell me and knowing she probably shouldn't, I wondered if it was possible that my own emotions had played so nakedly across my face at her age, and if they had, had I learned to mask them, or was I still that transparent? She finally gave in.

"His name's Seth," she said.

"And he's older?" I prompted. "He's driving?"

"You have to promise to not tell," she pleaded, clearly already regretting saying his name.

"Oh, honey—"

"Aunt Cora, please, you have to promise. Dad will kill him. He was crazy last night."

"Okay, I promise I won't tell your father."

Letty wasn't stupid.

"You can't tell Mom, either," she said.

I thought fast. I wanted to be her confidante, but if she told me something Ali needed to know, I was going to tell her. I made up my mind to lie.

"All right," I said.

"Say it."

"I promise."

She sighed, believing me. "Okay. He'll be sixteen next month, but he's driving already because he lives so far out."

"Wow, and his parents let him?"

"He just lives with his dad. It's his own car, so I guess he doesn't care. Or, well, I guess he doesn't even really live with his dad anymore."

"Where's his mother?"

"I—I don't know."

She'd clearly never asked. How well did she know this kid?

"Where does he live, then?"

She shrugged and bit her lip. "He's been staying with friends a lot."

I filed that away to come back to later. "So, okay, Seth asks you to this party . . . then what?"

"Well . . ." She stopped speaking and looked up at the ceiling. "See, I knew Mom wouldn't let me stay out late, so I said I was staying at Em's."

She looked at me as if gauging what she could tell me next and then went on in a rush. "And then the cops got called and busted the party, and I told them about Dad and they came to pick me up."

I suppressed a smile. There was an awful lot missing between deciding to lie about staying at Emily's and her parents picking her up.

"What did they have to say?"

"Oh my God, it was unbelievable! It was like he went nuts, and he went through all my stuff. He tore up my whole room, every-thing, went through my clothes, and my drawers, and even all my shoes and boots. And he flipped my mattress up, like I was hiding drugs or something. He took my cell, and my purse, and all my notes, and my diary—"

"And what is he going to find in those?"

She looked down at her knees. "It's not going to be good."

"About Seth?"

She nodded. I tucked my hair behind my ear and peered out the front window to make sure Ali wasn't pulling up. Letty looked fearfully over her shoulder.

"It's okay," I said. "She's not back yet. But listen, Letty, what's going on with Seth? Is he your boyfriend?"

She nodded and wouldn't look at me. I had to ask, but I didn't want to.

"Are you having sex, Letty?" I said it softly, but she still jumped. When she met my eyes the answer was clear, and she looked terrified. "Okay," I said, grasping her hands.

"When did this start?" I asked.

She shook her head. "Just last night," she whispered.

"Oh, Letty." I closed my eyes for a moment, just feeling her hand in mine, trying to adjust to the new reality of who this child now was. It had already happened, couldn't be changed now. When I opened them again she still looked exactly the same. Scared.

"Are you okay?" I asked. "Was it . . . okay?"

I wasn't even sure what I was asking for. I certainly didn't want details. I didn't want to know if she liked it, if Seth was a skillful fifteen-year-old lover.

She looked down, unable to meet my eyes.

"I guess."

I cast back to myself at sixteen, losing my virginity in my own bed at home after school, feeling like sixteen was so old. Some friends had said it hurt, some had said it hadn't. It had for me, but not horribly, not as much as I'd built it up. The boy was a short-term boyfriend, though of course I'd thought it was love at the time. I tried to remember the things I'd felt, the things I was worried about.

"Letty? Did you use birth control?"

She nodded, and I almost shouted *Amen* out loud. I had not, despite knowing all about it, despite being terrified of getting pregnant.

"You're pretty young, honey," I said.

"Almost all my friends have already done it," she said defiantly, but I wasn't buying it.

"Really? At fourteen, all of your friends are having sex already? Is Emily?"

"No. I mean, not all of them, probably, but a lot of them. I'm gonna be fifteen soon."

"I know, sweetie, I remember. It's still pretty young. Are you in love?"

She seemed surprised I'd asked, and for a moment appeared at a loss for what to say. "I—yes, I am," she said.

"Is he a nice guy? Do you go to school with him?" I was trying very hard to not allow my frustration to creep into my voice, to keep her talking and open. I knew I was being traitorous—there was no way I wasn't going to talk to Ali about it—but at least I knew I was doing it for her own good. Which, in itself, made me squirm. I'd rarely ever done anything for my own good, much less anyone else's.

"He's a sophomore," she said. "We have lunch together."

Wow. Lunch together. Romantic. I resisted saying it aloud. "How long have you known him?"

"I don't know, a while."

"And where is he today? What happened to him last night?"

"I don't know," she practically wailed. "Dad took my cell, and I tried to call him when Mom left but there's no answer, and I don't even know if he got home."

A flash of light caught my eye, and I looked over her shoulder to see Ali's car pull into the lot. "Okay, get yourself together, honey, your mom's back."

She looked panicked and grabbed my arm. "Aunt Cora, you can't tell her anything I said, you promised. You can't tell."

I nodded. "Okay, come on now, come on. Get to work."

She scrambled off the stool and was in the storeroom by the time Ali came in, bearing subs. She was surprised to see me but smiled wearily. "Hey, I wish you'd told me you were coming, I'd have gotten you a sub. You can split mine with me."

I waved her off. "No, I already ate."

"All right. Letty!" she called. "Come get lunch!"

She looked at me shrewdly.

"You talk to her?" she asked.

I wanted to grab her arms and blurt out, *Oh my God she has a boyfriend and thinks she's in love and she had sex last night!* But I managed to keep my mouth shut and just nodded as Letty joined us. She held her hand out for her sub, and Ali looked at her for a moment before giving it to her. Letty turned away and started back toward the storeroom.

"You're welcome," Ali said to her retreating back.

"Thank you," came Letty's sullen reply. I heard the storeroom door slam and whistled softly.

Ali sat on the stool and groaned, dropping her head in her hands. "Oh God, Cora, what am I going to do?"

"What happened?" I asked, certain I knew more than she did at the moment.

"Benny has lost his mind," she said.

That I hadn't been expecting. "What do you mean?"

"Well, after he picked me up he accused me of being a bad mother, basically blamed this whole thing on me because I work at the store, and indicated that he'd been miserable for years, because he's responsible, not only for everything in our lives, but for everyone in the state of Florida."

I looked at her in amazement. "Where did all that come from?"

"I have no idea. And then, you should have seen him with Letty, Cora. Five o'clock in the morning, and he's tearing up her room, like she's a criminal. And Letty, you should have seen her—" She stopped with a gasp. "Oh! And you would never guess what she had in her bag. Thongs. Fourteen years old, and the girl is wearing thongs. She went and bought them herself. What the hell is she doing wearing thongs, Cora?"

"Avoiding panty lines?"

She gave me a look.

"Sorry," I said. "Did you ask her?"

She shook her head. "No. It was so late, and I just wanted Benny to calm down and let us all get some sleep. She looked . . ."

"What?"

"When we picked her up, she was a wreck, hair all over the place, way too much makeup. When we got home, Benny made her go change and wash up, and when she came back in the room she was wearing her old pajamas. And they should have made her look younger, but, Cora, I swear, she looked like some little Lolita. It was embarrassing. Benny flipped. He was just—a stranger, he was like someone I didn't even know."

"So what did she have to say? Did you talk to her this morning?"

"Not yet. I don't even know what to say. She's grounded, of course. She's not going out of our sight—oh, that's the other thing," she said, interrupting herself again. "I'm supposed to drive her to school and pick her up every day."

"What about the store?"

"Well, since apparently he doesn't think I should be working here anyway, I'm just supposed to close it up when I go to get her in the afternoon."

"Why can't he do it?"

She sighed and began pulling tomatoes off her sub. "He's on days. Really, it's not that big a deal. The school's only ten minutes away, if that. And I don't want him working nights. It was just that we didn't even *talk* about it."

She suddenly looked at me with narrowed eyes, a plump, deep red tomato slice hanging from the tips of her fingers. I used to love tomatoes. I hadn't had them in months; too much potassium. Some PKD patients had too little potassium, and I envied them their tomatoes the way I used to envy happy, intact families.

"You know, there are a lot of things he's not talking about," Ali continued, oblivious to my tomato obsession. "He never told me he was thinking about going back to being a street cop, he never told me he has these horrible feelings about me. God, Cora, I was convinced we had a really good marriage until just this week. What the hell is going on?"

She laid the glistening tomato slice down on top of the others she'd pulled from the sandwich, and I was tempted to pick them up, en masse, and stuff them in my mouth. I restrained myself and tried to concentrate on my friend rather than her lunch.

"I don't know. Midlife crisis? Stress in general? Ali, you do have a good marriage; you have a great marriage. I don't know exactly what's going on with Benny, but I do know he's been madly in love with you since he was fourteen years old. Try not to worry too much about this. He'll pull it together. He's just having a tough week, being back in his old job and everything. Hey, maybe that's it? Maybe he's not sure he made the right decision?"

"Maybe," she said slowly. "You don't think . . ."

"No," I said. "I don't." And I didn't. If there was one thing Benny had proven it was that he could fully commit to something, and once he did he wouldn't be swayed. I knew he was committed to Ali. He'd never have an affair.

Her face cleared, and she gave a little laugh. "No, of course not."

"So are you going to talk to her together?" I asked, unwilling to spill my info with Letty eating her sub in the storeroom. The least I could do was wait to betray her until Ali and I were alone, but I would rather she told her mother herself.

"When I get her home, we're going to have one long, honest talk. And the honesty part better be coming from her."

"So the big thing is that she lied about staying over at Emily's?"

Ali took a big bite out of the sandwich and shook her head. "I'm not going to go over us doing the same thing at her age—"

"No, no, I wasn't going to say that," I said, though of course I was. I was also going to reference the boy she broke up with Benny for when she was fifteen. The boy she'd lost her virginity to . . . at fifteen. A boy she'd said she was in love with, who'd said he was in love with her.

"Can I still take her up today?"

Ali looked at me incredulously. "Of course not. This is really serious, Cora. I can't just reward her the very next day—"

"Mom, please?" Letty said from the door of the storeroom. I had no idea how long she'd been standing there.

Ali glared at her. "Absolutely not. Are you finished with your lunch? There are fifteen instruments back there for the elementary school that need to be unpacked and checked. You can start on that."

"Mom—" Letty started.

"Go," Ali said, with such hardness in her voice that I was embarrassed.

Letty fled back to the storeroom, and Ali wrapped up the remains of her sub. She hadn't eaten much.

"I don't know what to do with her," she said. "I don't know what to do with *him*. I don't know much, do I?" she asked with a rueful laugh.

"Hey," I said, "why don't you let me help? Just hear me out for a second. Let me take Letty. Let me get her up in the air and talk to her, find out what's going on, and get her out of your hair for a while. You both need a break from each other. In fact, I can keep her for the night, and you can talk to Benny."

"No, Benny would kill me. He's reading all these notes—"

"Yeah, Letty mentioned that. Her diary, too, huh? Was that really necessary?"

She shrugged. "He was just determined. What did you want me to do? Tackle him? I got him calmed down eventually, but, he was just . . . a different person. Or, maybe, he was the same person he's always been; I've just never seen that side. He was the big cop, you know? And maybe he's right. Maybe I've spoiled her, or haven't been paying as much attention as I should."

"Ali, what are you supposed to do? Follow her around every day? Come on."

"You don't understand, Cora."

"Okay, well, help me. I'll be Mom for the night."

Neither of us spoke for a moment. It was the closest we'd ever come to a head-on talk about our shared parentage. She was quiet for a long time, and I let the silence stand. I could take it; Ali had never been able to. I watched her while she looked for something to settle her gaze on.

"I'll bring her back safely," I promised.

She looked at me as though she doubted I'd bring her back at all, but then she raised her eyebrows and nodded curtly.

"All right," she said, her voice perfectly calm, a touch of challenge in it. "Take her. You're right. I need to talk to Benny, and Letty being there is just going to keep him angry all night." She looked at her watch. "If y'all leave right this second you'll have time to grab a few things from the house. You sure you want to do this?"

She had no idea how much. I wanted it even more than I wanted the tomatoes. When I first broached the subject, I had some vague idea that I wanted Letty to know me, to see me at my airborne best. But now, after recognizing my hair on her—albeit a better version of my hair—I realized that I wanted to see *her* in my world. I wanted to see Letty airborne, to see what else we had in common.

"Of course," I said, trying to keep my eagerness out of my voice, and not succeeding entirely.

Ali stared hard at me for another moment, not breaking her gaze when she called Letty's name. The storeroom door opened, and Letty poked her head out.

"What?" she asked, on guard, as if waiting for her next humiliation.

Ali finally looked away from me.

"You're going to stay with Cora tonight. You have about twenty minutes before your father gets ho—"

But Letty was already out of sight. She burst back through the doorway with schoolbooks and folders in her hands. "Let's go, let's go," she said, breathless.

I grabbed my keys. "See you, Al."

"You're welcome," Ali yelled at her daughter as we ran through the front door.

Letty's "Thanks, Mom!" was yelled back to a closing door, and I was doubtful that Ali heard it at all.

I gave the situation an appropriate sense of urgency and floored it all the way to Ali's house, taking corners and curves hard enough that Letty held on to the dashboard. I was concerned for Letty, of course; I didn't want her to have to deal with an angry Benny.

But I was just as concerned for myself. Benny and I had rarely had any open confrontations, but our relationship had always been tenuous, pulling Ali back and forth between us just as often as we gladly handed her off to each other.

I didn't want to start that sort of psychological tug-of-war with Letty. Not now, not when it mattered so much.

I pulled up outside their house and stopped in the street. "Make it fast," I said as Letty leaped out. She did. Within less than five minutes she was back in the car, a big cotton flowered bag gripped to her chest and her eyes scanning the street for Benny's patrol car.

I pulled away and she sank low in the seat as we drove out of the neighborhood, but we didn't pass him, and as we drew closer to my home the atmosphere in the car lightened considerably. I could practically hear her breathing easier.

"How did you do that?" she asked.

"What?"

"Get her to let me come over?"

"Oh, hey, I'm an old pro with your mom," I said, brushing it off. I wasn't going to talk to her about Ali's own problems with Benny. That was up to Ali if she ever wanted to talk to Letty about it. "You can dump your stuff in the guest room, and then, you feel like going flying?"

"Seriously?" she asked.

I laughed at her incredulity, the shock of going from the certainty of a Saturday night filled with her father yelling at her to going flying.

"Seriously," I confirmed.

And I felt, for the first time, what mothers must be reaching for when they have children to begin with. Letty practically glowed with love and appreciation for me, and it was more powerful than the gratitude of a friend, or the longing of a lover. It filled me like water, such deep and perfect satisfaction that I turned my head away from her rather than risk her seeing the rapture of it on my face.

7

A L I

I took my time closing. Benny hadn't called when he got home as he sometimes did, asking me to pick up something to grill for dinner, or just to check in to see how the day had gone. At each half hour I envisioned what he was doing.

First half hour, getting showered and changed, then out to the birds, small chores around the house, maybe, and then he'd have opened the safe to go through all of Letty's notes and her diary. The fact that he'd felt the need to put them in his safe made me even more uncomfortable than the fact that he'd taken them to begin with.

I pictured him girding himself, working out how he would confront her with whatever he found, quizzing . . . no, interrogating her, with me standing by, tacitly approving by my silence. But I'd had no practice with this particular Benny. Supposedly this Benny had been known to criminals, but he was not known to his family.

And despite the fact that I, too, was angry with Letty for lying, was frightened that I hadn't known where she was and had believed her to be safe when she quite likely wasn't, I didn't believe that either of us had deserved Benny's reaction to it.

I was almost an hour later closing than usual, and as I turned the lock on the back door I heard the store phone ringing. Confirming my certainty that it had been Benny, my cell phone rang as I was getting into the car. I didn't answer.

What an odd feeling it was for me to be nervous driving home. I'd always looked forward to seeing Benny, even when he was in one of his down times. I knew that other women spent their lives feeling the way I was feeling now, and I'd always been grateful that I'd never felt it.

But the fear soon turned into something else. Much like in the truck out to Golden Gate the night before, I turned angry. And by the time I pulled into the driveway, not only was I furious for feeling forced into this nervousness and uncertainty, but I practically rushed to the door, ready to confront Benny for being overbearing and cruel.

But when I opened the door, he wasn't waiting for us as I expected him to be. Instead, I found him in our bedroom, lying down, a cool, damp washcloth over his eyes.

"Hey," I said softly, slowly approaching him. "Benny, are you okay?"

He didn't raise the washcloth to look at me, he just shook his head, and I realized with a drop in my stomach that Benny had been crying. I sank to my knees beside the bed and pushed the washcloth up to his forehead.

"Sweetheart, what's going on?" For the first time it crossed my mind that something was truly, terribly wrong with my husband. "What?"

He scrubbed the washcloth across his face and sat up, swinging his knees over the edge of the bed and holding his head in his hands.

"Oh, Ali," he said, his voice gravelly, almost anguished. "I don't know what's wrong with me. I just can't get that kid out of my head."

It took me a moment to figure out who he was talking about.

"Jasper?" I asked.

"Todd, yes, Todd Jasper," he snapped at me, as if we'd been having a conversation about Todd Jasper all along.

"Can you talk to me?" I asked, feeling as anguished as he sounded. A certainty stole over me that something was going to change, something neither of us could prevent.

"I don't know. Last month I started having dreams about him, nightmares . . . horrible things, you don't even want to know, the house blowing up, what would have happened to him, to his body. And I thought once I went back to the street that I'd stop having them. But I haven't. I—"

He broke off and slammed his fist down on the nightstand, making me jump. "Dammit," he swore, and then he ran his hands down his face as though clearing cobwebs away.

"Benny, I didn't know. Why wouldn't you tell me?"

"They're *dreams*, Ali, what was I going to say? Come crying to you like a child?" He looked over at the bedroom door and then back at me. "Where's Letty?" he asked.

"I sent her home with Cora," I said, no longer nervous about it. "I thought we needed to talk alone."

His face darkened, and he rose from the edge of the bed. "You should have checked with me first. I tried to call. Where were you?"

"I must have been locking up," I said. "Now, look, can we talk about these dreams?"

He shook his head. "I don't want to talk about it. I know what I have to do, Ali. I have to get this family back on track. I'm going to take a shower," he said, standing. "And then we'll go pick her up."

"No," I said.

"Oh, yes," he said, starting for the bathroom. It was as though the previous few minutes hadn't even happened.

"No," I said, more forcefully. "You and I are going to figure out what's going on, tonight, together, and without Letty. She's fine where she is."

He turned around and strode toward me so quickly that I involuntarily backed up a step, but he reached past me and grabbed the stack of notes he'd piled on the nightstand in his hand. I hadn't even noticed them when I walked in. They were all opened, pressed flat and neatly stacked.

"Letty is not fine," he shouted. "Our daughter is a foul-mouthed little slut. I couldn't help Todd Jasper, but I'll be damned if I'm not going to do my duty by my own daughter."

I gasped and tried to pull the notes out of his hand, but he held on, and I only succeeded at tearing several of them, leaving me with pieces in my hands. "What are you talking about? How can you say that?"

He threw them on the bed. "Read them," he said, "and then you can tell me about how our daughter's fine."

And with that, he stalked off to the bathroom, leaving me

clutching the torn paper. The bathroom door slammed, and I gathered the notes up and went to the living room, where I curled into a corner of the sofa and read them while the shower ran.

He was certainly right about "foul-mouthed." The notes in her handwriting were filled with swear words, and the notes back to her, from her friends, were just as bad. But it was the sex talk that sickened me. Letty and her friends were not only explicit, but so casual as to appear offhand about their experiences.

But as I more carefully noted the names, I realized that Letty was rarely the instigator of these discussions, and I didn't recognize the girls' names, or sometimes just initials, on the notes. The ones to and from Emily were filled with just as many swear words, but the sex talk was limited to vague suppositions, and it was in these notes that Letty's words rang most true.

The other notes, the ones to and from girls I didn't know, seemed full of bravado more than anything else. But the ones that really surprised me were the ones from a boy, apparently Letty's boyfriend, Seth.

Of course. Of course she had a boyfriend. That was who she went to the party with, and the girls from the notes were probably there, too. In fact, there was even a note about the party from Seth. Yes, the plan was there, to say she was staying at Emily's, and to stay the night with Seth.

I felt sick. I'd never even heard his name before; he wasn't one of the kids Letty had grown up with.

By the time Benny arrived in the living room, his wet hair slicked back, slipping his belt into his jeans, I was over my shock and prepared for how this was going to go. I remained seated, the notes refolded and in my purse this time.

"You ready?" he asked, hardly glancing at me.

"No," I said. "We need to talk."

"We need to talk to Letitia," he said.

"No, I think we need to talk to each other first." I motioned to the other side of the sofa. "Please sit down and talk to me."

"Ali, get up and in the—"

"Okay, stop right there," I said. "For the past two months you've been talking to me like an errant child, and I'm not going to stand for it. It's not how we've ever run our relationship before and it's not going to change now."

"The way we've run our relationship before is the cause of this," he said, not sitting down, but at least not still moving toward the door. "I have to get control back before it all falls apart."

And, like Letty's notes to her best childhood friend, Emily, this finally rang true. Control. That was what Benny had been after. He looked away, raising his fingers to his temples.

"Okay," I said slowly, reasoning it out as I talked. "So you're feeling out of control. What else is out of control, Benny? Me? Letty?"

"That's going to change," he said.

I stared at him, this man I first kissed when I was fifteen years old.

"You've been horrible to me and your daughter for weeks. You've changed jobs without discussing it with me; you've accused me of being a bad mother, a bad wife; you've refused to discuss having another baby, something I want more than anything and that you acted like you wanted for years; and you've got Letty too terrified to even come home. It seems to me that *you're* the one out of control here, Benny."

"I'm not going to discuss having another baby when we can't control the one we have!"

"She's not a baby!" I yelled back, matching his volume, tired of being on the receiving end. "They grow up, Benny, they grow up and they lie and they test you and they do things that make you crazy. That's what they do. That's not a reason to turn into a dictator, and it's not a reason to not have another one."

"Well, I think it is." He clenched his hands, looking for something to do with them, his face red and mottled.

I should have been terrified for him. He looked like someone about to have a heart attack, or a stroke. But instead, I was terrified *of* him.

"I'm not going to stay here when you're this angry, and I'm not going to expose Letty to it, either," I said, my voice trembling.

"If you walk out that door, Ali, don't be so sure that it's going to be open when you decide to come back."

I shook all the way over to Cora's.

LETTY

She knew she had a huge stupid grin on her face, but she just didn't care. The very worst day of her life was so completely the best day ever now. She and her mom had flown to Arizona to visit her grandparents when she was, like, seven, and then her whole class flew to Washington, D.C., last year for their eighth-grade class trip, but she'd never been in one of these little planes before.

The only thing she could compare it to was when they'd go to Busch Gardens and go on the roller coasters. Not because it was so scary, but because she felt so light in the middle, like she was filled with helium, and she couldn't stop grinning.

"How you doing?" Aunt Cora called over to her, and all she could do was grin and nod her head, peering down through the windows to look at the water below.

"Put your hands on," Aunt Cora said, tilting her head toward the steering wheel thing in front of Letty. It was going up and down and turning the same way hers was.

She laughed and shook her head. "No way. I'll crash us," she said.

"No, you won't. I'll have control the whole time. Come on, it's fun."

Letty touched the wheel with her fingers and pulled them back quickly when it moved, laughing. Aunt Cora laughed, too.

"Okay," she said, more to herself than to Aunt Cora, and she lightly wrapped her hands around the sides. And she knew that she wasn't flying the plane, but oh, man, it almost felt like she was. She gripped it a little firmer, and it was like she could feel everything around them, like her whole body was set up to do this one thing.

"Want to go up a little?" Aunt Cora asked, and she nodded, not looking at her.

She knew Aunt Cora was in control, but now that she was touching the wheel she felt like she'd better watch where they were going.

"Okay, just pull back a little, like this," Aunt Cora said, pulling the wheel toward her, real slow and smooth.

She pushed it away again, and they leveled out.

"Really?" Letty asked, breathless.

Aunt Cora nodded. "Yeah, go on, I'm right here, I won't let it go too far."

So she pulled it a little toward her; it was harder than she thought, but she didn't want to give it too much and jerk them up into the sun or anything, so she just kept steady, and there it came, and they were going up!

She laughed out loud, screaming a little, and Aunt Cora was laughing along with her again, and she had never, ever, not once in her life, not with Seth, or her mom and dad, or Emily, ever felt so exactly perfect in her whole life.

She couldn't stop talking about it on the way home, and Aunt Cora was all happy and acting like she knew just how it felt. When they got back to the house, Aunt Cora said she was really tired and wanted to lie down, but Letty was so hyped up that she wanted to do something, and she figured it would be nice if she cleaned the pool as a surprise.

So when Aunt Cora closed her door, she found the stuff in the garage and got to work, and just as she was finishing up and thinking about diving in, she heard a car out front.

What if her dad had changed his mind and come to get her? She went out the patio screen door and walked around the side of the house to peer at the driveway.

It wasn't her dad, it was her mom, and she watched her sit in the car, her head on the steering wheel, for a minute before she approached, looking down the street to make sure her dad wasn't right behind.

Her mom jumped when she got to the window, like she'd scared her, and then she rolled the window down. She was crying, but she was mad at the same time.

"Go inside, Letty," she said, wiping her eyes. "I'll be there in a minute."

"Okay," Letty said, and all the good feelings from the flying just drained away. She went inside and curled up on the bed in the guest room.

Her mom didn't come in for a long time.

CORA

Letty woke me by sitting gingerly on the edge of my bed. I had no idea how long I had slept, but the room was gloomy and my thoughts muddled, so I had clearly been out longer than I would have preferred.

"Hey," she whispered.

I sat up and ran my hands through my hair, hoping that I didn't look like pure hell in front of her.

"Hey, yourself," I said. "Sorry I conked out on you. Are you starving?"

She shook her head. "Mom's here."

"She is? Is everything okay?"

"She's in the pool. She told me to not bother you."

"She's in the pool? It's filthy."

"I cleaned it. The chemicals were way off, so it's still really cloudy, but it should be okay by tomorrow. I turned on the pump and everything."

"How do you know how to do all that?"

She shrugged, a proud little tight smile on her face. "It's one of my chores. Dad showed me how to do it all."

"Nice job, thanks, Letty. So, how long has she been here?"

"Maybe an hour, but she was crying when she got here."

That woke me up.

"All right, why don't you give us a few minutes, and then change into your suit; we'll all go for a swim, and maybe we'll walk down to the beach for sunset?"

"Okay." She stood and walked toward the door but paused for a moment, turning back to me with a troubled look on her face. "Aunt Cora? Did you tell her?"

I'd been thinking about Ali and Benny, and it took me a moment to remember what Letty was talking about. But I recalled Seth soon enough and shook my head.

"No, I didn't tell her. Don't worry, this isn't about you. I know it must seem like it, but it's not."

I'd meant the words to comfort her, but it was clear from the look on her face that I had only worried her further. She turned away, and I heard the guest room door close a moment later. When I got out to the pool, Ali was on a green rubber float, her eyes closed. I slipped into the cool, cloudy water, my nose filling with the odor of the chemicals Letty had so recently dumped into the water.

I swam out to the float as Ali opened her eyes.

"What's going on?" I asked, skipping the niceties.

"Oh, Cora, I had no idea." Her voice was bleak.

"What?" I insisted.

She glanced toward the house.

"She's in the guest room. I told her to give us a few minutes."

"I think I just left Benny."

I gripped the edge of the float, staring at her in shock. This I had not ever expected. It simply wasn't possible.

"No," I said. "Get over here."

I swam, one-armed, for the steps, dragging the float behind me. She stared at the screen overhead and let me pull her to the edge without protest. I got out and wrapped myself in a towel and then held one out for her, but she didn't move. She simply looked at the colorful beach towel hanging from my hands, her face slack, as if she had no idea what it might be for.

"Come on, Ali. Get out of the pool."

She clumsily flopped off the float and walked into the cocoon of the towel, finally settling it around her waist and sitting on the edge of a lounge chair. I dragged a patio chair over and sat in front of her, staring at her until she finally looked at me.

"Now. What do you mean you left him?"

"I mean, well, I don't know that I *left* him, for good. But I'm not going back until he gets some help."

"What happened?"

"He scared me, Cora."

I gaped at her. I couldn't imagine Benny frightening anyone, but once she told me the whole story I was a little afraid of him myself, and Ali had always been more afraid of confrontation than I was.

She looked past me, out toward the areca palms that shaded the patio, crowding closer every year, their copper and green fronds pressing against the screen, desperate to get in and take over the pool.

"So, I left."

I reached out and took her hand in mine. "You did the right thing, Ali. I'm so sorry, but listen, Benny loves you, and you love him, and he'll get help, okay?"

She nodded, but she looked miserable. I felt terrible for her, and I also felt sorry for Benny. But I certainly wasn't going to admit it.

"Hey, Ali, Benny's a bit of an anachronism, don't you think? I think he sort of sees the world in a really idealistic way. It's no wonder he became a cop; he wants everything to be in order, to make sense. And when something like this happens, something that doesn't make any sense to him, the death of a boy who was just like him, I bet it freaks him out. Moving back to being a street cop is probably going to be really good for him. He hasn't had an outlet for this . . . what? Moral outrage?"

Ali gave a small laugh, but she was listening.

"I'd be willing to bet that he just needs some action in his life, a way to feel like he's really helping. Benny's not a naturally angry guy, and he loves you so much. It'll calm down, you'll see."

"Mom?" Letty's voice came from a crack in the sliding glass door, sounding young and scared.

Ali said, "In a minute, Let," at the same time I said, "It's okay, come on out."

I don't know that I was louder than Ali, but Letty wasn't about to sit in the house any longer, and she rumbled the slider open as soon as the "okay" was out of my mouth, approaching her mother cautiously.

"Hey, punkin," Ali said, patting the lounge.

Letty looked at me quickly.

"Sit down," I said, giving her a reassuring smile.

She lowered herself onto the edge of the lounge slowly, looking between us as if certain she was about to be set upon and interrogated.

"What's going on?" Letty asked.

"Everything's fine," Ali said. "We're going to stay here for a few days, give us all a break from each other."

Letty looked back and forth between us in panic. "What do you mean? What's Dad doing?"

"Don't worry, Letty," Ali said, but it was clear that Letty was going to worry. "Everything is going to stay the same, Dad's going to go to work, you're going to go to school, I'm going to run the store. We're just going to stay with Cora for a bit . . . if that's okay?" Ali looked at me as if suddenly aware that she'd never asked if they could stay, as if she had to.

"Of course," I said. "It's going to be fun."

"You're still grounded," Ali told Letty, who appeared even more confused.

"Why can't we go home?" she asked. "Did Dad . . . did he tell us to leave?"

"No, not at all," Ali reassured her. "Your dad is under a lot of stress at work, and we both think it's a good idea if he can get into the routine of this new job without worrying about us."

None of us were fooled by Ali's light tone, and Letty kept that worried furrow between her young eyes for the rest of the weekend, despite my attempts to snap her out of it.

Ali took Letty to school on Monday, and I picked her up, taking her to the airfield to cheer her up. She wasn't the only one who needed the distraction. Dr. MacKinnon had called with my appointment with the vascular surgeon to have my graft put in place, and I was in sore need of something to take my mind off it.

MacKinnon thought a visit to the dialysis center would be just the thing. I told him he had an interesting sense of humor, but on Wednesday I found myself changing clothes three times, as if I were going on a first date, and driving to the dialysis center across from the hospital.

I sat in the parking lot for more than half an hour looking at the center and fantasizing about going to the coffee shop across the street for a contraband espresso instead. I'd quit caffeine as abruptly as I'd quit potato chips, and I wasn't sure which I missed more on most days. But when considering basic quality of life— and staring at that facility from the parking lot made me consider hard—coffee won, hands down.

The center was painted a dusky pink, an odd sunset of a building that held me mesmerized, envisioning the shadowy goings-on within it.

Nobody entered and nobody exited for the thirty minutes I sat there. I'd hoped to get a glimpse of a human, some living breathing thing I could use as a barometer of what to expect, but nothing moved until I finally did.

Research, I told myself. *Go do your research. It's all black and white. Knowledge is the only thing in our control.*

And so I went.

The social worker gave me the tour. She was lovely, and informative, and encouraged me to come back the next week to sit in on a patient meeting. And she was careful to not overwhelm me.

And I wanted to shake her.

Because I wanted, *needed,* to be overwhelmed, because I knew how to be obsessive, and I knew how to use information as a way to hide, and if ever there was a time I wanted to hide, it was right then.

The scale across from the front desk was like something you'd see in a veterinarian's office, and I stepped on its shiny metal surface briefly, felt the change under my shoes, felt the chill of it radiating up my ankles, then stepped off it to follow the social worker into the main room of the center. The room with the chairs, the machines.

The people.

The chairs were arranged in groups of four, a *pod*, the social worker said, like the patients were happy peas. There was one empty pod toward the back, and I followed her to it, trying to not stare at the people in the chairs, all of them covered to the neck in blankets, as we passed. It was quiet, individual televisions attached to the chairs turned low, technicians tapping keyboards.

One woman knitted, and a young man in a baseball cap read, iPod buds firmly planted in his ears. Everyone else appeared to be either watching TV or sleeping, and I wondered how I would fill my time, unable to even get up to use the bathroom or walk around. I didn't see myself taking up knitting.

As the social worker pointed out the features of the chair to me (heated, massage), I felt eyes on me and turned to find the young man in the hat gazing at me frankly, sweeping up and down my frame. Had I been younger, or even simply looked better, I might have thought he was checking me out, but no, this was just the standard fellow patient assessment.

We were the youngest two patients in the room, aside from a woman in the first pod who had fallen asleep, two framed photos on the tray in front of her. He, of course, wondered what was wrong with me, and I couldn't help but wonder what was wrong with him.

"Cora?" the social worker prodded me, and I realized that I hadn't heard anything she'd said for several minutes. She was gesturing at the chair.

"Sorry," I said, trying to concentrate.

"You'll have the same team every time, you'll have the same chair, the same dialyzer. Everything is computerized, and your information will be automatically sent to Dr. MacKinnon as well as to your insurance."

She smiled and nodded at me as if expecting something in return.

"That's . . . efficient," I said.

She tilted her head at me, and I struggled to recall her name.

"Dee," I finally said, "he's so young . . ."

Her eyes never left my face. "Yes."

I didn't continue. I didn't want to know, and it was obvious that she wouldn't tell me anyway. I supposed I should have been grateful for that; at least they took patient confidentiality seriously.

"Would you like to meet the dietitian today?" Dee asked gently.

I realized, abruptly, and with gratitude, that Dee was very, very good at her job. I was—had been—good at my job, and I knew the signs. And Dee had them. She'd paid attention; she'd adjusted her tone of voice and amount of information; she'd let me feel in control.

I needed that.

"No," I said. "Thank you, though."

"Okay. We're here for anything you need, any questions you have; any time you want to stop back in, we're here."

It should have been reassuring, and yet it filled me with dread.

"I have a lot of information for you, cookbooks, and information packets, and, oh, just about anything you might have questions about. Why don't you grab a seat, and I'll get it all together for you?"

"Okay," I said, smiling at a tired-looking woman in the reception area and taking a chair next to the door.

"Picking up?' the woman asked as Dee left.

"Oh, no," I said, leaving it at that. She wasn't deterred.

"Getting information? For you?"

I cleared my throat and looked toward the hallway Dee had disappeared down.

"Yes. For me."

"When will you start?"

"Don't really know," I said, shaking my head.

The woman tilted her head to the side and studied me, then smiled, leaned forward, and stuck her hand out. "I'm Susan. Brandon, my son, likes me to be here toward the end. When he was younger, we had a few problems when they disconnected. Now, well, now it's just a tradition, you know?"

I didn't, no, but I nodded and shook her hand, and said, "I'm Cora."

"Is this your first visit?"

"Yes, it is." And then, because she seemed to be waiting for me to make polite conversation, I asked, "Has Brandon been coming for long?"

"Oh, yes, since he was about seven. He's nineteen now; we just moved him over from the pediatric center last year. They're good here; we've only had a couple of problems, cramping, you know. And sometimes that just can't be helped. So, you haven't started yet? Got your access?"

"Uh, next week, a graft."

She appraised me again, as if she could see beneath my skin. "Anyone step up for a transplant yet?"

I laughed, shocked at her boldness, but I supposed when you'd been doing this for three days a week for twelve years, this might be a perfectly normal conversation to have.

"No. How about for Brandon?"

"Oh, yeah, we've gotten the call four times. None ever came through, though. I gave him one of mine when he was eleven, but he rejected at fifteen, so it's been back on hemo ever since."

I didn't laugh at that. Susan hooked her thumb toward the woman with the frames on her tray and lowered her voice.

"Flora, she's been called eight times. But no luck. Her girls—you'll see them when you leave, they wait outside with their grandmother—they're the most beautiful little things you've ever seen. Do you have children?"

"I—no, I don't," I replied.

She nodded. "It's tough on kids, watching parents go through this." She laughed a little. "'Course it's hard on parents watching their kids go through it, too."

Dee returned with a stack of pamphlets, and I thanked her and stood to leave. Susan looked at her watch and stood, too.

"Hey," she said, "why don't you come back and meet him before you go?"

"Oh, no," I said. "I don't want to disturb anyone."

"He'd really love it," she said. "It can get pretty boring for him here."

"Well, okay," I said, shrinking from it but unable to resist her hopeful expression. Dee patted my arm as I followed Susan back to the third pod. The technician looked up from her computer at us and smiled.

"We'll be about fifteen more minutes," she said softly, and Susan nodded.

"Thanks, Shelly. I want to introduce him to a new friend real quick."

"Okay," she said.

Brandon looked up expectantly as we approached, yanking his earbuds out by the cord.

"Brandon, this is Cora," Susan said. "She's going to start hemo soon. I thought she'd like to meet you."

He gave me that steady once-over again.

"I'm doing my orientation," I said, feeling the need to explain my presence.

He leaned his head back against the chair.

"Yeah, that's what I figured. You got that look."

I didn't ask what look, and he didn't elaborate.

"When do you start?"

"I'm not sure yet," I said. "They're doing my access next week."

"Well, when you start, try to get a chair next to me. I'll tell you everything you need to know."

I smiled at him, the ambassador of dialysis. His sullenness seemed more like simple fatigue to me now, something I could readily identify with.

"We're about ready," Shelly said pointedly.

"Okay, well, it was nice to meet you, Brandon."

"See you later," he said.

Susan walked me back to the corridor.

"Thanks," she said. "He's such a good kid, and he likes meeting new people."

"Well, good luck. I hope you get a good call soon and it works out."

"Oh, we will," she said. "I have to go, but listen, good luck to you, too, okay? This isn't the end, you know? You can have a whole happy life on dialysis; it's all in what you bring to it."

"Thanks," I said, trying for a smile, fearing that it appeared as little more than a grimace, and dropped it, raising a hand instead.

As I left I passed an older woman sitting on the bench outside, watching two little girls playing in the grass beside the center, their dark hair lifting in the breeze. She gave me a wave, and I waved back but hustled to the car, avoiding more conversation and thinking about Flora, the girls' mother who wouldn't allow them inside.

I slumped in the driver's seat, letting the heat that had built up envelop me, unable to start the car for a few minutes, thinking of Brandon, and Flora, and the community I was about to join against my will.

When I finally had the strength to start the car, I drove across the street to the coffee shop and had a double espresso.

8

A L I

Benny and I continued our fight on the phone for the first week, and I hovered close by when he had brief conversations with a subdued Letty, watching for any signs that he was taking his anger out on her. But eventually his tone gentled, and we started having short bursts of affectionate, playful banter that wove in and out of our more serious talks.

He started to drive past the store a couple of times a day in his cruiser. He never stopped, and I'd found myself watching for him, looking forward to it, raising my hand in a wave that he returned with a hesitant half salute of his own.

After almost two weeks had passed, he called me on my cell after work. I smiled involuntarily when I saw his name pop up on the phone display and answered before it had a chance to ring twice.

"Hey," I said.

"Hey, Al. How are you? Are you okay? How's Letty?" he asked in a rush, as if afraid I'd hang up.

"I'm fine, Letty's fine. How are you?"

"I'm doing okay. I just wanted to call to tell you that I've been doing a lot of thinking."

"Okay," I said cautiously.

"Well, I thought you should know," he said, pausing and taking a deep breath before continuing quickly, "I've set up an appointment with the department psychologist."

"Really? When?"

"He wants me to come in Tuesday and Thursday next week. It was the first time he could get me in."

"Twice?" I asked. "You told him what was happening?"

"Yeah, I told him, you know, as much as I could without going in for a full visit," he said.

"That's good, Benny. Are you still having the nightmares?"

He was silent for a moment, and then said, "Yeah. I'm not sleeping much, though. I miss you. I miss Letty."

"We miss you, too," I whispered.

"Is she there? Could I talk to her?"

"She and Cora walked down to the beach," I said, "but I'll have her call you later."

"Is she being good for you?" he asked. "Where she's supposed to be, and when?"

"She's doing fine. Don't worry, she's being punished appropriately."

Of course she wasn't, not really. I dropped her at school and Cora picked her up, and she didn't go anywhere without one or both of us, but she'd been flying again, and we'd been out to dinner a couple of times. She wasn't exactly suffering. I knew I was probably being too light on her.

"Of course. You—" He stopped and cleared his throat. "You were right to leave, Ali. You're a good example for Letty. You're a good mother to our daughter, the best I could have hoped for."

I closed my eyes, savoring the sound of his voice.

"Thank you," I said.

"I'm going to get it together, okay?"

"Okay. Why don't you call me after your appointment on Tuesday?"

"All right. And you call me whenever you want, doesn't matter what time it is."

That was more the Benny I knew, and when we hung up, I looked around my borrowed room at Cora's and took a deep, shaky breath. I never thought I'd be in this position, never thought I'd have left my home, left Benny, but then I'd never thought my gentle husband was capable of frightening me into leaving.

Thank God Cora was here. I didn't know what I would do with Letty, what I would do with myself. I changed into a bathing suit and inspected one of the old bikes in Cora's garage, pulling out a cobwebbed pump and plumping up the tires before throwing a towel and some water bottles into the basket and heading down to the beach after Letty and Cora.

When we were kids, we'd make this short trek almost every day, even in the rain. The beach was open season, always, trusted by us and by our parents. We'd drop our bikes next to the sea grapes, no need to lock them up, and when we actually had shoes on, they'd go next to the bikes.

I carefully locked Cora's bike onto the stand and pulled the removable basket off the handlebars, stuffing my flip-flops into it before heading down the walkway. The sand was still hot enough to hurt, and I hurried down to the water before looking around for Cora and Letty. They were nowhere to be seen, but I spotted Cora's beach quilt, an ancient, faded thing that made me smile with nostalgia.

I dropped my things and lay down on my back, pushing my sunglasses to the top of my head to get some sun on my face. When we were teenagers, the need for sunscreen had not yet appeared on our radar, and we drenched ourselves in baby oil and iodine, and, oddly enough, I'd not yet begun to be sorry for it.

In fact, considering we were in our forties, both Cora and I seemed to be holding up pretty well. Aside from her being a little sick and bloated on this visit, Cora still had the smile and personality of the girl I'd met on this very beach thirty years ago. She could still drive me crazy, too. I'd been trying to talk to her about Drew all week, but she'd avoided my questions and sought out ways to include Letty in our every conversation.

I should have been able to relax. It was quiet on the beach but for the soft, rhythmic rush of the Gulf meeting the edge of the beach and the occasional cry of a seagull. But my mind wouldn't settle, wouldn't accept this rare moment of quiet. I put my sunglasses back in place and sat up, scanning the beach for Cora and Letty again. I finally stood and waded out into the water. As I cooled off I spotted them, walking along the water's edge, back toward the quilt, and my breath caught at the sight of them.

Letty was almost as tall as Cora, and seeing them side by side, in bathing suits, brightly lit by the sun and framed by the blue backdrop of a cloudless sky, I realized that they could have been sisters, or, more accurately, mother and daughter.

They had the same shape: the slender neck, slim hips, long legs, the same hair, the same jawline. The few die-hards left on the beach faded from my sight, and I was suddenly alone except for those two women walking toward me. The current pushed lightly, and I let it take control of me, weaving back and forth with it, hypnotizing me with its rhythm, Cora and Letty like identical, hazy mirages in the distance.

As they drew closer I saw the differences, but now that I'd seen the similarities I couldn't pretend they weren't there. They split as they approached, Letty headed toward the quilt, Cora headed toward me.

"Hey," she called as she waded in. "I thought that was you. Glad you changed your mind."

I forced a smile to my face, seeing Letty in Cora's wide grin, in the light freckles across her chest, hearing her in Cora's voice.

"Yeah," I said. "I wanted to talk to Letty. You know, this thing with Benny has sort of taken the heat off her—"

"Oh no," she interrupted me. "If anything it's made her feel even worse. She thinks this is all her fault, you know."

I sighed. "Of course I know that, but there's only so much I can reassure her that it's not. And this was serious, Cora. There are things we need to talk about, things that were in those notes. If Benny and I weren't in the middle of this, I can tell you she sure wouldn't be having a day at the beach."

"Oh, Ali, let it go, huh? Look, her birthday is coming up, she's been beating herself up over something she doesn't understand and that isn't her fault, and—no, wait a second—she screwed up, and she's feeling pretty badly about it. I think if you wanted to punish her, you're doing fine. Just relax, huh?"

I laughed, I couldn't help it. She looked so earnest.

"All right, well, if you won't do it for her, then could you do it for me?"

"What do you mean?" I asked.

"Ali, I'm only here for a little while. I want to have some fun with you."

"Well, I'm sorry it doesn't happen to be a fun time in my life right now, Cora."

"I know. But, it's not a fun time in my life right now, either, and it's definitely not a fun time in Letty's life. So, since we're all not having a fun time in life together, couldn't we just forget about it for a few days? I'll be gone soon enough, you and Benny will work things out, and you can punish hell out of the girl. Lock her in the basement and feed her scraps. I'll send manacles."

I shook my head at her. "You're crazy."

But I listened.

And we did have fun. Cora picked Letty up from school and either took her back to her house to swim and do homework, or brought her to the store to work, and I even agreed to another trip to the airfield as a birthday treat.

But the most fun we had was when we walked down to the beach for the sunset each evening. The absence of the things that seemed to take up our time when we were at home—bills and grocery shopping for me, texting and Internet and television for Letty—turned into freedom to do something we hadn't done for a long time: We talked.

I had forgotten, at some point in the past few years, that I could have a fun conversation with my daughter, and she added a new dimension, a valid viewpoint, to the same conversations that Cora and I had been having for almost thirty years. I watched her, and listened, and was surprised by the fact that Letty was funny, as clever as Cora, and as thoughtful as Benny.

On Tuesday Benny called after his appointment with Dr. Weist. I didn't ask for a blow-by-blow account, though I was intensely curious. I thought he should have some sense of doing this as much for himself as for me and Letty, and respecting his privacy felt like an important part of that.

"What about Letty's birthday?" he asked.

"I thought we'd go out to dinner. Letty wants Emily to go, of course, and then I'll take the girls to the mall. I picked up a gift certificate for her from both of us."

"Thanks, I wasn't sure what to do. What about dinner?"

"We'd like you to come."

"Yeah?"

"Of course."

"Okay. All right, that's great. I'll see you tomorrow, then?"

"I'll see you tomorrow, Benny."

I had a date with my husband.

LETTY

Seth had been staying at the abandoned house in her neighborhood ever since the week after the party. The cops had towed his car because the tags were out of date, and even if he had the money to get it, he didn't think they'd let him take it, since he wasn't sixteen yet and didn't have insurance, so Scott was picking him up in the mornings.

They'd all skipped out at lunch a couple of times to go over to the house, but Scott never left her and Seth alone, so they didn't get to talk much.

Seth showed them how he slid a pane of glass out of the jalousie door in the carport. Then all he had to do was slip his hand in to unlock the door. He was showering in the mornings in the locker room at school when the swim team went in.

She didn't know what to do to help him, and she didn't even know why he couldn't go home. Whenever she started to ask him about it, he just got mad. Not at her, but just in general, and so she left him alone, and they mostly saw each other in the lunchroom and in the hall between classes.

At lunch on Tuesday she left the table when Seth went to get a soda and found Emily on the other side of the lunchroom, sitting with a couple of kids they'd gone to middle school with. Hardly anyone said hello to her, and even Emily looked like she didn't really want to talk. She sat down anyway.

"Are you still going to dinner with us tomorrow?"

Emily shrugged. "Why don't you take Seth?" she asked, looking at her like she was challenging her or something. Everyone at the table was staring at them.

"Come on, Em," she said, talking real soft so not everyone in the place could hear. "We always have our birthdays together."

Emily looked down at her plate.

"Fine," she said.

"We'll pick you up at six?"

"Yeah, okay. I didn't get you anything." She looked back up at her, like she was mad again all of a sudden.

"That's okay," Letty said. "Mom is giving me a gift certificate for the mall, so maybe we can go after. I'll share it with you."

Emily didn't say anything for a second, like she was thinking about it. "Okay," she finally said, and then she looked up over Letty's shoulder.

Seth put his hands on Letty's upper arms and squeezed, and she stood up right away.

"I'll see you later," she said, and Emily nodded, not saying anything to Seth, though to be fair, he didn't exactly say anything to her or anyone else at the table.

There were fifteen minutes left of lunch, and they went out to the courtyard, slipping around the back to sit on the low wall by the parking lot. There used to be bushes and flowers and stuff in the planters, but now there were mostly cigarette butts and trash.

"So, I have to go up to my cousin's place in Venice," he said. "I thought maybe you'd go with me."

"What? When?"

"Well, I figured you'd want me here for your birthday, even though I'm not invited to *dinner*, so I guess Thursday."

"What about school?"

He shrugged. "I don't have any tests or anything. It's just for the day."

"Seth? Can I ask you something, and just tell me, okay, don't get mad?"

He looked over her head for a minute and didn't answer, but then he finally looked at her and said, "Yeah, all right."

"Why can't you go home?"

He sighed, and she just wanted to hug him, to tell him everything would be okay, but if she did that he wouldn't answer, so she just looked at him, and he finally told her.

"My dad, he let this other guy move in, like a roommate you know? He took my room, and we don't get along so good, so I don't want to go back there anyway."

"He let him have your room?" she asked in disbelief.

"I was going to get out of there soon anyway," he said.

"But you can't keep staying at that house," she said. "What if you get caught?"

"Where else am I supposed to go? I won't get caught. Now, are you going to Venice with me or not?"

He leaned forward and kissed her, and she knew that she would go.

On her birthday her mom made pancakes for breakfast and was really nice when she dropped her off. When Aunt Cora picked her up that afternoon, her and Seth's plans were all worked out. She was wearing the necklace he got her for her birthday, and she could tell Aunt Cora noticed it right away, but she didn't say anything.

She'd taken her flying again the day before—an early birthday present, she'd said—and it was just as incredible as she had remembered it. She thought that maybe she could be a pilot when she got older, and she and Seth could have one of those houses in central Florida like John Travolta had, where you could keep your plane right by your house, like it was a car.

"Can we go by my house?" she asked. "Dad won't be home for hours, and I need more clothes."

She went straight to her parents' room first, leaving Aunt Cora to find something to drink in the fridge. She looked everywhere, under the bed, in the dresser, and finally found her purse and cell phone on top of his gun safe in the closet.

Aunt Cora came in just as she left the closet and stood, leaning in the doorway with a soda in her hand, looking around the bedroom. She didn't even seem at all suspicious of why Letty was in her parents' room.

"I'll grab some clothes," she said as she rushed past her.

Aunt Cora was still in her parents' room when she came back, staring at the framed articles and pictures on the Miracle Wall. She was standing really still, looking at the *People* cover, and she didn't even hear Letty come in. But she must have made some kind of noise, because Aunt Cora jumped a little and looked like she'd been caught doing something she wasn't supposed to.

She was pretty, Letty suddenly realized. Not, like, Barbie pretty, but just really naturally pretty, even though she'd gained weight and her face was a lot rounder than it was on the *People* cover.

"I can't believe how much you've grown up," Aunt Cora said, not moving from in front of the wall. Letty dropped her bag on the bed and went to stand next to her, both of them looking at the articles and pictures.

"Yeah," Letty said, looking at the cheesy studio photos, where she was in frilly dresses and posed with angel wings and big plastic letters. She couldn't believe she was ever so small. She realized that Aunt Cora was turned toward her, staring at her, but it just felt too weird to turn and look back at her, so she pretended she didn't notice.

She moved away from her a little, toward the corner, where the pictures and articles stopped. Her mom had stopped putting pictures up a few years ago. She didn't know why. Maybe because she always acted like it was so embarrassing. She could see out of the corner of her eye that Aunt Cora had stopped looking at her and was looking at the wall again.

"What do you think about all this?" Aunt Cora suddenly asked, waving her hand at the wall.

Letty shrugged. "I—I don't know. You mean the pictures?"

Aunt Cora turned around fully toward her then, like she was irritated or something and touched her on the shoulder.

"What?" Letty asked, finally looking at her.

"It's weird, right?" she asked.

Letty nodded.

"Look," Aunt Cora said, "I just want you to know that I am really proud to have been a part of this. I feel as though I did something really important in my life when I look at you, Letty."

Letty didn't know where to look. Aunt Cora stayed quiet and just looked at her.

"How come you never had kids?" Letty asked. It was something she'd always wondered, but she'd never even talked to her mom about it. Aunt Cora looked surprised.

"I guess I never thought it was necessary to complete my life," she said after a minute. "Not the way it was for your mother."

"But did you ever just want them?"

She looked over at the pictures again.

"No. Actually, no, I didn't. I never felt that urge, that deep desire to be a mother. I think that maybe because I knew your mom, knew what that real, deep-seated desire to have a child was from her for so long, that I realized that if I didn't feel it like that, I probably shouldn't do it."

When she finished, she looked at Letty with her eyebrows raised, like she was looking for her approval.

"Are you ever sorry?" Letty asked.

Aunt Cora smiled. "Sometimes," she said. "But then I hear about what you're doing, or your mom sends me a picture, and I know that my role in having children was the one that I chose."

Letty looked back at the photo, and she saw what Seth had seen, what Aunt Cora saw, and she was okay with it. She did look like her, and that wasn't exactly a bad thing.

"Do you think I could learn to fly planes?" she asked.

Aunt Cora laughed, like she was surprised again. Letty had never known she was so surprising.

"I don't see why not," Aunt Cora said. "It's work, a lot of homework. And it's expensive. Lessons are pricey, and you know how much fuel costs? And how much you use, just flying around the way we've done?"

"I could get a job," she said. Aunt Cora looked pleased.

"I think that's a great idea. Maybe your mom would like some help at the store? You know she worked there all through high school."

"Maybe," she said, but she didn't think her mom wanted help at the store, especially her help. "Do you think they'll get back together?" she asked, afraid to ask it, but more afraid not to.

"Get back together?" Aunt Cora repeated. "They're not apart, Letty. Stop worrying about your parents, okay? They're fine, and this has nothing to do with you."

Nothing to do with her? Then why had they been staying at Aunt Cora's for weeks? What was wrong? But there was definitely something, because Aunt Cora looked guilty, like she'd said something she shouldn't have.

"Letty," Aunt Cora said, and for one of the first times ever she talked to her like she was a little kid. "Sometimes parents just need a little time away from each other, that's all. It's going to be fine, I promise."

Letty stared at her. She hated it when people lied to her.

*　*　*

Her birthday dinner sucked.

Emily acted weird, and it was obvious to everyone that she didn't like Letty anymore. She didn't really know what to do about that. She had friends when she was a kid that she wasn't friends with anymore, but she'd always thought she and Emily would wind up being like her mom and Aunt Cora.

They even used to pretend to be them when they played. When Letty got her period first and it took Emily forever, they even thought that maybe she'd never get it and then Letty would have a baby for her when she wanted one. But she did finally get it, of course.

At dinner Emily mostly talked to Aunt Cora and her dad, and she watched her, thinking about the fact that she didn't even know that she and Seth had had sex. Only six months ago she would have sneaked into the bathroom right after to call and tell her, but it had been more than two weeks and they still hadn't even talked about it.

But her dad was the worst part of all of it. She could tell that he wanted to hug her, but he acted like he wasn't sure she would want to, and so they wound up sort of half-hugging, like the guys did at school. He didn't even give her a present. He said the gift certificate was from him, too, but she thought probably Mom had gotten that on her own. She didn't even want to go shopping after dinner anymore.

Her mom didn't say much during dinner, and then afterward, once half the restaurant sang "Happy Birthday," she and Emily went to the bathroom. They were in there for only a minute, and it was almost like they were going to start talking like they used to when Aunt Cora came in. Letty went back to the table, leaving Emily washing her hands.

The chairs were empty, and the waiter was already clearing the dishes. He nodded toward the front doors, and Letty could see her parents on the sidewalk, talking.

The front doors were double swinging doors with lots of little windows in them, and she got right up close to them and could hear a little bit.

They weren't even talking about her.

They were talking about having another baby.

"I've been giving it a lot of thought," her dad said. "And you're right. I was having a hard time separating Todd Jasper from all of this. I'm working on it. I'm willing to at least talk about it if you really want another baby."

"Really? Are you sure?"

Her mother had her hand on her chest, and she sounded super excited. Her dad put his hands on her shoulders, and she tilted her head up to look at him. They didn't look mad at each other at all anymore.

He took a really deep breath with his eyes closed, and then he leaned down and kissed her mom lightly on the lips.

"I've missed you."

He didn't say anything about Letty.

CORA

When Letty wasn't waiting in front of the school on Thursday afternoon, I wasn't worried. I leaned my head back against the seat and let my mind wander, allowing myself to pretend that this was my life, that I was waiting for my daughter to come out, even allowing myself a little motherly irritation at her for making me wait.

I didn't see any harm in it. Haven't we all pretended, just for a few minutes, to be living a different life?

After we'd dropped off a strangely subdued Emily, the shopping trip at the mall relegated to another time after Letty said she didn't want to go, we'd driven home in near silence. Ali went straight to bed, but Letty and I got some ice cream and sat on the sofa.

For a birthday it had seemed like a sadly noncelebratory evening, and I couldn't blame Letty for her downcast eyes, her downturned little mouth. She looked like any other sullen fifteen-year-old girl, but I had some empathy for her. There's always a point in childhood when you realize your birthday is just another day, no more or less magical than any other.

"I remember the day you were born," I said to her. "You were pretty angry about coming out into the world."

She seemed to consider this for a moment, and then, as she had so often this past week, asked me a question that made me think her mind was moving much faster than mine, leaping ahead three or four beats.

"Are Mom and Dad planning on having another baby?"

"What? Where'd you get that idea? Of course not!" I gaped at her, my spoonful of ice cream suspended halfway to my mouth.

She shook her head. "They were talking about a baby."

"Well, what baby? Maybe a friend is pregnant, maybe they're talking about you being the baby, maybe a lot of things. But believe me, if your mom was even considering having another baby, I'd be the first to know."

She'd only cocked an eyebrow at me, making her look far more knowledgeable than her fifteen years and making me question myself.

The stream of high school kids had slowed to a trickle, and only two other cars were waiting in the roundabout. I rubbed my arm, thinking of the operation to set up my access point tomorrow, knowing that I had to tell Ali that afternoon. It had gone on too long. I was nervous, of course, but relieved to finally get it out of the way.

I squinted up at the steps and checked my watch. It was nearly twenty minutes past when she was supposed to meet me. Ali had stressed the importance of her being on time and not making me wait, but I'd given her plenty of slack, assuming she was talking to her boyfriend.

Of course that was another thing I would need to talk to Ali about, but as Letty spent every second outside school with either me or her mother, I hadn't been overly concerned that she was seeing too much of him, or at least not enough that they could have sex again. I didn't think, despite the alarmist news media, that teens had resorted to having sex in school bathrooms just yet.

Though perhaps I was out of touch on that account. I would never know, and it was one thing I was certainly glad that I didn't have to ever find out about. The insanity around "rainbow" parties in the news a few years ago had been entirely enough for me.

I had told Letty the truth. Sometimes I regretted not having children, but, overall, whenever stories like those appeared in the news, I felt horrified and anxious and then relieved, knowing I wouldn't have to deal with it.

I finally turned off the car and got out, heading up the steps. The office had a few parents and kids in it, and I patiently waited my turn, keeping an eye on the hallway in case Letty walked by. The secretary finally met my eyes.

"May I help you?" she asked, resignation in her voice.

"I'm Cora Brooks. I'm supposed to pick Letitia Gutierrez up, but she hasn't come out yet."

The woman's gaze flicked to the clock on the wall, and then, as if agreeing that it had been long enough, asked me for my ID. She called Ali and got her permission to check Letty's attendance records and share the information with me. My cell phone went off just as the secretary nodded at something on her computer screen.

"Hey, Ali," I said, "just hang on." She was talking, but I tuned her out to listen to the secretary.

"She was here for her first class," she said, "and then it looks like she wasn't present for any after that."

I relayed that to Ali and then silently handed the phone to the secretary.

"We don't have the school locked down, Mrs. Gutierrez," the secretary explained, from her tone obviously having gone through this before. "Children skip class all the time. We can't possibly keep track of them all once they're out of elementary school. At the high school level we do our best, but there are simply too many of them."

She listened for another moment, handed me the phone without a word, and then made an announcement over the speaker system for Letty Gutierrez to report to the office.

"What's up?" I asked Ali.

"Oh my God, where the hell is she?"

"I don't know, Ali, I'm sorry." Her panic made me start to really worry for the first time. I just figured she'd skipped school and would show up acting innocent at any moment.

"Well, it's not your fault," she said, but she didn't sound completely convinced. She was silent for a minute. "Give me back to the secretary," she said.

"She wants to talk to you again," I said, holding the phone out. The secretary took a breath and sighed it out before taking it.

"Yes, Mrs. Gutierrez?" She started typing on her keyboard. "I can't give you any specific information about another student, but it doesn't appear that way." She handed the phone back to me.

"What?"

"I asked her to check Emily, to see if they skipped together, but it doesn't look like it. Of course not. Emily has always been smarter than my daughter, dammit. I wish I knew that kid's last name."

Though I knew more about Letty and Seth's relationship than Ali did, I'd never thought to ask his last name.

"Would you mind checking the house to see if she's there before I freak Benny out?" she asked.

"Of course not," I said.

I waited another ten minutes to see if Letty would respond to the announcement, but she didn't, so I headed to Ali's house. But Letty wasn't there, either. And while I talked with Ali on the phone I drove by Emily's, where nobody was home. Thinking she might have wanted to use the gift certificate she'd received for her birthday, I drove across the street to the mall and hunted through the stores she preferred, growing ever more disgusted at the clothing they marketed to teenage girls. As I sped through racks of half shirts and tiny shorts, Ali called again.

"I'm on my way; I left a note for her on the door. We can cover the mall faster together."

We met at the entrance to one of the anchor stores, and in tandem we searched the mall, even having security make an announcement for Letty to meet us at the information office. But if she was at the mall, she wasn't coming forward.

"What should I do?" Ali asked, turning toward me in the parking lot. "Should I call Benny, or should I wait?"

What I wanted to say was that I was sure Letty was simply being difficult, punishing her parents, and maybe even me, for her lousy birthday and she was likely right that second over at Seth's house . . . playing house. I couldn't keep Letty's secret anymore.

"I have to tell you something," I said, unlocking my car doors and motioning to her to sit inside. Just the hour that the car had been sitting in the lot had been enough to spike the temperature well over a hundred, and I lowered myself onto the old vinyl gingerly and blasted the air.

"Now, Letty did not want me to tell you this—"

"Cora, come on, just tell me, I'm worried enough as it is."

"Okay. The night you picked Letty up at that party . . . she had sex. Letty and Seth slept together."

"Oh my God." Ali looked as if someone had hit her in the stomach, her face paling.

"I'm sorry—"

"How could you have not told me?" she said, turning on me, the color coming back now, her cheeks flushed with anger. "How dare you withhold this kind of information from me? You had no right, none. I don't know what's wrong with you these days, Cora, but ever since you've been back you've been acting like—" She stopped for a moment, searching for her next words. I had no idea what she would say, either, but I was giving her the time to figure it out.

"We're not talking the way we always have," she finally finished. "I know that's my fault. Letty's been with us practically every second, so I'm not blaming you. But it feels like you'd rather talk to her than to me these days, anyway. Are you mad at me or something?"

I shook my head and reached out to take her hand, but she pulled it away. "No, of course not, Ali," I said. "I was just waiting for the right time—"

"There is no right time," she said. "Do you know where she is? Is she okay?"

"Of course I don't know where she is," I defended myself. "I would tell you. You've had enough to worry about with Benny, and she was with us every second she wasn't at school, so I figured that, for now, while she was grounded anyway, she was safe. I'm sure she's okay. I imagine she and Seth skipped school. She's probably at his house."

"Do you know where he lives?"

"If I did we'd have already been over there," I said. "Now look, if I had any idea where she was, I would tell you. Stop acting like I've kidnapped your daughter."

We glared at each other. I had never argued with Ali about Letty. I'd never even considered asserting my maternal rights. I had none. We weren't co-mothers. And I had never felt that more pointedly than I did now.

Ali finally slumped back in her seat and covered her face with her hands.

"I can't believe she's having sex," she whispered, and then groaned, as if saying the words physically hurt her. "What did she say?"

I repeated the conversation, making sure to lead off with the fact that Letty had assured me that they'd used a condom, and finishing with her assertion that they were in love. Ali snorted at that.

"Please," she said. "She's a child, a *child*. In love." She groaned again, then took a deep breath, and when she spoke again, she sounded uncertain. "Is she, was she okay?"

"I asked," I said quietly. "She said she was, but who knows. I don't think she'd have told me if she wasn't. I'm shocked that she told me as much as she did."

"Why didn't she tell me?" Ali asked, pain in her voice. "I don't understand. She's always been so open with me."

She looked at me, bewildered, but I didn't have much of an answer for her.

"I imagine she thought she'd get in even more trouble than she already was," I said. "And I think she was afraid that you'd tell Benny."

Ali rolled her eyes toward the roof of the car. "Oh my God, Benny's going to kill this kid," she said.

"Letty or Seth?"

She sighed. "Both, I imagine. Okay, so she's in love, she's mad that she's grounded and can't see him, so they took the day off school so they could spend time together. Ugh. You'd think they would have been smart enough to get back to school in time for you to pick her up."

I shrugged. Yes, I would have thought Letty was smarter than that, too, but a new idea crossed my mind.

"I wonder if she's doing this on purpose," I said.

"Why? She must know she has our attention the last couple of weeks," she said.

"Well, maybe not. Last night, after you went to bed, Letty said she overheard you and Benny talking about having another baby."

Ali gasped, her hand flying to her mouth.

"I told her she must have misunderstood."

She tilted her head back against the seat and stared up at the sagging headliner. "Oh, this is just not at all how I pictured this. I was waiting until this thing with Benny worked itself out before I mentioned it to you."

"Did she hear correctly? Are you really thinking about doing it again?" I asked. She lifted her head up and looked at me.

"Yeah," she said with a small smile. "I am. Actually, I'm doing more than thinking about it. I really want to do it. Last night, Benny said we could talk about it. He was against it at first, but I guess not having us there made him give it some more thought. And I'm—I think we're going to go home this weekend. Benny says he feels much better now that he's talking with Dr. Weist, and I'm ready. I've missed him so much. So, yeah, I want another baby. What do you think?"

"Wow, *that's* what I think," I said with a laugh. "I don't know, I guess I'm not sure what to think. You'd go through it all again? I just don't think I could do it."

"Well, we have nine embryos left. I've been paying to keep—"

"Whoa," I said, holding my hand up, "wait a second. Still have embryos left? Mine?" I stared at her wide-eyed, dismay filling my belly, making me nauseated.

Ali looked taken aback. "Well, ours, I mean, mine and Benny's . . . yes, yours, I guess."

"Oh no, no, Ali, you can't!"

"Why not?" she asked, clearly shocked at my reaction.

"They can't possibly still be good," I protested, certain that my shock was greater than hers. It had never crossed my mind that she might want to use the original embryos. How could that be possible? I'd never imagined that Ali would have continued to pay for storage of them for this many years. I'd also never thought about what would be done with them if she decided to stop paying to store them.

What did they do with them?

"I think they could," Ali said. "An Israeli woman gave birth from twelve-year-old embies, and in 2006 a Spanish woman gave birth from thirteen-year-old embryos. They're saying there's no telling how long they could remain viable. I mean, I know it's a long shot, but it was a long shot to begin with and we did it."

She was glowing as if she were already pregnant. I tried to rein my feelings in. I had to tell her, of course, but neither of us would have the time we needed to discuss it, not while we still didn't know where Letty was.

"Okay, we should talk about this, we *will* talk about this. But first, what are we doing about Letty?" I asked.

"Oh God, I don't know," she said. "Okay, let's call some of her friends. Damn, I wish Benny hadn't taken her cell phone away. Hey, let's grab her cell phone. It's in my closet. I bet this guy's number is in it." She looked triumphant.

"Good idea," I agreed. "I'll meet you there."

"No," she said, "I don't want Benny to realize anything is wrong yet. I'll grab the phone and meet you back at your place."

I drove her back to her car, wishing I could feel as relieved as she clearly did. Before she got out she reached over and squeezed my arm. "It's going to be okay," she said, and I nodded and smiled automatically, then drove home with the nausea in my belly returning.

Now, not only did I have to tell her how sick I was and how sick the child I had made for her might get, but I got to crush her dreams of having another one.

9

ALI

I managed to get home before Benny and didn't bother to turn the car off, leaving it running in the driveway like a burglar. The house had the stale air of a home without a family, and an overwhelming sense of sadness stole over me as I dashed into our bedroom.

I groped along the top of the gun safe, assuming my hand would quickly connect with Letty's purse, but all I got was some dust. I stood back and craned my neck to get a better view and couldn't see it. I'd watched him put it up there. I jumped once, twice, and it was definitely not there. I looked around the closet, wondering why he'd moved it.

I looked through the rest of the house, but it definitely wasn't there, and I finally gave up and headed back to Cora's.

She was in the guest room when I got back to her house, looking through the closet. She turned as I walked in, her face somber.

"Some of her stuff is gone," she said.

"What do you mean?" I asked, gazing into the closet with her. I was the one who took her to school, and she hadn't had anything but her backpack. But now that I thought of it, it had looked more full than usual.

"Well, what the hell?" I asked, baffled.

"I don't know. She left plenty of things, so I don't think she actually ran away, but other stuff is definitely gone, so I don't know, maybe she did and just didn't want it to look like it? Or, her bathing suit isn't hanging in the shower anymore, and her beach towel is gone, too, so maybe they just went to the beach and lost track of time," Cora said. "Did you find her cell phone?"

"No," I said, still looking at the closet. "It was in our closet, but Benny must have moved it."

"Your closet in your room?" Cora asked.

I just looked at her.

"She went in your room when we went to the house to pick up some of her clothes on Tuesday," she said.

"Oh, I am just going to kill her," I said, running out of the room and grabbing the phone, dialing her number with shaking fingers.

"Answer, answer, answer," I pleaded softly as Letty's phone rang . . . and rang. At the sound of her voice, her recorded voice, I still felt enormous relief. At least there was this tether to her, taken on purpose, evidence that she was doing this by choice, not hauled along somewhere against her will.

"Letty, it's Mom," I said, willing myself to remain calm. "I need you to call me immediately. I get it. There's been a lot of tension, a lot of fighting with all of us, Dad, me, you. But I need to know that you're okay. I've not said anything to your dad yet, but, Let, I'm going to have to soon if I don't hear from you. I'm at Cora's, and my cell is on. I'll give you . . ." I looked at my watch and calculated how far I could push it with Benny. "Until seven o'clock. If I don't hear from you by then, I'll have to get your father involved. And you know what that means. I know about Seth, I know—everything, and it will be—" The tone sounded that I had run out of time, and I jabbed the off button in irritation.

Cora was leaning against the sofa when I turned around. I shook my head.

"She didn't answer," I said.

"I'm really sorry," Cora said, her face sorrowful, accentuating how bloated and tired she looked. "I honestly didn't think she was going to run away, I thought she was just trying to get some attention."

I sighed. "It's certainly not your fault. I told her to call by seven or I would have to tell Benny."

"What will he do?" Cora asked.

"Depends," I said. "He'll do as much as he can, you know, legally. If this kid is old enough, he'll try to charge him with whatever he can. I'm going to try Emily again."

I dialed Emily's, and her mother answered. My relief at speaking to another mother I knew was only slightly greater than my humiliation at calling her over my daughter's transgressions twice in one month.

"Hi, Jean, it's Ali. How are you?" I asked, forcing myself to slow down and be civil.

"Oh, hi, Ali," she answered. "Emily had a nice time last night."

"Well, it was lovely to see her. I was actually calling to see if she was home? I'm looking for a friend of Letty's and thought she might know him," I said, trying to keep my tone light.

"Emily's not here." Jean said, sounding a little puzzled and a lot curious. I hated it. We'd been close when the girls were little, but we'd drifted apart while the girls stayed friends—although when I looked back over the past several months, I had seen Emily less and less. I didn't know why I hadn't noticed it before.

"Does she have a cell phone?" I asked, and Jean laughed.

"Who doesn't?" she replied, giving me the number. But she wasn't ready to let me go just yet.

"Is everything okay?" she asked.

"I think so," I said, cautious of telling her too much before I knew anything.

"Well," she said, then hesitated.

"What, Jean?"

"I just . . . I've been worried, you know, at some of the things Emily has said . . ."

"Okay. Like what?"

"Just, things, you know the way girls are."

She laughed. I stayed silent, letting her twist in the uncomfortable quiet, knowing she would crack. She cleared her throat, and I heard ice falling into a glass.

"I don't guess the girls have been very close this year, that's all. There's a boyfriend, I hear?"

I was suddenly very, very tired, and no longer cared that Jean might think I had lost all control over my daughter. The thing was, apparently I had. My concern won out over my pride.

"Jean? Pardon me for being blunt, but my daughter seems to have run away. I don't know this boy at all. His name is Seth, and if there's anything, anything at all, no matter how minute or un-substantiated, I wish you would just tell me, because I need to find my daughter."

Now it was her turn to be silent. I waited. When she spoke again, there was no false concern in her voice, only the urgency of one panicked mother to another, and it no longer mattered that we had grown so far apart.

"Okay, let's see . . . yes, I know his name is Seth, but I don't know a last name. Hang on, let me get to her room. She might have it on her computer; she has no idea I know the password." I heard a door opening and then fingers on a keyboard, but she kept talking while she worked. "All I know is that from what Emily has told me—now keep in mind this is an adolescent girl who might be a little hurt that her friend is moving away from her—"

"I get it, thank you," I said.

"Okay, so she says that Letty started hanging out with a real party crowd, older kids, she hardly talks to any freshmen any-more. Their other friends from middle school all seem to be mad at her for dumping them. Emily says she's one of the only ones who still talks to her. She wasn't going to go on the birthday dinner, but I made her." Her fingers stopped tapping.

"No, I'm not seeing a Seth on her MySpace page," she said. "I'll check her e-mail."

I was impressed. Not only did I not know if Letty even had a MySpace page, I certainly wouldn't have been savvy enough to have discovered her passwords. And, to be honest, I still held the belief that my daughter deserved a certain amount of privacy. But I was reconsidering that.

"Nope," Jean said. "I've got nothing but e-mail from Letty

where she mentions Seth, and . . ." More tapping. "No good information there, just talk about parties, kissing, the usual. Okay, let me think for a minute, see if there's anything else on here that might be useful."

"Thank you, Jean," I said quietly.

"Parents have to stick together these days, don't we?" she murmured, still working on the computer.

"I guess so," I said, but she wasn't really listening at that point.

Finally she sighed. "Ali, I'm sorry, but there's just not much here. I tell you what, wait for about ten minutes. I'll call Emily and tell her to be honest with you when you call. I assure you, she'll tell you what she knows." Her voice had turned dark. I believed her.

And as I hung up I had to question my own parenting. In any other situation, Jean's level of involvement in Emily's life would have been horrifying to me. But perhaps that was what was called for. The things I was going on to Cora about, insisting how things were different now, how I had to be more strict, perhaps I was only skating across the surface of what being a parent now meant.

All I knew was that Emily was going to be at home that night, and my daughter might not.

I kept an eye on the clock and called Emily after ten minutes had gone by. When she answered, she sounded nervous.

"Hello?"

"Hi, Emily, it's Ali."

"Oh, hi," she said.

"Your mom talked to you?" I asked.

"Yeah. What do you want me to say?"

"I don't want you to say anything that's not true," I said, trying to put her at ease. "I promise I won't tell Letty that we talked, okay? I just need to know that she's okay, and since she hasn't talked to me about this boy she's seeing, I really kind of need someone to do it for her."

"Okay. Well, his name is Seth Caple, he's a sophomore, and he lives out in the Estates."

I was scribbling down notes as she talked. "Do you have his number?" I asked.

"No, but I might be able to find someone who does, if you want." But she sounded doubtful.

"That would be great," I said. "So, what else can you tell me about Letty and Seth? Did you see them today at school? Did she talk about running away?"

She hesitated. "No-oo, she never said anything. But I'm not surprised."

"Really? Why?" It took everything I had to not just yell at her, *Tell me what I need to know!* But I didn't want to frighten the information right out of her, make her freeze up like a bunny.

"She just got, really into him, you know? And she liked that whole crowd; she was trying to be more like them. She acted like the rest of us were just big babies or something. And, I mean, I don't know if you know but, they do drugs and stuff, and someone told me that Seth sells, too."

"Seth sells drugs?" I repeated, glancing at Cora, who bit her lip.

Emily started backpedaling immediately. "Well, I just heard it, I've never seen him do anything."

"Okay, I'm going to try to find him now that I have a last name, but, Emily, if you could find anyone who might have his number, I'd sure like to get it, okay?"

"Um, okay," she said.

"And if you think of anything else, let me know, please? And if Letty calls you—"

Emily laughed a bitter laugh from a friend who'd been dumped. I felt sorry for her, and angry at my daughter. Emily had been a good friend to Letty for years, and she'd been hurt by Letty's callous disregard. I couldn't blame her for being bitter.

"Well, if she does, would you tell her to call me, please? And then let me know she called?"

"Okay," Emily said, "I'm sure she's fine. She's just, you know, out partying or something."

"Thanks, Emily," I said, hanging up. I knew she said it to make me feel better, but it certainly didn't. I turned to Cora, who was already sitting in front of her computer, and gave her Seth's name. We turned up plenty of Seth Caples, but none who appeared to be the right age or geographic region.

Finally we checked for just his last name and Golden Gate Estates and found three Caples. We printed out directions and headed out, me driving and Cora navigating.

"So what are we going to do?" Cora asked. "Just walk up and ring the bell?"

"You have a better idea?" I asked.

"I guess not," she answered.

"I can't believe she's doing this to me," I said.

"And yet you want to do it again."

I laughed. "You sound like Benny."

"Benny's a smart guy." I shot her a look, and she amended it.

"Usually. Benny is *usually* a smart guy. So, what have y'all been talking about?"

"I guess there's not a whole lot to talk about. I'm still cautious, I suppose."

"That's certainly understandable."

"Yeah, and I've been thinking a lot about what you said."

"Really?" she asked. I laughed.

"Why do you sound surprised?" I asked. "Have I not been listening to your advice for more than half my life?"

"I thought you'd spent more than half your life ignoring my advice," she said with a grin.

"No, not true. Sometimes it just takes a while to sink in that you're usually right."

"So what was this brilliant advice I gave that has finally sunk in?"

"In all fairness, I never said it was *brilliant.*"

"Okay, okay, point taken. What was this vaguely coherent advice I gave?"

"I don't remember your exact words, but you said something about Benny being an anachronism, an idealist?"

"I remember," she said.

"You said that as soon as he had an outlet he would calm down, and I should be patient with that. He has an innocence about him, doesn't he? A cop, for heaven's sake. But he's innocent about a lot of other things. And, honestly, it's one of the things that I love about him. It was one of the reasons I fell in love with him to begin with, that innocent determination and belief that he could make things right. And you know what? This is going to sound so crazy, and you're the only one I would admit this to . . ." I trailed off.

"Ali, come on, you're killing me!" she prodded me with a laugh.

"Well, when I saw him at the restaurant, I really *saw* him, like for the first time in years and years. And you know what?"

"What?"

"He's really cute."

"Oh, good Lord," Cora said, beginning to laugh in earnest.

"He is," I insisted, making her laugh even harder until I finally slapped her on the knee, laughing myself now.

"Okay," she said, catching her breath. "Yeah, he is, I guess."

"I just, I saw him the way he really is. He really turned into a handsome man, and he's kind, and he's funny, and he knows his job. And he's a good man going through a hard time. I think I did the right thing by leaving, and now *he's* doing the right thing, just like he always does. It's . . . comforting. I suppose we just both needed a break. And you were right; I need to be patient with that."

"So that's a good thing, right? Have you told him all this?"

"I would have, but then our daughter went and ran away." I sighed. "But it got him to really give some thought to the baby, so maybe there's a bright side to it all."

"Oh?"

I could practically feel Cora tense up.

"All right, let's have it. What do you have against this?"

"I don't have anything against you wanting another baby, Ali," she said, but it wasn't how it sounded. "Or, maybe, I don't know. Why now? It would be such a long time between kids. Do you really want to have a teenager, be going through this again, when you're in your fifties?"

"I always wanted more kids, Cora. I wanted ten kids, twelve. I wanted my own little army of kids," I said, and now, so many years after being so grateful for Letty, the grief of it overwhelmed me again. "It's not fair, it's just not fair."

"No, of course it's not. It's not fair."

"And there are a lot of women having babies at my age. Hell, I'd be on top of a trend for the first time in my life."

Cora looked out the window for a minute before she spoke, her voice soft. "Ali, what if it doesn't work? What if the embryos are . . . bad?"

"But I can at least try. I want a full sibling for Letty. And look, I've gone through the heartbreak before, I can handle it if it happens again, but if it doesn't, then I have a chance for another beautiful baby. And I want it, Cora, I really do. Why do you think I've kept them for so long?"

"I never thought about it."

"Really? You never thought about them? Waiting there?"

"No," she said, and I didn't know what I heard in her voice, if it was shame, or regret, or something else entirely. "No, not like that. I guess I thought they just . . . faded away. I guess I didn't give them much thought at all."

"No, there are tons of them out there. There are even embryo adoptions now. You can donate them to other couples, donate them to science. Or destroy them. I couldn't do that. I guess a lot of other people can't do it either, because a lot of them are abandoned."

"Abandoned?"

"Well, they just stop paying. And, I suppose, try to forget about them. Don't look at me like that. I understand the temptation of it, okay? It's not as easy as people make it. If you've never been the one looking at the forms, then you couldn't possibly understand. But that's part of it. At least I won't be wasting all of our work. I'll be giving them a chance."

"What if they're all good?"

"Viable."

"Okay, what if they're all viable? Are you going to implant them all?"

"Transfer them all. You hope for one to implant."

"Whatever, Ali. You know what I'm asking. What will you do if you transfer some and it works? What about the rest of them?"

"I don't know," I admitted. "Maybe I'll let them be adopted?"

Cora visibly paled.

"What would you have me do, Cora? Destroy them?"

"I don't know," she said, shaking her head. "I just don't know. Yes, I guess that's what would have to happen."

"Why would it *have* to happen?" I asked, staring at her in disbelief.

"And if it doesn't work?" she asked. "If they're not good, viable? Would you keep going? Get a new donor?"

I frowned. I didn't want to think that far ahead. I believed, I really did, that at least one of those embryos was destined to be my baby. I could feel a personality out there, waiting for me to claim it, waiting to become my baby.

"I don't know," I answered. "It's so expensive . . . I just don't know. But what is your hesitation? Are you sorry you did this to begin with?"

"No, no of course not," she cried. "I love Letty, you know that."

"I know, but something is definitely different on this trip, Cora.

All of this, with Letty and Benny, I mean, you're taking it all so personally . . ."

A thought occurred to me, something that now seemed obvious, why she was home, why she seemed bloated, tired, overly attentive to Letty. I couldn't believe I'd been so stupid.

"Cora," I said, nearly breathless with it. "Cora, are you pregnant?"

She just stared at me for a moment, and I felt delightfully smug, as if I had discovered her secret. But then she laughed, covering her mouth when it turned into a groan.

"What, Cora? What's going on?"

"No, I'm not pregnant, Ali. And, you can't use the embryos. Nobody can. I—Ali this isn't easy. I, ah, I have a problem." Cora cleared her throat and wiped her hands across her face, then spoke in a rush, her voice flat as if she'd rehearsed it too many times. "I have polycystic kidney disease, Ali. I'm losing my kidneys. I have to go on dialysis very soon, and if I don't get a kidney transplant I will be on it for the rest of my life."

I eased to a stop at a red light and turned in my seat, speechless.

She nodded. "Yeah," she said softly. "Definitely *not* pregnant."

The light changed, but I couldn't seem to move. There wasn't a car behind me, and Cora finally just pointed to the light. I faced forward and accelerated slowly.

"Where are we going?" I asked, aware that we were coming up on one of the streets on our directions.

"You're going to go left at the next light."

We were both talking as though we were in church, the music on the radio providing a strange, modern background to an atmosphere that had so suddenly grown reverential and cautious.

I eased into the left lane and took the turn.

"Right at the next street," she said. "You okay?"

"Hang on," I said, making the right. It was a long street, ending in a cul-de-sac, and I drove slowly, barely touching the gas pedal. "Okay," I said, finally able to form a thought. "What do we do? What has to happen? You need a kidney? Is that the deal? How does it work?"

"Oh, Ali, no," she said. "You don't understand—" We both jumped when her cell phone rang. She picked it up and gave a little gasp, holding it out for me to see the Caller ID.

"It's Letty!"

"Okay, answer it, answer it," I said. "Don't tell her you're with me, she might hang up."

She quickly flipped it open and said, "Hello?"

She listened and then turned toward me before saying, "No, no, she's out looking for you. Letty, where are you?" She was quiet again for a moment.

"Are you okay?" she asked, and then listened and nodded at me, making me press my hand to my chest in relief. I pulled around the curve of the cul-de-sac and stopped the car, turning the radio off.

"Of course," Cora said, making frantic scribbling motions at me. I dug in the console for a pen and a notepad, and she quickly wrote down an address, and then wrote *VENICE* in big letters and underlined it before turning the notepad toward me.

"No, I don't think she's called your dad yet," she said. "Yes, I do, Letty, I have to tell her. I have to at least tell her you're okay. No, there's no argument about—"

I could hear Letty talking on the other end, panic in her voice.

"No," Cora said, raising her voice to cut through whatever pro-testations Letty was making. "No, just stay there. It will take me less than two hours, just stay right there, don't move, okay? Order something to eat, and I'll pay for it when I get there."

She pointed north, and I took off for the entrance to I-75, headed toward Venice and my child.

CORA

Letty had sounded about seven years old, and my chest actually hurt when I heard her. Ali took off for I-75 like a rocket, and I was reminded of the road trips we'd taken in high school, giggling and singing at the tops of our lungs up the road, waves of heat shimmering before us.

I told Ali everything Letty had said, repeating it several times before she calmed down enough that I wasn't afraid for our lives as she sped through traffic.

"Okay," she said, "I'll drive by and drop you off so she doesn't see me and run."

"Okay," I said, unable to manage a clever retort about rescue missions and undercover ops the way I once might have. Not only was I afraid of the fact that Ali only had half of the information she needed right now, but I was also afraid for Letty. I had thought

Ali had been overreacting about Letty, but now I realized that she had been exactly right to panic.

Once we got past Lehigh Acres, Ali reached over and gripped my arm.

"All right," she said. "Now, let's talk about this. Start over, okay? I need to know everything."

I sighed and leaned my head against the window, the glass chilly from the air-conditioning, belying the heat just an eighth of an inch away.

"I have kidney disease," I said, my voice dull. I could say it no other way. "Autosomal dominant polycystic kidney disease. PKD. It is irreversible, it has progressed quickly, and tomorrow morning I have to go in and have a tube installed in my arm that they will stick needles in to remove all my blood, clean it, and put it back in, three times a week."

"But, Cora, are you—are they sure? I mean, have you gotten a second, third, *sixth* opinion? When did this happen? Why didn't you tell me? Who else knows?"

I lifted my head off the glass and smiled at her. "They are sure. I've had plenty of opinions, and they all say the same thing. It's a little tough to argue when even I can see the images."

"Why? What's on the images?" she asked, fear in her voice. I didn't blame her. It scared me when I read about it, to picture it, but then seeing it on the ultrasound images, well, it was worse than I had prepared myself for. For about a month I had obsessively researched, and there are images and heartbreaking stories seared into my mind that I will never forget.

I'd stopped the research after that month and started concentrating on living my life until the inevitability of the hemodialysis stopped me.

"It's, well, it's really pretty awful, Ali."

"Are you in pain?" she asked, taking her eyes off the road every few seconds.

"Drive, please," I said, pointing toward the road in front of us. "Sometimes it's uncomfortable, yes. It's hard to be still for long. They, the kidneys, grow larger . . . because of the cysts."

"Oh."

"Yeah. You getting a mental image?"

"I think so."

"Well, try to block it now. I try to not visualize it anymore. It's more important to know what it does than what it looks like."

"And what does it do?" she asked.

"It kills your kidney function," I said. "No kidney function means your body can't clean all the toxins out of it, and if you can't clean the toxins out, you die. It's really pretty simple."

"So the dialysis . . . wait, you said you were going *tomorrow*?"

I sighed.

"I know. I've been trying to find a way to tell you, a time. I'm sorry. It's the reason I came, it's why I'm here, to tell you. And look, tomorrow's not a big deal, okay? It's not for the dialysis, it's just to get the access for the dialysis put in place. It's really not a big deal."

"How long have you known?" she asked, and there was no disguising the hurt in her voice.

"Six months," I said, aware that it wasn't a good answer. And, technically, I had known something was wrong for much longer than that. I just hadn't known what. I heard her draw in a long, slow breath and assumed that a torrent of angry words was going to come riding along on the exhale. But I was wrong.

"Okay," she said evenly, accepting it, but I was willing to bet I was going to hear more about it later. "So, you go in the morning . . . oh my God, and here I've just been going on and on about all of our stupid problems. How could you stand it? And now I've dragged you out—"

"It's been wonderful," I said.

She laughed. "Oh, clearly. This has been great fun for you, I'm sure."

"Not fun, maybe, but it has been good for me, being able to spend time with you, with Letty, get to know her a little more."

"Stop, Cora, you're scaring me," she said. "You sound like you think you're going to die, like this was a good-bye trip or something. We're going to fix this, okay? Okay?"

"Okay," I agreed.

"So, what has to be done? The thing tomorrow, when is that?"

"I'm supposed to be there at seven in the morning. Keith doesn't have a flying lesson until nine, so he's going to take me, and bring me home the next day. But I'm supposed to have someone check in on me—"

"Well, Keith isn't taking you, I am. And I'm taking you home, and I'm staying there until you're better."

"It will be fine, really, it's not a big deal. They basically connect an artery to a vein by sticking a tube in my arm," I said, holding my arm out, tracing a loop along the inside of my elbow. "It will be the spot where they put the needles in for the dialysis."

She looked down quickly at my arm and then met my eyes before she looked back at the road.

"What, the tube sticks out?"

"No, no, both ends are in the arm."

"Okay," she said, and I could tell that it made her feel better, the idea that I would not have things sticking out of me, all signs of illness contained, hidden within my body. I didn't point out that it didn't make me any less sick, but that would be evident enough in time, and if it made her feel better about things now, so be it.

"What then?" she asked.

I shrugged. "When my blood tests get to a certain point, I go on dialysis. Three times a week for three to five hours."

"Well, that doesn't sound so bad," she said, hopefully.

"It's better than the alternative," I agreed with her.

"But it's better to get a kidney, isn't it?" she asked.

"Well, sure," I said. "For most people. Some people aren't good candidates."

"Are you?"

"I don't know. I haven't gotten that far along. I don't know why I wouldn't be, but that's something to look at down the line. Right now I'm just coming to grips with going on hemodialysis."

"But if you can do it earlier, then why wouldn't you? What do we need to do?" she asked. "How do we do it? I assume I have to get tested, all that, but hey, I figure if I could carry one of your eggs to term in my body, a kidney should be a snap, right?"

And here was the tough part, as if it hadn't been tough enough for both of us up until then. Because now she was determined Ali, Ali who would just forge ahead and make things better, Ali who had gotten through all of her heartbreaks and had plowed ahead and had a successful pregnancy and a healthy baby, and by God, if she could do that, she could do anything.

But she couldn't do this.

"It's not quite as simple as that," I said. "You can't give me a kidney, Ali."

"No, actually, I can," she said. "This is how this works, how this friendship has always worked and always will work. I'll go with you tomorrow and while they're doing their thing with your arm I'll get the information—"

"No, Ali," I interrupted her. "You don't understand. You have to keep both of your kidneys, and"—I took a deep breath—"you can't use the embryos."

"Why?" she asked. "What does that have to do with it?"

I pressed my lips together as if I'd just applied lipstick, afraid to say it.

"It's hereditary, Ali," I finally said softly. "It's hereditary. Even if you were a match, you can't give me a kidney because if Letty has it, you're going to need it for her. And you can't bring another baby into this world with my genes."

A small noise escaped her. And this time it was I who reached across the console and gripped her arm.

"I'm sorry," I whispered. "I am so, so sorry, Ali. I didn't know, you know that, right? I didn't know, I had no idea."

She was silent.

"Ali? Oh, please, please talk to me," I pleaded. "Oh, God, I couldn't stand to tell you, I'm so sorry."

"Just," she said, holding her hand out as if she were going to pat me on the knee, but she didn't touch me. "Just hold on, okay, just, give me a second here. I just need a second."

"Okay," I said. "Do you want to—do you want to pull off the road for a minute?"

"Shhh," she said.

"Okay." I nodded my head, agreeing with her. I needed to shut up. I was just about to go into a hysterical babbling of apologies and long-winded explanations. I stared ahead at the road, occasionally looking over at her. She kept her eyes forward, driving with extraordinary concentration now.

When she finally spoke, her voice was very calm.

"What are the odds?" she asked.

"Fifty percent," I answered.

She nodded and was silent again for several minutes.

"How do we find out?"

"There's a genetic test," I said. "If she has it, it doesn't mean she'll develop the disease—"

"Stop."

"Okay."

She drummed her fingers on the steering wheel and made the humming noise again. I didn't look at her.

"Okay," she finally said. "There's a genetic test."

"Yes."

"But what does it tell you?"

"It tells you if she has the gene, my gene."

"Okay. And if she does?"

"It only says she has the gene. Nothing can tell you if she will eventually develop the disease or not."

"Eventually?"

"If she does develop it, it likely wouldn't start until her thirties or forties."

"She couldn't have it now?" she asked, and I heard the edge in her voice, heard the as-yet-unspoken accusation that if I'd known, why hadn't I told her earlier.

"It would be very, very rare, incredibly rare, for this particular kind to begin at her age," I said.

"Uh-huh," she said. "So a fifty percent chance."

"Yes."

"All right, so we'll get the test."

"I will, of course, pay for whatever needs to be done," I said, but I regretted it as soon as it was out of my mouth. This was what she was finally able to sink her anger into.

"Well, yes, obviously that's my major concern," she said, giving me a look I'd never seen directed my way before. "Yes, that was exactly what I wanted you to say."

"No, Ali, I just thought—"

"You wait six months to tell me that my daughter might have this disease, but it takes seconds for you to reassure me that it won't hurt my pocketbook. Good to know you've got your priorities straight here."

"I know, I know," I said. "It was the wrong thing to say. Please, I am so sorry."

She put her hand over her mouth, and when I dared to look at her, I saw that tears were spilling over it.

"Oh, Cora," she finally said, wiping her face. "I'm so sorry, I am so sorry you're so sick."

"No, I'm sorry," I said, handing her tissues from my purse, using some myself. "I'm sorry I waited, I'm sorry I—I'm just sorry for all of it."

"I know," she said, sniffing, then blowing out a long sigh. "All right, so, we need to get ourselves together and go get Letty. Not a word to her, okay?"

"Of course not," I said. "No, we just need to get her home."

"Right," she said. "We get her home, and then we figure out the rest."

10

ALI

By the time we got to Venice I had convinced myself that Letty didn't have any little ticking time bomb genes in her perfect young body. Fifty percent.

Back in my twenties, when all my friends were getting pregnant, there was much discussion of how to influence the sex of the baby. Everything from eating meat for a boy and sweets for a girl, to the position on the compass the woman is lying in during conception, was bandied about and either sworn by or dismissed.

One friend, desperate for a boy, was convinced that having sex on even days ensured a girl, and odd days assured a boy. I've never been a particularly superstitious woman, and I wasn't going for it, but she continued to insist that it was scientifically proven, and that the odds were impressive.

"Okay, what are the odds?" I'd asked.

"Fifty percent!" she exclaimed, which made me nearly breathless with laughter. I never could get her to understand that her odds were fifty percent no matter what, as there were only two choices, but she had sex on odd dates and she did, by God, have a boy.

Those odds had seemed so frivolous to me then. It wasn't even statistically interesting. Besides, actually being pregnant and deciphering the odds meant so little to me. I was *pregnant*. Who cared whether it was a boy or a girl? It was a *baby*! I was one hundred percent pregnant, and that was all I cared about.

But now fifty percent really meant something. Like the choice between boy and girl, there were only two choices: good gene or bad gene. I suppose had the actual sex of a baby meant anything to me, I would have already understood the importance of that fifty percent. I felt badly for laughing at my friend.

Fifty percent.

By the time we took the exit that would take us down to the beach in Venice, it was all that was in my head.

I wasn't thinking much about Cora. I simply could not absorb the knowledge of her illness into a mind so full of concern for my daughter. I'd thought I could protect her by grounding her. The morbid absurdity of it was infuriating.

Even the reason we were going to pick her up had escaped me. What did it matter? All that mattered was that I got her home and got that test. Everything else would just have to wait: Benny, Cora, even the embryos.

I felt a twinge at that, an extra niggling grief trying to worm itself into the anxiety over Letty, but I snuffed it out. Fifty percent.

I looked over at Cora. She looked more miserable than I felt. I wanted to help, but there was nothing I could say. She was right. As soon as I realized that Letty might, just might, need a kidney one day, I immediately felt a hoarding instinct kick in. There was Benny, of course, but kidneys rejected, I knew that. What if I gave Cora one, betting on Benny being able to provide if Letty got ill, and then Letty's body rejected Benny's? What if she had the gene, *did* develop the disease, and by that time, what? Her forties, like Cora? What if by that time Benny wasn't healthy anymore, or even alive? What if none of us were matches for either of them?

There were too many *ifs* to take a chance. I was her mother, and this was exactly what I was here for. It had never crossed my mind that I might have to allow my friend to suffer in order to save my child.

But I would. It wasn't even a question, no hesitation.

But what I didn't feel, and it was something that I couldn't articulate to her right now—but I would, once I could think straight again, I would—was the need to assign blame. I did not blame Cora for this. The only enduring emotion I would ever feel when it came to Letty and Cora was gratitude.

There had been other emotions that popped their heads in over the years—the most recent, on this trip, being a cautious and uncomfortable jealousy. But even now, oddly, especially now, I felt a nearly overwhelming tide of gratitude for the fact that I had a daughter to begin with.

I reached over and grasped her hand, and she held on. We stayed like that until it was time to turn onto the road leading to the restaurant where Letty waited for her Aunt Cora to come save her.

I drove past it quickly, hoping Letty wasn't so sharp-eyed and paranoid that she would recognize my car and disappear, then turned into a hotel parking lot.

"If you don't find her right away, call me, okay?" I asked.

She nodded. "Of course. I'll be right back with her."

I nodded, watching her retreating back as far as I could, hoping that Letty would be where she'd said she would be.

I kept an eye on the sidewalk and prayed, but when I saw Cora come around the corner of the hotel and Letty wasn't with her I cried out loud and jumped out of the car, running to meet her. She held her hand up, stopping me, and then slung Letty's backpack off her shoulder, holding it out to me.

I backed up to the car, looking around for my daughter, and grabbed the backpack as soon as Cora was close enough. "What happened?"

"It's okay," Cora said. "She's in the restaurant. She isn't finished eating, so I told her I'd drop her pack in the car. Look, we both need to eat anyway. Why don't I go back in, and I'll take the seat across from her, and it'll pretty effectively block her view of the door, plus I'll be talking to her so she won't be looking for you. She's less likely to run if we're all in public, and she'd have to get by you anyway."

I leaned against the car in relief. I'd have agreed to anything.

"Okay," I said. "How does she look? Is she all right?"

Cora smiled and grasped my arms lightly. "Honey, she's fine, just fine, okay? She's been gone for a day, not a week. Everything is going be okay. Give me a minute, and then come get your daughter."

I closed my eyes for a moment and bit my lip, then leaned against her for a moment. Finally I pulled back.

"*Our* daughter," I said. "That's what she is, Cora. Only a mother does all this. Thank you."

She didn't answer. She just shook her head and turned away. I slung Letty's pack into the trunk and patiently counted to one hundred before I headed toward the restaurant. The closer I got the faster I went, and when I hit the door I nearly plowed over the hostess who had kindly opened it for me.

I saw her immediately, and despite Cora's good intentions and newly bloated body, she still wasn't enough to block my daughter from seeing me. Her face fell instantly and she was on her feet, and I braced myself, like a football player, to block her attempt to get past me.

But to my amazement and relief, rather than flying past me she nearly knocked me down flinging herself into my arms.

"Hey," I said, stroking her hair. "Okay, all right." I looked over her head at Cora and mouthed *It's okay* at her.

"Come on, sweetie," I said. "Let's go to the ladies' room, huh?" She nodded her head against my collarbone and we made our way, with her clinging to me all the while, through the swinging door and into the blessedly empty restroom. I leaned against the counter, feeling the pool of water on it soaking through my jeans, and Letty leaned against me.

I grabbed some paper towels, pulling her hair out of her face and scrubbing her tears away.

"All right, now here's what's going to happen: You're going to wash your face and pull yourself together, you're going to stop worrying about anything, we're going to go out there and we're all going to have something to eat, and then we're going to drive home and you'll tell me about it all, okay? It's time to come clean, sweetie, and I promise you're going to feel better about it when you're all done."

She started to say something, but then she just nodded and whispered, "Okay."

"I'm going to step outside the door and give you a minute."

"Okay," she said again.

When I opened the door, she was already running water in the sink. I leaned against the wall just outside the door and took a deep breath. I could see Cora just around the corner, occasionally taking a look over her shoulder, could hear the water in the restroom running, and thought about the fact that Benny was likely sitting at home waiting for the phone call I'd promised him.

For just this second the ratty little hallway outside the bathroom was my only refuge. I enjoyed it while it lasted. Cora caught my eye, and I held up a finger to indicate we'd just be a moment, and then the bathroom door opened, and my cell phone rang.

I knew it was Benny even before checking the screen and quickly hit the mute button—I couldn't talk to him yet. I checked Letty's face, making her give me a tentative smile before I winked at her and led her back to the table.

"Hey," Cora said brightly, as if we'd just arrived for a lunch date. "I ordered us a couple of salads; I hope that's okay?"

"That will be great," I said, meeting her eyes across the table. "Thanks."

She nodded and looked down at the table. Letty's eyes were on the old laminate tabletop also, and I gave in to it for a moment as well, gazing at the advertisement for desserts propped up by the salt and pepper shakers, wishing Cora had ordered a giant slab of gooey chocolate cake for me rather than a salad.

We maintained a solemn and exhausted silence until the food

came and then ate in silence, paid the bill in silence, and all filed
out of the restaurant without a word. I handed the keys to Cora
and she led the way to the car, with Letty and me following behind. Letty slipped her hand into mine, and even at fifteen, at my
height and a woman's weight, it still felt the same way it felt when
she was six: as though all the trust in the world were caught in the
palm of my hand.

Letty and I got in the backseat and Cora drove. It was full dark
now, and Letty leaned against me and fell asleep with me stroking
her hair. The drive home seemed shorter and was a lot less emotional than the drive up, and I walked Letty right into the house
and steered her toward the bathroom.

"Shower up and get into bed," I said. "I'll be in to check on you
in a few minutes."

"Okay," she said, her voice cracking slightly as I turned away.
"Mom?"

"Yeah, honey?"

"I'm so sorry," she said, nearly a whimper.

"Okay, don't get all upset again. I'm just glad you're home, I'm
glad you're okay, and I want you to get cleaned up and in bed."

If it was a relief to me to go into autopilot mom-mode, then it
was also clearly a relief for her. For the first time in a long time,
something I'd not noticed until now, Letty seemed happy to simply
be the child in the relationship, amenable to being told what to
do.

But I felt no sense of triumph at the realization, only a deepen-
ing fear that I had lost some knowledge of who my daughter was
without even noticing. With Letty in the bathroom I looked for
Cora, finding her dropping Letty's things in the guest room.

"Thanks, Cora," I said.

"No problem," she said. "How's she doing?"

"Weird," I answered with a laugh. "I don't know, like she's ten and happy to be ten."

"She's happy to be with her mother," she said. "She feels safe with you."

"She feels safe with you, too. You're the one she called."

"Only because I can't ground her for the rest of her life."

"Maybe. But, there's no question that the two of you have become closer on this trip."

Cora sank down onto the edge of the bed and closed her eyes for a moment.

"Are you okay?" I immediately asked, dropping to my knees in front of her. "Are you in pain?"

She laughed. "Oh, well, I have no idea how to answer that right now. No, no, I'm not in pain. I'm all right. Tired. I'm just constantly tired."

"You too, into bed. You have a big day tomorrow. I'll be taking you, no arguments."

"I'm not Letty. You don't need to mother me, Ali."

"Someone has to," I said.

She didn't argue either. With Letty in the shower and Cora washing up in her bathroom, I took a moment to sit on the sofa and collect my thoughts, but it was no use. I heard the far-off sound of Letty's cell phone, the phone she'd taken out of our closet.

I rushed to the guest room and grabbed it from her purse, flipping it open before the call was lost.

"Hello?"

"Letty?"

"This is Letty's mother. Is this Seth?" I could hear my voice shaking a little and was surprised and infuriated with myself that I was afraid of talking to a teenage boy.

There was a long moment of silence.

"Uh, yeah. Is— Where's Letty?"

"Letty is home, with me. Where are you, Seth? What happened today?"

"She's okay?"

"She's upset, but she's here. Now I want to know about you. What exactly did you think you were doing taking my daughter to Venice? You do know that she's fifteen? That her father is a police officer?"

"I—I know, yeah, I do know."

"So what did you do to my daughter that had her calling in a panic for me to come get her?"

"I didn't do anything, I swear, I didn't. I got—I screwed up."

I didn't know this kid, but there was real fear in his voice. "What do you mean, you screwed up? What's going on?"

"I can't—" He broke off into a frustrated groan. "I'm—they're holding me. I was just trying to get hold of Letty so I could tell her I was okay. I knew she had to be worried."

"What do you mean? Who's holding you?"

"Well, you know, I mean, the cops, you know?"

"Great, that's great. What happened? Why are they holding you? Have they charged you with anything? Where are your parents?"

He blew out his breath hard enough into the phone that I pulled Letty's cell away from my ear. "Seth?"

"Yeah."

"Have you called your parents? I'm sure they're worried about you."

"Oh man. No, no my parents aren't worried about me. But hey—hey, uh, Mrs. Gutierrez?"

I had always told Letty's friends to call me *Ali*. But I wasn't willing to do that this time, not like this. *Mrs. Gutierrez* was fine.

"Could you just tell Letty, just tell her that I'm sorry, I didn't mean to leave her alone there, and I thought I'd be back quick, and—"

"Seth. Seth, listen to me: Do your parents know you're in jail?"

"No! No, man, shit. Look, I mean, I'm sorry I cussed, okay? No, they won't be able to find my parents. It's just not—it's not gonna happen, okay?"

His voice had climbed high, betraying his fear, and I couldn't help myself.

"What can I do to help you, Seth? Why can't they contact your parents?"

"My mom hasn't been around for, what? Fifteen years? And my dad—my dad wanted me gone anyway, okay? He's sure as hell not going to answer the phone or do anything to get me out. So, look, I'm really sorry about everything. Please tell Letty that I love her—"

We were both shocked into silence at that.

"Okay, so, sorry," he said.

"Tell me where you're at, Seth," I said, but he had already hung up.

"Mom?"

I closed Letty's phone and turned to her. I didn't know how long she had been there. She was in her ancient Hello Kitty pajamas. When we picked her up from the party and she'd changed into them at home, I had been shocked at how obscene she had suddenly looked in them. They were too small, years too small, and had been washed so many times the fabric had thinned to something between lace and fog.

Everything about her that night had been tawdry: her hair dry and slept on, her expression rebellious and pouting, her posture loose-limbed, her arms and legs too long and splayed in the pseudosexual manner of fourteen-year-old models.

Tonight, the pajamas were the same, but everything else was different. Her hair was still damp, combed tightly back into a low ponytail in a sprung scrunchy; her face was scrubbed clean of make-up, her eyes were wide and scared, and she held herself closely together, as if prepared for cold.

My little girl broke my heart, but I made a mental note to discard the Hello Kitty pajamas once she had changed out of them.

"Yeah, honey?"

"Was that . . . ?"

"Come on in and sit down. It's time for you to tell me what's been going on."

I kicked my shoes off and scooted up on the bed, against the headboard, and patted the bed next to me. She came hesitantly, but at last she came and she talked, settling against me and telling me about how much she felt she'd changed in comparison to the kids she went to middle school with, how she met Seth in the courtyard at lunch, how they'd fallen in love, and then, God help me, that they had slept together the night of the party.

"And . . ." I couldn't frame what I wanted to ask her properly. "Are you okay? Was it . . . painful? Were you scared?"

"You're not mad?"

"Oh, I don't know that I'd say that," I said. "I am. I think you're much too young—"

"How old were you?"

"That's not the point."

She pulled away so she could look me in the eye. "Why not?"

"Because it was a different time, a long time ago, and because I know a lot more now than I did then. I was too young, too, and I was pressured into it. I was afraid, of a lot of things, making him mad for one. And I thought I was older than I really was."

"Mom."

I sighed. "I was fifteen, Letty, but older than you. You were technically still fourteen."

"Was it Dad?"

"This conversation isn't about me, Letty. It's about you. We'll talk more about me one day, but not tonight. Now, were you pressured?"

She shook her head. "Not really. I mean, I didn't really want it to happen there, like that, but I did want to do it—sorry. I did want to, with him, and I told him I did."

What was I supposed to do? It was already over, there was no going back. I wanted, more than anything, to wail and protest that she was too young enough times that it would somehow make a difference in the universe and I could turn the clock back. But at no time during my life had that ever worked, and I'd tried it plenty. So I took a deep breath and continued to ask the questions that the situation called for.

"And did you use protection?"

"Mom," she said, a thin hint of a whine creeping back into her voice.

"Did you?"

"We used a condom, okay?"

"And was that the only time?"

"Well, yeah, remember? You grounded me."

"You skipped school today. You might have skipped every day for the past few weeks for all I know."

"But I didn't."

"Okay."

"Was that him on the phone?"

"It was, and I'll let you know what he said, but I want to hear the rest. Why did you run away, and what happened in Venice?"

Letty looked away from me, her face turning crimson.

"Letty. It's time to be honest with me."

"You're going to be mad."

"I'm already mad. But you're home, you're okay, and we're going to work this out."

She looked at me speculatively for a moment, gauging whether I was telling the truth, and then she took a deep breath, sighing it out before she started, resignation heavy in her voice.

"Seth wanted to go see his cousin."

"Did you plan this?" I asked, unable to keep myself from interrupting.

"He asked me to go a couple of days ago," she said, then fell silent, waiting for me to fire another question at her. I restrained myself, and she started again. "So we were just supposed to go up for a few hours, to the beach where they have all the shark's teeth, you know? And then we were going to come right back. But there were a bunch of people there and everyone was drinking, and when we went back to his cousin's place, they took off—"

"Who took off?"

"Seth and Jimmy, his cousin."

"Were they drinking?"

"Everyone was drinking, Mom."

"Were you?"

Letty looked away from me.

"Yes. But I only had a beer, that was all."

"Okay, keep going."

"So they left, and then Jimmy's roommate was trying to get me to drink more. They were playing beer pong, and—"

"How old is Jimmy?" I asked. I wanted to find Jimmy and his roommate and wring their necks.

"I don't know, maybe twenty?"

"And his roommate?"

"Mom," she protested.

"All right. So he wanted you to play a drinking game?"

"Yeah, but I was getting nervous about what time it was, and Seth wasn't back, so I went into the bedroom and tried to call him, but he didn't answer. And then Jimmy's roommate came in the bedroom, and . . ."

"And what, sweetie?" I asked softly, praying silently that nothing like what I was envisioning happened.

"He was trying to, you know, kiss me and everything."

My hands curled into fists, and I breathed deeply, trying to hide my fury. Grown men feeding my daughter alcohol, coming on to her; I got a little taste of how out of control Benny felt.

Letty rushed forward. "But I got away."

"Got away? Did you have to fight? Did he hurt you?"

"No, Mom, I just, you know, I screamed, and someone came to the door, and I got out and ran to the bathroom and locked the door."

"Well, how far did he get?"

"He just—kissed me," she said, in a near whisper.

"Are you sure, Letty? If anything else happened, I need to know. Everything will be okay, but I need to know."

"No," she said, sounding stronger. "He scared me. He held on to me, my arms, when he was trying to kiss me, but nothing else happened. It just scared me."

I stared at her, trying to decide if she was telling me the truth. I thought she was.

"Okay," I said. "So how did you get out?"

"I stayed in the bathroom for a while, and after I heard him go in the living room I went back to the bedroom, locked the door, and then went out the window."

"Good girl," I said, so relieved by her escape that I forgot to be angry with her.

"I can handle myself, you know," she said, her voice filled with bravado.

"You should have never been in the situation to begin with," I said. "And jumping out of a window isn't *handling* yourself. I'm glad you did it, but knowing how to handle yourself means keeping yourself out of questionable situations to begin with. Skipping school, lying to me and your father, and leaving town with a boy we've never met is *not* handling yourself well. It's immature, and . . ." I trailed off when Cora appeared in the doorway.

As I had been lecturing Letty I had forgotten about Cora, about why she was here, about the *fifty percent*. I stared at my daughter, all of my anger draining out of me as I considered how irrevocably things might change soon.

"Everything okay in here?" Cora asked.

"It's fine," I said quietly. "We're fine."

"Okay. Good night, Letty."

"'Night, Aunt Cora," Letty said, looking from me to Cora rapidly, aware that something had changed.

I took a deep breath as Cora turned away.

"Okay, we'll talk more about this tomorrow," I said. "But I think I'm done for the night. And you need to get to sleep."

I reached out and pulled her toward me, and, surprised, she let me hold her against me, breathe in the warm scent of shampoo and soap and girl. For the moment I was just happy to have her here, safe, for as long as I could keep her that way. I finally pulled away and stood, dizzy and fatigued with emotion.

"Wait, Mom," Letty said, reaching for my hand and tugging me back. I sank down on the edge of the bed. "Are you . . . are you and Dad planning on having a baby?"

"What makes you say that?" I asked, trying to ascertain what exactly she had heard.

"I heard you talking after dinner last night," she said, then fell silent, waiting for me to fill her in.

"If your father and I decide to add to our family, we will discuss it with you together at an appropriate time," I said.

"Well—I don't think you should," Letty said, the words coming quickly, defiantly, as if she had stored them up for a moment when she felt brave enough to say them.

"Why is that?" I asked, truly curious.

"Mom, I mean . . ." Letty's eyebrows pinched together and she leaned forward, pulling her knees up and wrapping her arms around them.

"What, Letty? You obviously have something to say about this."

"Okay, well, you had all those problems and all those miscarriages and then you had me, and all those articles, you know? You always talked about how hard it was, losing all those babies, and how it was so hard on you and Dad, and how grateful you were that you finally had me. And then you even did it again and it didn't work and—you know, Aunt Cora is happy to not even have one baby. Why aren't you happy anymore with just me?"

I started to speak, but Letty was determined to have her say.

"And you're too old, and if you did get pregnant and had a baby you're going to do the same thing to it that you did to me, and I just don't think it's fair."

"You don't think it was fair? What did I do to you?" I asked.

"God, Mom, everywhere I went everyone knew all about me. All my friends knew everything, about me being conceived and everything about you, and how you didn't have good eggs, and their mothers would all ask me questions and, it was just, really . . ."

"Embarrassing?"

"Yeah, it was totally embarrassing, for, like, ever. And even, you know, all the stories, and the stuff on your wall, it's all still there, and so even now, even when I'm fifteen, if people come over to the house they see all that stuff, and I just don't think you should have another baby if it's, like, this whole big thing that lasts for years and years. And it would be even worse now because the baby would also have to grow up with you and Dad so much older than all its friends' parents and it would just be another thing making it a freak."

"Letty, my God, did you think you were a freak?"

I pressed my hand over my heart, suddenly unable to breathe.

"Well, yeah, I was. It's not like you guys just did it and had me and people who needed to know, knew. You had to tell the whole world about it. I mean, I'm sorry, but it's weird to be, like, seven years old and be talking to my friends' moms about sperm."

"But we were so happy," I said, leaning forward, taking her hands in mine. "Don't you understand? We were so, so happy to have you. Of course we wanted to tell the whole world. You were a miracle, Letty, a perfect, beautiful little miracle."

Letty shrugged and looked away.

"Well, isn't one miracle enough?"

LETTY

She might have gone too far. Her mom just stared at her, like she didn't even know who she was. And she still didn't know what Seth had said. She should have asked about that first.

"Mom?"

Her mother just shook her head and pressed her lips together.

"Mom, what did Seth say?"

She knew it might just get her angry again, but she had to ask. It took her mom a minute to change gears, and Letty could tell she was still distracted. She answered, but it was like she was across the room; her voice sounded faraway, sad.

"Oh. Okay. Well, it sounds as though he's in trouble. He didn't say he was arrested, but they're holding him until they can find his parents. From what he said, that's not going to happen."

"He's in jail?" Letty asked, surprised, but not completely shocked.

"I didn't say that. It sounded to me like they were holding him to turn over to his parents."

"But, Mom, his dad didn't even want him in the house. He won't do anything. Mom, we have to do something," she pleaded, panicking at the thought of him in jail, or wherever he was being held.

"Oh, honey, there's nothing we can do," her mom said.

"Call Dad," she said, realizing how crazy it was. Her dad, especially in the mood he'd been in lately, would sooner hit Seth than help him. "He's a cop, he can make them let him go."

"Letty!"

"Mom," she begged. "Please, we have to do something. They could, they could keep him until he's eighteen if nobody does anything, couldn't they?"

"I don't know. I guess it depends on what happened, Letty, I just don't know enough about it. Luckily, for me and for her, I haven't had to pick *my* child up from jail."

Letty knew it was supposed to make her feel ashamed, and she did, but it didn't change the fact that Seth was in trouble.

"You must have an idea about what he did to get picked up," her mother said.

Letty didn't say anything for a minute.

"Letty? This isn't the time to get silent on me. Now, you found it easy enough to express your thoughts a moment ago. So let's have it."

Letty looked down at her hands, one holding the other, the tiny turquoise ring her father had given her when she was little now relegated to her pinkie finger. It was now really too tight on even that, and she began twisting it off as she spoke, avoiding her mom's gaze.

"I think he might sell some pot once in a while," she finally admitted. "He's not, you know, a dealer or anything. I think he was just trying to make some money so he could afford his car."

"Oh, Letty, are you serious?"

"But if *he'd* been doing anything, then they would have arrested him, right? So I think his stupid cousin is the one who did something, and Seth was just with him, you know? Mom, please, you have to help me."

"Letty, he's safe, okay? He's safe for the night, and I'm not going to call your father, explain all of this to him, and then expect him to do something for the boy who slept with his daughter, persuaded her to run away with him, and is possibly a pot dealer. Think that's really a good idea?"

"No," she whispered.

"All right." Her mother sighed, rubbing her forehead and getting up off the bed. "You need to get to sleep. I *am* going to call your father to pick you up and take you to school in the morning."

"Why?" Letty asked.

"I have something important to take care of with Cora, and I can't leave you here by yourself."

"What are you doing?"

"Nothing for you to worry about. Cora is going to have a small medical procedure. It's not a big deal, but I want to take her and be there if she needs anything."

"What do you mean? What's wrong with her?"

"There's nothing wrong with her, it's just a small, personal thing."

That meant woman stuff. Or cosmetic stuff. She was probably going to have Botox or something. Letty was disappointed. She'd thought Aunt Cora would be one of those women who refused to do stuff like that.

"I'm not going to tell your dad about any of this tonight, so you just act like you went to school today and everything is fine, understood? I'll talk to him about it when things have calmed down a little."

Letty stared up at her. "I—won't he be mad that I pretended nothing happened?"

Her father had always been big on a lie of omission still being a big, fat lie.

"I imagine he will, but I'll take care of that. He won't be mad at *you*."

That was a first. They were always, *always*, together against her.

She got under the covers, and her mother bent down and kissed her on the forehead before she turned out the light and left, leaving the door cracked a little bit. Aunt Cora's guest bed was bigger than hers at home, and the pillow was soft. Her hair was still a little damp from the shower, and it felt cool against her cheek. She closed her eyes, realizing how happy she was to be here, falling safely asleep, rather than in Venice, fighting off Jimmy's roommate.

She was fine being fifteen that night.

CORA

I was out of the shower and waiting on the sofa when Ali finally came out of Letty's room. She looked shell-shocked, and I poured her a glass of wine; she drank half of it in a couple of quick swallows, placing it back on the coffee table hard enough to make us both jump.

"Sorry," she said, checking the glass and the table for damage.

"It's fine," I said. "Everything okay in there?"

She looked at me, her eyes wide, disbelief stamped on her face.

"Cora," she said, speaking slowly, "I have no idea who that person is. Who is that kid? Because I barely recognize her. When did this happen?"

"I guess around the same time we grew up? Fifteen? Sound familiar?"

She leaned back into the sofa. "Oh, Cora, were we that young at fifteen, though? We were more mature, weren't we? Tell me we were."

"If you say so."

Ali sipped on her wine. "So, I need to call Benny, I'll have him pick her up for school, we'll get you checked in and settled, and then I guess I'm going to have to talk to him about all of this."

"What about Letty? What do you want to tell her about me?" I asked. I understood the need to figure out the best way to tell her not only what was happening, but what her interest in it might be. I'd hoped we wouldn't have to do it so quickly, but here it was, upon us.

Ali held her glass of wine against her forehead for a moment, rolling it back and forth, cooling herself. "I guess Benny and I will talk to her after school," she said. "I think I'd just like to tell her about you first, okay?"

"What will you tell her about getting blood drawn for the tests?"

"I'll think about that. From what you said, if she has it, she has it and there's nothing that knowing any sooner will gain us?"

I shook my head. "No, I'm sorry. Of course if she does carry it, she'll want to know for her own children—"

Ali laughed. "Oh, God, tell me that's a long way off. This is as much as I can stand for ten years or so."

"Well, that could be one way."

"What?"

"If she's sexually active, you need to get her to the doctor."

"Cora, I am not ready for this," she said.

"I know, but apparently she is. Or, I guess it doesn't matter if she is or not, she's there. So you take her to the doctor for her first exam, get to have all the talks, birth control, STD prevention, all the fun stuff. Maybe *they* could draw blood and order the tests.

She'll never know what she's being tested for, and if she's negative, she'll never have to worry about it."

Ali was nodding. "It might work. What about Benny, though? I don't see any reason to tell him that she's no longer a virgin, do you? I don't think that's need-to-know information—God, this is so weird."

"Which part?" I asked. It had all been weird for me for months, though with my access surgery in less than ten hours it was becoming more real every moment.

"You spend the first part of their lives as a unit, you know? I never kept anything from Benny about Letty, and I know he never kept anything from me. Even if we told her it was a secret, we told each other. But now, it's like I'm moving a little more toward Letty being allowed to keep some things from Benny, for everyone's good. Does he really need to know that she's had sex? I wouldn't have wanted my father to know, and I don't see any reason why he should have."

I hardly knew what to say. After all, I'd never had a father to know whether I'd had sex. And Barbara had never had to deal with a co-parent of any kind. Who knows what my biological mother would have thought? If I hadn't been having sex by fifteen, she probably would have wondered what was wrong with me. It wasn't a dilemma I'd ever had to consider, or even thought I might have to consider. And so I hadn't.

"I don't know, Ali," I said, but she gave a sharp laugh, and I realized she wasn't finished.

"And Letty," she continued. "I've spent most of her life being so open with her. I thought it was the right thing. She knows more than she should about her conception. I *burdened* her with that knowledge, and I never even knew it. And now I'm not telling her about this . . . this thing that might affect her more than how she was conceived ever would. I'm keeping things from Benny, I'm keeping things from Letty. I don't know what to do."

Ali was shaking her head.

"I—I don't know, either, Al," I said, desperate to say something helpful. "I guess I can see both sides of it. I suppose if I had to make the decision, I probably wouldn't tell Benny about Letty, I mean, about the sex part. But I don't want to tell you to lie to your husband, either. And Letty, you know, that's your decision, and I—I just, I don't know—"

I stopped babbling when she turned to me and cocked her head to the side.

"You don't know?" she asked. "*You* don't know? Well, hell, Cora, if you don't know, who am I supposed to ask?"

I looked at her uncertainly. But then she put her wine down and scooted close to me, taking my hand in hers and peering intently at me.

"Hey, listen, you don't need to fix anything here, okay? I'm just talking out loud, trying to get a feel of this new thing. I'll figure it out. But all you need to do is think about how to get well. We're going to figure that one out together. And I have a feeling, a good feeling, that one of my wine-soaked kidneys is going to clean its act up and find a new home with you. I think Letty's fine. So stop worrying about it, all right?"

They were less the words of optimism than of worry deferred, but if she was going to give me permission to not think about it for a day or two, then I was going to take her up on it. Maybe she was right. Maybe Letty was fine.

And maybe when I went in tomorrow they'd discover that it had all been a big mistake, and Keith and I would go back to the airport and fly for the rest of the day. But I wasn't counting on it.

As Ali went to the patio to call Benny, I crawled into bed and stared into the dark for an hour, lightly caressing my still unscarred arm, tracing my fingers over the veins, feeling for my pulse, the steady current inside my body finally lulling me to sleep, where I dreamed of the winds in Africa, the turbines in New York, and the feel of the air beneath my plane.

In my dreams, I controlled them all.

11

A L I

"I thought you were going to call me," Benny said, sounding petulant.

I knew that he had no idea of everything I'd been through in the past eight hours, but it still irritated me. What had been so hard about his night? He probably sat on the sofa, ordered Chinese food, and watched TV all night. While I'd had to drive to Venice to pick up our errant daughter and found out she might be carrying a ticking time bomb and was sleeping with a possible pot dealer who was in custody. Not to mention the fact that my best friend had a life-threatening disease.

"What do you call this? Here I am, calling you, right now."

"Okay," he said slowly. "Everything all right?"

"No, nothing is all right. Cora is ill, Benny."

In trying to explain Cora's kidney disease I realized how little about it I truly knew, and vowed to begin educating myself so that not only could I help Cora more efficiently, but I'd be prepared . . . just in case.

"She'll be going in to get the access point for the dialysis put in place in the morning, so could you please pick Letty up here and take her to school?"

"Of course," he said, sounding apalled. "Ali, I'm so sorry. Cora always seemed so . . . healthy. Annoyingly healthy, you know? Vibrant, I guess, always *there*."

"She's still here, she's still vibrant, but she needs a little help."

"I just—I don't know what to say. Do you want me to take the day off tomorrow? I can drop Letty at school and come to the hospital to wait with you."

"No, you need to go to work, Benny. We'll be okay. I'll pick Letty up from school and we'll go back to the hospital," I said.

"Ali. I love you so much; you do know that, don't you?"

"I do."

"Are we . . . okay?"

"We're going to be fine."

We both sat quietly for a moment, listening to each other breathe, relaxing back into our together space, the place where we were one, a unit.

"I'll see you tomorrow," he finally said. "Both of you try to get some sleep, and tell Cora I'm thinking about her, and we'll be there for her."

"Thank you, Benny. Good night."

"Good night, sweet dreams," he said, the same thing he said to me every night before I fell asleep.

I checked on Letty, cracking the door wider to make sure she was there, to make sure she was sleeping and not lying awake, worrying. She was curled on her side, her hair slipping over her face, only the tip of her nose and chin visible. The sound of her regular breathing made me aware of how tired I was, and I quickly got ready for bed.

Cora was already asleep when I finally slipped under the comforter. Or if she was awake she didn't want me to know. As exhausted as I was, there was no sleep for me that night, and I watched the clock, aware of what kind of day I was facing, unable to slow my mind down.

I was up first in the morning, taking my shower before I woke Letty for hers. I sat on the edge of her bed, my hair wrapped in a towel, and laid my hand lightly on her shoulder.

"Come on, sweetie, time for school."

She woke slowly but didn't give me any trouble getting up, and I woke Cora before heading to the kitchen to make breakfast. Cora couldn't eat before her surgery, but I wanted to make sure Letty had a good meal in her. It was going to be a long day for everyone.

When Benny arrived, we hugged for a long moment in the driveway before he came in and ate while we waited for Letty.

"How's Cora?" he asked. "Should I . . . talk to her?"

"She's in the shower," I said. "Don't worry. I think she's fine with being left alone for now. I'll let her know you're thinking about her. I just told Letty I had things to take care of with Cora today. So just talk about light things on the way to school, okay? Or better yet, don't talk at all, just let her pick the radio station and listen to her sing the whole way."

He laughed. "It's not really one of her talents, is it?"

"I'm sure she has others," I said, grinning at him. "They'll show up . . . one day."

When Letty came out of the guest room, shining and young and ready for school, she ran as soon as she saw Benny, throwing her arms around him. They left for school with Benny carrying her backpack and her chattering about possibly taking flying lessons over the summer. I didn't know why I'd been worried about her confessing what had happened the day before.

Keith, who had taught Cora how to fly so long ago, arrived soon after they left, and I gave him coffee while we waited for Cora to emerge from the bedroom, explaining that I would follow behind them to the hospital, and that I would pick Cora up the next day. In the nature of a particular type of kind man everywhere, he seemed relieved to have someone to share in this responsibility, as if afraid he was going to say or do the wrong thing at exactly the wrong moment.

When Cora appeared with a small overnight bag, I was amazed at how collected she appeared. You'd have thought she was just heading out for a little road trip, and maybe she'd stay the night if her destination held enough interest for her. She kissed Keith on the cheek, and he blushed, his cheeks turning pink above his beard.

"Can you even have coffee?" I asked, my hand already on a mug for her.

She shook her head. "I don't think so. I've never been much of a coffee fan anyway. Would you mind braiding my hair for me?"

"Of course," I said, already on my way around the counter.

"We'll just be a minute," Cora said to Keith, laying a hand on his arm briefly, before following me. She sat on the stool and let me comb her hair. "You don't have to be so gentle," she murmured as I delicately drew her hair back from her face.

"Well, I want to be," I said. "How did you sleep?"

"Surprisingly well," she said. "I don't want you to worry, Ali. This is a very simple operation. They're just opening up my arm, not my chest."

"I understand that," I said. "But I can't help thinking about why you're doing it in the first place."

She shrugged. "Can't be helped," she said, closing her eyes.

"Doesn't mean I have to be happy about it." I tugged a little more insistently on her hair.

She smiled a little and opened up one eye to peek at me, then closed it again. "I suppose not."

"I'm going to get as much information on transplants as I can today," I said. "If there's anything I can get done while I'm there, like blood tests or anything, I'm going to go ahead. Benny, too."

"You might want to check with him first. He's liable to run screaming if you just set upon him with needles and a scalpel."

"Benny will happily sit in one spot and let them do anything they want to him for you."

She was quiet for a second, and I could feel her head wanting to tilt forward, to cast her gaze down. I tugged gently and made her meet my eyes in the mirror.

"He'll do anything he can for you, Cora, he's already said so."

"That's because you haven't told him about Letty yet," she said.

*   *   *

As I followed Keith and Cora in my car I could see Cora through the back window, waving her hands in the air. She was telling stories, passionate about her life, as she always was. The only thing I'd ever been passionate about was becoming a mother. There was no question that becoming pregnant through in vitro had been difficult. In fact, *difficult* did not do it justice; there was no one word complex enough to describe it.

But it served as a focus for me. All that had once been out of my control became fixable, with schedules, and shots, and tests, and for the first time, I was passing tests. Maybe they weren't pregnancy tests, but they were tests indicating I was ready for pregnancy, and I was passing. I had a plan.

I grieved the loss of the plan as much as I grieved the loss of the embryos. The time between a miscarriage and the start of the next series of procedures to get my uterus ready for transfer was lost time, crazy-making time. My schedule was gone, my plan gone. But then it would start again, and I could feed the hope again.

I always imagined that the way Cora felt about her job, traveling around, trying to get people to put wind turbines on their land, was the way I felt during those hopeful, scheduled, planned times. Once she found her calling, she was always fertile, always up and excited about her life, creating energy. She had things scheduled for years in advance, and most of her plans came to fruition.

If any big things fell through for her, if she had any heartbreaks, like my miscarriages, she kept them to herself, and despite what I knew of her early years, I considered her charmed. There were times, I was ashamed to admit, that I'd resented her for it.

There were times, despite my desperate love for my husband and my child and my home, and even for Florida itself, that I resented her for being able to travel all over the world. I'd never even had a passport. And not only had she traveled all over the world, she could do so *on her own*. She wasn't just taken places, she could fly there herself.

And there she was, being driven to have an operation designed to eventually marry her to a machine for the rest of her life, completely changing everything about her life that she was passionate about. I could still see her through the back window, acting as if she were on her way to the airport to jet off to Kuala Lumpur. Cora could make anything sound exciting.

It was very difficult to realize that your friend was a better person than you, and to know that you'd been suspicious of that fact for most of your life. I wanted to believe that I brought something to the table, and I thought I'd gotten the opportunity. The only person in the world who could have stopped me from lying right down on the table and insisting they take my kidney now was Letty.

Though they weren't close, Benny had a brother, and if I were down to one kidney and Benny needed one, I thought he would likely step up. But this was Letty. Everything of mine was for her, as was everything of Benny's. The fact that Cora had gone through everything she had in order to provide me with the very thing that might keep her from getting a transplant made me feel drenched in panicked selfishness.

We'd know soon enough. I consoled myself with that. There was so much I had to do in the meantime. I had no idea how long a genetic test could take, and I would use that time to research everything I could about PKD, not only for Letty, but for Cora, too.

I could feel the panic start to lift. Like my IVF years, once I had a plan, I could handle it. Of course, *handle it* meant different things to different people, and I was aware that at times during the in vitro there were people who didn't think I was handling it so well.

At the hospital we waited. And waited some more. And finally I met Cora's nephrologist, who had stopped in to check on her and talk to the vascular surgeon. Once he got there, things moved pretty quickly. As they prepared to take Cora away, she told Keith good-bye, asking him to keep an eye out for her next week, that if there was one thing she knew she wanted to do after this was over, it was to fly.

I gave him my cell phone number and took his and promised to call as things progressed. When they wheeled her away, I laid a hand on Dr. MacKinnon's arm.

"Could I speak to you for a moment?"

He checked his watch and then said, "Sure," folding his arms around a clipboard and looking very doctorly.

"From what I understand, Cora is going to wind up needing a kidney transplant," I said, hoping he would simply continue my thought process on his own. He just tilted his head to the side and waited me out. I'd never been good at that game.

"And I told her, immediately, that I would do it. But there might be an issue with my daughter. You see, she was conceived with Cora's egg. She is, technically, Cora's biological child."

He shook his head. "Well, you just can't do it even if you are a match, then, can you?"

The speed with which he comprehended the situation astonished me. And the definite tone of his reply took me aback.

"I—well, I don't know. We don't even know if Letty, my daughter, inherited this."

He motioned me over to a couple of chairs in the corner. They sat at a ninety-degree angle to each other, and our knees touched when we sat. He leaned toward me and spoke quietly.

"I can't talk to you about Cora's case specifically. However, if your daughter has a biological parent who has PKD, then you have to work under the assumption that she does have the gene. I have two children, and as far as I'm concerned, any of my donateable organs are stamped with their names."

I nodded. "Absolutely, yes, that's just how I feel. And Cora feels that way, too."

"But Cora has a better chance at being a match with your daughter than you do. And even that's not guaranteed. Everyone seems to think organs can just be tossed around between people like footballs, but matches can sometimes be difficult to come by, even in families."

"I already know we're a good blood-type match. We had to be for her to donate eggs."

"They look at more than blood type. Your antigens need to be as good a match as possible. And they'll cross-match, to see if she might reject a kidney due to protein or cellular differences."

"Well, we still want to test Letty—"

He held his hand up. "Tested as a match for Cora?"

"No, to see if she has the gene."

"Have you spoken to anyone about genetic testing yet?"

"No, not yet. I just found out about all this—"

"Okay, then before you get any further in this process you have some things to think about."

He pulled out his BlackBerry and expertly thumbed some information up on it. He placed it on his clipboard and pulled a business card out, turning it over to copy the information on the BlackBerry onto it.

"This is a genetic counselor," he said, putting the BlackBerry away and handing me the card. "I strongly suggest you contact her as soon as possible. Let her know that I've referred you."

I took the card and finally made my point. "Listen, we already know what to do," I said. "Once we get the results back, if they're negative, then I'll definitely be a donor for Cora. I want to get as much information as I can, so that when we get the results, I can just be ready to move ahead quickly."

He stared down at his clipboard for a moment, then looked up at me, emotion I couldn't read on his face. Pity, impatience, something I didn't expect.

"It doesn't work like that," he said. "You *must* speak to a counselor first. I'm not qualified to give you any advice here, but you need to make sure that you even want the tests done to begin with."

"Why wouldn't we want the tests done?" I asked in surprise.

"Well, for one thing, it changes nothing for your daughter. There is no cure for PKD, and no medication to slow its onset, *if* she even has it."

"But Cora—"

"*And*," he interrupted, "there are other ramifications of genetic testing. Like what the knowledge of a disease waiting in the wings for you does to your psyche. The only thing we could do for your daughter right now, *if* she even has the gene and until she shows signs, would be to give you dietary guidelines. And regular ultrasounds. That's it."

He reached over and tapped my knee. "Call the counselor before you do anything," he said, and stood. "I'll be around to check on Cora later," he said, leaving me there with the business card burning in my hand.

Just as I started putting everything he had said into some sort of context, Benny arrived.

"Hey, sweetheart," he said, pulling me up into his arms. It felt good to be back in that space with him. "Okay," he said as we sat down. "So what's going on? Is she in there already?"

I nodded and looked at my watch. "I imagine they're putting her under right about now."

He looked at his watch, too, and I knew he was setting himself up to be organized throughout the rest of the day.

"Any indication of how long it's going to take?" he asked.

"No. It's really not a dangerous operation. The risk of it is in the anesthesia. I'm sure she'll be just fine with this part; it's the disease as a whole that's concerning."

"What's the bottom line on this? Is it fatal or something?"

"There's no cure. She said people can live for years and years on dialysis, but don't people die all the time waiting for a kidney?"

He shrugged. "No idea, really. It's not something that's ever been on my radar before except to sign my organ donor card, you know? What about the guy, the boyfriend?"

"They broke up, remember?"

"Well, so what is it you're thinking, Ali?" he asked, his voice low and serious, pained already.

I took a deep breath. Here we go.

"Of course I immediately told her that I wanted to give her one of mine—"

"Ali! How could you not have talked to me about this?"

"Just hold on before you say anything else, Benny. You need to hear the rest," I said.

I turned the chair toward him, our knees mingling, my hands on his legs.

"I don't think I can give her a kidney."

"Is she too far along?" he asked, his sympathy kicking in quickly on the heels of relief.

"No. The kind of disease she has, polycystic kidney disease, it's hereditary."

He didn't get it for a moment. He just looked at me, and as realization dawned across his face I felt my heart break over it all over again.

"Letty," he whispered.

I nodded. "Now let me tell you the rest before you get too upset, okay? Obviously we're going to be doing a lot of research, and we'll learn about all the details, but here's what I know so far." I couldn't get the words out fast enough. Benny's eyes were huge, and he was holding himself together, but I needed to give him something to grab on to quickly.

"There's a chance she doesn't have it at all, and even if she does carry the gene, it doesn't mean she'll ever develop it."

He ran his hand across his face. "So what are you saying here? What are the chances?"

"It's fifty-fifty."

"So what are we going to do?"

"The way this thing works is that it doesn't usually show up until the thirties. And until there are some symptoms . . . You know what, honey? I don't know. I just don't know enough about it, and I'm going to tell you something that's wrong and—"

"Hey," he said, reaching over and grabbing my arms just above the elbow. "Okay, it's all right. Just slow down. Come on."

I took a deep breath. "Oh, Benny, I just can't believe this is happening."

"Well, maybe it's not. There are tests, right? We'll get the tests, we'll find out for sure, and maybe . . . what?" he asked, trailing off as I shook my head.

"There is a genetic test, you know, testing her DNA. But there are problems, things to think about, with testing her. We have to figure out what to tell her, and I guess we'd all have to get tested to see if we're even matches, any of us, for Cora and for Letty, before we do anything."

"So we'll do it. Who gives a crap about the problems? We'll just deal with them. If it's expensive, we have good insurance, and we can take care of the rest. Isn't it better to know?"

I held the counselor's card out to him. "We have to go see her before we make any decisions about this."

He took the card and pulled his cell phone out.

"You're calling now?" I asked.

"I don't feel like agonizing over this any longer than I have to, do you?"

"I—I guess not."

He stared at me for a minute.

"Are you telling me everything?"

I hated this part of him being a cop. When he turned that calm suspicion on me, I always got defensive. Benny, as far as I could tell, had never taken on either the "good cop" or the "bad cop" persona. He fluctuated between the two, being exactly what a person needed at any given moment, lulling you into feeling understood, practically handing him the information he'd use to hang you with.

"No, but I will, and none of it is as important as getting this appointment, so go ahead and do that," I said. He alternated watching me and punching the numbers into his phone. I leaned against the corner and stared at the faded pastel print on the wall while he made the appointment, trying to figure out what to tell him and what I should keep to myself.

"Okay," he said, hanging up. "We're going in next Thursday. And you think—what? That we shouldn't tell Letty anything?"

"We're going to have to tell her about Cora, of course," I said. "Though I don't see any reason to fill her in on how serious it is yet. It would just scare her, and she's really going to go through enough. What do you think?"

He nodded. "Hell, I'm sorry *I* even know. I'm scared. You know, I thought Cora looked bad. Is this why?"

"Yeah. She told me she'd been sick, but I never thought it was something like this."

"Letty," he said, nothing else, and I knew we were both picturing Letty looking the way Cora did.

"Speaking of Letty," I said. "She skipped school yesterday."

He sighed heavily and tipped his head back against the wall. "I thought you were making sure she got there in the mornings."

"I did, Benny. She left with her boyfriend—"

"Oh, great. This is the guy from the notes?" he asked, snapping his head back up.

"Seth, yes. The guy from the notes."

"That's it. I don't care what you say about her growing up. I'm putting a stop to this today. Under no circumstances is she to see this kid again."

"I'm not sure she should either, Benny, but there's a problem with him, and, to be honest, I'm concerned."

"You're concerned about *him*?"

"They went to Venice yesterday. Apparently he went to do something with his cousin, the cousin got arrested, and Seth is in custody. He's a minor and they have to release him to his parents, but he says his mother hasn't been seen in years and his father won't go get him, if they've even been able to find him."

"Venice? What the hell is she doing taking off to Venice?"

I sat back down in the chair. "I think she was trying to get our attention, punish us, I don't know."

"Get our attention? Having to pick her up at three in the morning didn't get our attention? What the hell is going through her mind? Punish us? For what? Spoiling her? Keeping a roof over her head, food on the table?"

"She is no more spoiled than any of her friends, Benny, and a lot less spoiled than a lot of kids in this town. Things are different now. Her parents don't pick tomatoes for a living. We have the means to give her the same things all these other kids have. What do you want to do? Dress her in rags?"

"She doesn't have to dress in rags, but she doesn't have to—"

"Benny, Benny, hang on. Let's think about what's really important here, okay?"

To my surprise, he stopped talking and looked at me in desperation.

"One of our dearest friends, the woman who gave us our child, is gravely ill. It's possible our daughter will eventually be, too.

And there's a young man she cares about who's in trouble, and who we might be able to help. We're doing what we can for Cora. We're here, and we're willing to learn about what we can do for her. Same for Letty. There's not much else we can do right now, Benny. So, I know you, and you need something to do. You said you wanted to help kids like Todd Jasper? Well, here's your chance. This kid clearly needs help, Benny. See what you can find out about this boy."

I could practically see the wheels turning, the plan falling into place, his determination to not forget Todd, the one boy he hadn't been there to help, the chance to possibly make up for that.

"What's happening for Letty at school today? She have any tests you know about or anything?" he asked.

"Not that I'm aware of."

He nodded and took a look at his watch. "All right. I'll look into it, but that doesn't mean I approve of her seeing him."

"Of course," I said.

He sighed and gripped the arms of his chair before pushing himself up.

"I'll go home and get ready for work and go talk to her before I head in," he said. "I'll check out the records, see if he's in the system yet."

His relief at having something concrete, something he was good at, to do, was nearly palpable. I wished for that kind of task, something I could throw my physical self into. He kissed me before striding off, leaving me to wait, and think.

LETTY

Everyone turned around and looked at her when the intercom blared her name. For a second she was just happy to get out of class, but she knew they were all thinking it had to do with Seth. Everyone had been asking her where he was, and she just had to say she didn't know.

It killed her to not have her cell phone again, though she guessed he didn't have his either if he was in some juvenile detention center or something. But they had to at least let him make calls, right? She was thinking that maybe she would go to the school counselor's office, but then what if they found out Seth wasn't living at home?

Mom wouldn't help, but maybe she could talk to Aunt Cora alone and she might do something. Even if it was just find out where he was and if he was okay. Letty had been making notes in her spiral about where they were in Venice, and his cousin's name, and anything else she could think of so she wouldn't forget anything, when they called her to the office.

It wasn't until she was out the door that she got scared about why they were calling her.

The doors to the office were always propped open, so she saw the cop before he saw her. His back was to her at first, but then he turned to the side a little and she saw it was her dad. She still wasn't used to seeing him in his uniform, and he had never, ever, not one single time, showed up at her school.

His being there made her more nervous than if it had been a whole room full of cops.

He still hadn't seen her, and she looked toward the front doors, considering just walking right out then and running for the mall, an easy place to hide. But then she thought about what he might actually be doing there, and only one thing came to mind: Something must have happened to her mom.

She ran the last few yards, and when he saw her, he had such a weird look on his face that she thought for sure she was right.

"What's wrong?" she asked, already in his arms.

"Hey, nothing's wrong," he said, but he leaned down and kissed the top of her head, and she couldn't remember the last time he'd done that. He let her go and looked at the secretary. "Is there an empty office?"

She shook her head. "No, but you can talk in the library. Letty knows where it is."

They walked down the hall, and Letty was glad she had her biology book to press against her stomach, because she definitely felt like she was going to get sick. She wished he would just start talking instead of making her wait.

But they finally got to the library and she took him to the back, where they kept all the old computer stuff. A couple of the guys who had been at the party watched them go by. She ignored them, but her dad must have given them his cop stare or something, because they got up and left right away.

She dropped her books on the table and sat down after her dad did.

"What's wrong?" she asked again.

He pulled his little notebook out of his shirt pocket and sat with his silver pen in his hand.

"There's nothing wrong, really," he said. "Nothing you need to worry about, okay?"

He gave her a hard look, like he was trying to stick *okay* in her brain. She nodded.

"Now, your mom already told me about you skipping school yesterday—"

He held his hand up as she opened her mouth to defend herself. She was glad he stopped her, because she really didn't know what she was going to say.

"We'll deal with that. We'll talk about it later. I'm not happy about it, no. But your mom told me about Seth. He's in some trouble, right? Your mom seems to feel as though he doesn't have anyone to help him. So, as long as things aren't out of control, I thought I'd see what I could do."

"I—really?" she asked.

"Is this a decent guy, Letty? You need to tell me now, because if I stick my neck out and find out he's a jerk to you or involved in something heavy, then I'm going to be pretty ticked off. I don't want to regret this, and I don't want you to, either."

"No," she said quickly. "Oh, Dad, I don't know what's happening."

"All right, we're going to figure it out. I already know what he told your mother. I want to hear about the two of you first. How long have you two been . . . together?"

She could tell it was hard for him to ask her like that. And it was definitely hard to answer, but if anyone could really help, he could. So she just told him the truth, and told him everything she knew about Seth's dad having some guy move into the house and Seth leaving, and about him sleeping in his car, and at friends', and in the house down the street.

"The gray and white house?" he asked. She nodded, and he sighed and rubbed his forehead really hard. "He do any damage in there? Vandalize anything, steal anything?"

"No! I mean—I don't think so. It was just for a few days. Dad, he's not a criminal, he's not."

"Technically he is, Letty. He broke into a house and squatted there. In our own neighborhood. That's against the law, and that makes him a criminal. You should have told me."

"You would have had him arrested. You wouldn't have helped him. He didn't have anywhere else to go, Dad. What was he supposed to do?"

"He could have stayed with friends—"

"He did, as long as he could. Parents don't just let someone move in without trying to find out what's going on."

"What was going on that was so bad?" he asked. "Did his father hit him? Was there other abuse?"

"I don't know," she admitted. "He would never take me to his house. I think he was embarrassed. I mean, I know they don't have much money, and I didn't want to ask and, you know, make him feel bad."

He nodded then, like he really did get it. He made another note on his note card. "Okay, now tell me everything you remember about Venice: names, addresses, anything you can think of."

She pulled her spiral out and pushed it across the table to him, opening it up to the page she'd been making notes on.

"Good girl," he murmured with a funny smile, ripping it out of the notebook as he studied it and sliding the spiral back across the table to her. She told him everything she could remember, and he made notes next to hers as she talked.

When she finished, he asked, "Nothing else? Nothing you're holding back because you think you might get in trouble? It's not a trick question, Letty. I can't say that I won't get upset, even angry, but listen . . ."

He scooted his chair over next to hers and leaned toward her, placing his hands on either side of her face and making sure she was looking right at him. "Letty, no matter what has happened, no matter what you've done, no matter what you'll ever do, I love you more than anything else in my life, and I always will. You know that, don't you?"

"Dad?" she asked. It looked like he might start to cry. He was scaring her. "Are you okay?"

He tilted his head and looked up at the ceiling, taking a deep breath. "I am fine, sweetie," he said after he looked at her again. "I just want to make sure that you know that you don't have to do everything yourself, okay? It's all right to let me and your mom worry about things sometimes. When you have a problem, or one of your friends needs help, you can talk to us."

"I know," she whispered.

He scooted back and looked away, up the hall of bookshelves. He had his chin tilted up, and he looked about a million miles away. Her mom would always tease him and say he was thinking deep thoughts. Letty didn't know what to do, so she just stayed quiet.

He started talking again, but he didn't look at her.

"You know, I met your mother in middle school. We were in P.E. together, and we were playing softball. I pitched her an easy hit, and she plowed it right at me, and I fell in love with her. Right then, just like that. I don't know why her hitting that ball did it. It was a long time before she loved me back."

He looked at her then.

"So, how much does this guy mean to you, Letty?"

She wanted to be able to act like she understood what he was saying about her mom. She did think it was really cool that they met so long ago, and that they were even together back then. But then they went and got married right out of high school. Just the thought of it all as a whole freaked her out. She loved Seth, but she didn't look at him and see marriage and babies like her mom and dad did, not even in a house with a plane next to it.

"I think I love him, Dad, I do, but . . . I don't want to get married or anything."

"Well, that's good, because when all this is over, I'm going to have to think about whether you're going to be seeing him at all."

She began to protest, but he held his hand up.

"Look, I want a lot of things for you, Letty. I want you to be a good student, I want you to be smart and stay out of trouble, and I want you to go to college. But I want you to enjoy your life, too.

I want you to love and be loved by a good person. But I don't want you to think that because your mother and I met and married so young that you're supposed to do that, too, and I certainly don't want you seeing someone who's already in this much trouble at this age."

"Dad, he's just . . ." She trailed off with a sigh. "He's my first boyfriend. I mean, aren't you supposed to move on from them anyway? They're your 'first love,' right? Like, you look back on them later."

He laughed. "Well, yeah, only I'm still with my first love. I'm just as in love with your mother as I was when I was fourteen, no matter what problems we might be having right now. She had—she'll tell you sometime, I guess—she had other boyfriends. And, maybe I wasn't even her first love. I don't know."

He stopped talking then, but not like he wanted her to say anything, more like he was just thinking, or remembering, so she stayed quiet.

"You're a smart kid, Letty," he finally said, slapping his hand lightly on the table and then leaning over and kissing her cheek.

"I'm going to go see what I can do about this boy, okay? If we can help him, we will."

She didn't know what to say. She realized that she hardly ever said *thank you* to her parents, because she wanted to say it now, and she knew it was what she should say, but it seemed so hard. She nodded and looked down at her ballet flats.

He waited a moment and then stood up, pulling her cell from his pocket and handing it to her.

"Keep it on. If you get in trouble with anyone, you have them call me. I'll stop in the office before I leave to make sure they know you're allowed to accept phone calls today. Put it on vibrate and if it goes off in class, you get up and leave right away. Don't disrupt things."

"Okay," she said, turning it on and clipping it to her pocket.

He hesitated for a minute as if he wanted to say something else, but then he just patted her shoulder and turned to go. She took a deep breath.

"Dad?"

He turned around.

"Thank you."

CORA

I woke once, twice. The third time I felt like humming. Not because I felt so wonderful, I certainly did not. But there was a buzzing in my ears, in my head, a certain tone that, for some obscure reason, I wanted to match, and I began to hum. Or I thought I was humming, but when someone said my name, I opened my mouth to respond to them and never stopped humming. Or thinking I was.

Within a few moments I recalled where I was and made an effort to focus my eyes. Two nurses were standing by the bed, both of them talking, one over the other.

"Hi, Cora, everything is okay."

"You're all right, Cora, everything went just fine."

"Can you look at me, Cora?"

"Can you squeeze my hand?"

I did have a moment in which I was frightened. I remembered the last second of consciousness, realizing that they were shoving a tube down my throat, and then I was out, and now this. The humming faded away, and I was filled with gratefulness to these wonderful women who were standing by me, as if I were the only patient they had, reassuring me, so well, so quickly. I tried to speak, to tell them, *Thank you, thank you so much, what wonderful, nurturing women you are, what angels.*

The drugs were doing their job very, very well.

But of course my voice didn't work just yet, and as I came more fully out from under the anesthesia my angels drifted away and were not at my bedside by the time I could say *thank you*. A different nurse smiled kindly at me and took my vital signs.

Ali was waiting in my room when they wheeled me in, and she just winked at me as they got me situated, staying well out of the way until the nurses decided everything was just right and left the room. Then she leaned over the silver railing and kissed me on the forehead with a loud smack. If I could have laughed, I would have.

"How you feeling?" she asked, pulling a chair up and holding my hand under the rail.

"All right," I croaked. "Doesn't hurt."

She grinned at me, and we both said, "Yet," at the same time.

"You want the TV on?"

"No. Drew?"

She held up her cell phone. "Called and left a message that it went fine, and I said I'd call again as soon as you were coherent. Are you coherent?"

"Not really. Give . . . a minute."

"Okay," she said, her voice growing softer. "Relax. You can close your eyes if you want to."

That sounded good. So I did. Just as I shut them, the first twinges in my arm made themselves known.

When I woke again, Ali was still sitting in the chair, but her eyes were closed and she was breathing evenly enough that I didn't think she was just resting. We both jumped when her cell phone rang, and she scrambled to get it, casting a quick glance at me and grimacing.

"Hello?"

I wasn't particularly interested in who was on the phone. I was, however, very interested in the water on the nightstand and figured out the buttons to push to raise my bed and leaned over toward it.

Ali waved at me to stop and leaped up to help, putting her hand over the mouthpiece.

"You up to talking?" she asked. "It's Drew."

I held my hand out eagerly, croaking, "Hey," into the phone, waiting to hear his voice, surprised by my need.

"How you doing?" he asked, his voice filled with worry.

"I'm okay," I said. "A little sore."

"Know where I'm at?"

"Where?"

"Atlanta. I'll be there in a few hours, assuming we get out in time."

"Really? Are you crazy?"

"Just about you," he said.

"Goofball."

"Should I rent a car or take a taxi?"

"Take a taxi," I said, but Ali held her hand out for the phone, and I handed it over.

"What time are you getting in?" she asked him, writing it down on the notepad on the nightstand. "The airport's only twenty minutes from here. I'll have just enough time to get you before I have to pick Letty up at school."

She handed the phone back to me just as the nurse and the vascular surgeon entered. We said our good-byes, and I suffered through an exam. The surgeon was pleased.

"You'll be ready to go in the morning," he assured me. "I'll stop to check on you, but everything looks good. The things we talked about stand; no pressure on it, keep it clean, et cetera. I'll want to see you in the office in a few days."

I thanked him, and Ali followed them out, to talk about me in the hall, I imagined. It made me smile. How wonderful to be taken care of, how lovely to have people who cared about you so much, who hopped planes to fly across the country, who closed their business in order to attend to you.

My smile slowly faded. It was lovely, wasn't it? It was lovely when you had the flu. Lovely when you were having a baby, though of course I wouldn't know about that. Lovely, right this second, trying to believe that this was it, just this one little, easy surgery. It's my *arm*, for heaven's sake, just a couple little slices and a tube in my arm.

But what is this little surgery for? What does it usher in?

That wasn't so lovely. It wasn't so lovely to think about other people taking care of you when you weren't going to recover. It wasn't so lovely when you realized that those same people might be doing it for years. That this was just the beginning of a life like this. Sitting here, unable to go anywhere.

Waiting for health.

And it would never come.

12

ALI

Drew was nothing like what I'd expected, and yet he was clearly perfect for Cora. As hippie as she was, he was straitlaced, and older than I'd anticipated. He arrived in a blue oxford button-down, navy blazer, and khakis, rimless glasses resting on small ears, and closely cropped hair, silvering nicely on the sides. He could have been anyone, any trim executive on a business trip.

But there were clues to his life in academia, a looseness in the way he moved, a round metal pendant on a leather cord around his neck, and a ready smile despite the underlying reason for his trip. We held each other longer than most people who'd never met would have, two people who shared a common love and worry for another.

He grabbed his bag and squinted as we walked out to the car. I had a spare pair of Benny's sunglasses in the car, and I handed them to him as we sped along the long curve of the airport exit.

He laughed apologetically as he took them. "Thank you," he said, settling them over his own glasses. "So? How is she?"

"She's good, you know, physically," I said, turning onto the back road to I-75. "It's all so scary." I glanced at him quickly. "God, that sounded narcissistic, didn't it? I imagine it's a lot scarier for her than it is for me. I just—Cora's never made me worry before, you know? I guess I'm not used to it."

"I understand. She always took care of me, too," he said. "I never realized how skewed our relationship was on that front until this. I admit it was frustrating at first."

I laughed. "I know. Isn't that strange? It's like when your mother was sick when you were a kid. You just wanted her to get up and make you dinner, right? How dare she feel bad when you're hungry?"

He laughed, too, but it was subdued. "Well, you'd think I'd have gotten on the bandwagon a little faster. I'm still ashamed of that. Not that I ignored it, but I think it was just too much to take in. It was diagnosed so quickly. She was tired; her back and her sides hurt; she was bloated. She went in because she thought maybe she was starting perimenopause. She wasn't even going to go, but I finally convinced her that there were things that could be done, hormone replacements, supplements to make her feel better. Who knew she'd come back with this?"

His head swiveled as we passed a panther crossing sign, and he looked at me in astonishment. "Are you serious?" he asked, as if I'd personally planted the signs.

"Yep," I said. "Although I have to admit that I've lived here my entire life and never caught sight of one in the wild."

Despite that, he watched the sides of the road carefully even after we merged onto I-75.

"She tells me you want to donate," he said, his voice barely audible over the noise of the road.

"Of course I do," I said. "But did she tell you . . . everything else?"

I had no idea what Cora had told him. I assumed she'd been honest about Letty, I assumed she was as open about our situation as I was, but over the years I'd stopped asking when she mentioned a new boyfriend. It had started to feel uncomfortably selfish somehow, to follow every announcement of a new relationship with questions about how much she'd mentioned me and Letty.

He smiled at me. "I don't know," he said, catching me by surprise with the clear tease in his voice. "Why don't you tell me everything, and I'll let you know?"

I laughed. "Forget it. Some things have to stay just between friends. We keep each other's secrets, always have."

"Well, she told me about Letty, that she donated eggs to you and your husband so you could have her. And that she loves you all very much."

I wanted to say that we loved her, too, so much, but I couldn't trust myself to speak.

"And yes, she told me about it being hereditary. I understand that you can't do it. It must have been an agonizing decision."

"I am not positive that I can't do it," I said. "My husband and I have an appointment with a genetic counselor next week. We're thinking about having Letty tested to see if she has the gene or not. If she doesn't, I could do it, I would do it . . ."

"Ah," he said, and I shot him another glance.

"What? I mean, I know there are considerations; we don't even know if we're a match, lots of stuff to think about."

I swerved down our exit too quickly, making Drew grip the handle on the door a little more tightly.

"She said you couldn't donate," I said, probing cautiously.

"Well, we're not a match. I got tested immediately. But even if we were, there would be some things to consider. I'm a hemophiliac," he said matter-of-factly, and I immediately slowed down.

Just what I needed. A car wreck in which Drew's kneecap split open and he bled to death. It felt as if everyone around me were fragile as sea foam, breaking apart at the slightest breeze, tatters across the sand.

Only Benny remained as solid in real life as I had always believed he was, though I was beginning to grow uneasy about the possibility of little time bombs within any of us, waiting for the moment that their ticking would grow loud enough to hear. I didn't say a word, but at the stoplight at the base of the exit I sighed and lowered my forehead to the top of the steering wheel for a moment.

"I know," he said quietly.

"There's nobody else?" I asked. "Nobody close enough to offer, to ask?"

"She has students who love her, but she says they're too young to understand the ramifications."

Something started to gnaw at me, something in between all the information, a sinuous suspicion, threading its way through my mind. As the light turned green I said, "Why is she coming up with all these excuses?"

"What do you mean?"

"The first thing she said when I told her I wanted to donate was that I couldn't because of Letty. You can't . . . I know that's not something you can help, but now students, she says they're too young. What's she waiting for? Who would be a perfect candidate for her?"

He bit his lower lip. "I can see what you're getting at, but I don't know how it changes anything. She doesn't want to die, I'm certain of that. And her students—it's not as if any have come forward specifically and offered. There's been talk, rumors, but what is she supposed to do? Ask directly?"

"Why not?" I asked. "Or you could."

He leaned his head against the window and stared out at the old cemetery flashing by us, overhung with oaks dripping moss, only turning back to me once it had been replaced with a view of the neighboring trailer park.

"I have. The ones I thought might be serious. None of them were willing to take it to the next stage. Don't tell her. She expressly forbade me to approach anyone."

"Is there any way I could help?" I asked, visions of healthy young college students in my head: quick smiles, able bodies, extra-plump pink kidneys.

"I don't know," he said. "There's one girl. She's still a possibility. I'm keeping in touch with her by e-mail. I'm trying to be careful, not push her too much." He pressed the heels of his hands against his forehead, as if holding back more pain than his head could possibly contain.

"Well, keep on her," I said, "and if you think it might help, I'll talk to her."

"Yeah," he said, nodding, his voice hoarse. "I think she just needs some time. Most people are on dialysis for years before there's even the possibility of a kidney. It seems like Cora's kind of flighty, impulsive, but she's really quite methodical. I think she's just trying to get through one stage at a time. It's easy for us to jump ahead when we're not the one going through it."

"I suppose," I said, knowing he was right.

"We're going straight there?" Drew asked.

"If you want," I said.

"Please."

We didn't speak the rest of the drive to the hospital. When I walked him to the door of Cora's room, I hung back, allowing him to go in alone. The door closed slowly, and I heard Cora cry out in pleasure just before it shut completely. I waited for a moment, but then made my way down the hall to the small waiting area outside the elevators and pulled my cell phone out of my purse.

Benny didn't answer, and I called home to check messages, but there was nothing. I settled in to wait until I thought Drew and Cora had had enough time to talk alone. I wanted to see her before I had to pick Letty up from school in a few minutes, but just as I fitted my cell phone back into my purse it rang.

"Hello," I answered quickly, assuming it was Benny calling me back.

"Ali? It's Tim, uh, where you at, honey?"

The only reason I knew I was still breathing was that aside from Tim's voice in my ear, the only thing I could hear was my breath rasping in and out. Tim was a friend, a cop friend, a former partner of Benny's.

And there was only one reason for him to call me.

"Tim? Tim?" I asked, as if he weren't talking, as if I couldn't hear him. He went silent for a moment, forcing my own silence.

"Ali," he said slowly, keeping me from doing anything but concentrating on his voice "Benny's been shot."

*   *   *

Not just shot—but shot three times.

All I got to see of him was a blood-soaked gurney surrounded by a medical team flying by, racing into surgery. I never had a chance to call out to him, and I don't know if I could have produced sound even if they'd stopped right in front of me to let me see the damage.

Tim arrived within seconds of the ambulance and sought me out amid the sea of uniforms in the hall outside surgery and clasped me to him, his bulletproof vest unwieldy under my arms, his fear-laced sweat acrid in my nose.

He held me still for a moment, an embrace I would have normally felt trapped in. I pretended, for a split second, that it was Benny's arms holding me upright, and strength flooded me like adrenaline, forcing my legs to straighten, my shoulders to rise. I didn't know if it was me pulling away, or Tim letting go, or a combination of those things, but I found myself standing upright and alone, a three-foot-wide cushion of air around me like an emotional no-fly zone.

"What can I do? What do you need?" Tim asked, leading me to a small waiting room. Energy practically vibrated off him, and I realized that he was desperate to do something, anything. Like Benny, he was built for action, and as cops began to fill the hall that same energy made me feel as if I might drown in it.

I thought quickly, ticked off a mental list of what might get lost in the next twenty-four hours. Only one thing came to mind.

"Letty, oh God," I said, the image of her standing in front of the school waiting for me to pick her up sliding over the memory of the blood-spattered gurney.

"Where is she?" Tim asked, seizing on it. "I'll go get her, or I'll send someone for her."

"No, no, I think it would be better to have someone else pick her up," I said, already dialing Emily's mother. I couldn't have Tim pick Letty up. His nervous energy, his fury, and worry, and barely contained need to *do* something would only frighten Letty more than she was going to be to begin with.

"Jean," I said, not even giving her a moment to finish her greeting. "There's been an accident and Benny's been hurt. I'm at the hospital. Could you possibly pick up Letty at school?"

"Oh my God," Jean breathed, but then her efficiency kicked in, as I had counted on. "Of course. What do I say?"

I remembered this, the way we had, during those short toddler years, compared notes on what to tell our kids, making sure our own thoughts were in order before presenting them to our, or each other's, children. The mommy bond was one I'd been surprised to find existed, and one I hadn't realized I'd missed so much.

"Don't say anything, please. Once you pick her up, tell her to call me and I'll tell her."

"Was he . . . was it a car accident?"

"No, he was—Benny was shot."

Jean gasped but remained silent, waiting for me to continue.

"He's going into surgery now, and that's as much as I know."

"Oh, Ali. Okay, okay, where am I going? Should she be at the hospital?"

I recoiled at the thought. No, there was no reason to subject her to . . . *this*—the jumpy cops, the surgeons and nurses and the smell of blood and fear. There were still some things I could control, and if I could help it, she wasn't going to be here for this part of it.

"Could you take her back to your place? She'd probably need to spend the night. Is that okay?"

"Of course. She's welcome here for as long as you need. I'm out the door. Keep me posted."

"Thanks, Jean," I said, hanging up.

"You got someone? Because I can go get her, I'm happy to go get her," Tim said, standing, ready for anything I might point him toward, like a retriever.

"It's okay," I said. "My friend will pick her up. I need to call her."

"Okay, you tell her that he's going to be fine, you know? He's a hell of a tough cop and he's going to come through this . . ." He trailed off and looked away from me, toward the three cops who stood in a huddle in the hall, his shoulders hunched forward. I could have fitted myself into that space again and it might have helped, a little. I turned away from him and dialed.

"Tell me you're on your way," she answered the phone. "Because if I have to listen to the marching band murder Eminem one more time, I really might spontaneously combust or something."

I wanted to be able to laugh for her, if for nothing else than to put off her inevitable fear for as long as I could. But I could not manage it. At least my voice didn't shake when I spoke.

"Sweetie, Emily's mom is going to pick you up. She'll be there soon."

Her tone changed immediately. "Is Aunt Cora all right?"

I had forgotten about Cora. Completely forgotten the fact that she was the reason I'd been at the hospital to begin with. Leaving her to have some alone time with Drew seemed like weeks ago. I seized on it, relieved to have an opportunity to put off telling her that her father had been shot, to put off not just having her hear it, but put off having to say the words myself.

"Cora's okay, she's resting, but I got hung up here. Jean should be there in a few minutes, so call me the second you're in the car, okay?"

"Mom, I wish you hadn't called her. I could have found another way home," she said, peevish now. Which was fine. Peevish was normal, and I even smiled a little.

"Just call me when she gets there, all right, honey? I love you," I said, my voice breaking. I punched the off button quickly, hoping she didn't catch it.

"Hey, Ali," Tim said quietly. "I thought I'd try to see where he is, you know, where they're at, and then I'd go give blood."

I nodded. It was what the department usually did when one of their own had been hurt. They arrived, in uniform, in plainclothes, in the cutoffs and T-shirts they were wearing to cut the lawn, in whatever they had on when they got the news, to roll up their sleeves and give blood, the only thing they could do. The little room would soon be swarming with people trying to support me, and the thought of it made me dizzy. I'd been on these hospital visits myself, called by Benny when a colleague had been in a car accident, or, as had happened twice in his career, when they had been shot.

Both of those cops had died, and everyone had gathered around their wives before they'd even passed away, as if they already knew.

I wasn't ready to be treated like a widow.

LETTY

She hung up with her mom and wished her dad would call. She wanted to know what was happening, if he'd found Seth's dad, if he'd gotten any information about getting him out of Venice.

But she mostly just wanted to be able to talk to Seth, to let him know that someone was doing something for him.

She didn't think a lot of people had ever gone out of their way to do anything for him before, and she was proud that she had the kind of father who would. It made her feel safer, like he really meant it when he said she could tell him about any problem. She thought that maybe Seth could be like that, if he had someone like her dad to show him how.

Emily's mom didn't take long. She could see Jean's face through the windshield, looking all worried with her eyebrows hiked up way high. She didn't see Emily in the passenger seat, and she was surprised at how much that hurt.

But when she opened the door, she saw Emily in the backseat, biting her lower lip, looking like a little miniature Jean. They used to make fun of her mom, how protective she was, but now it was like Emily was turning into her. She didn't know why they were so worried about her waiting a little long to be picked up. She wasn't six years old or anything.

"Hey, Jean," she said, climbing in and dropping her bag on the floor. Emily leaned forward and put her hand on Letty's shoulder.

"Are you okay, Let?" she asked, nearly breathless as her mom pulled away from the school.

She had been feeling bad about Emily, about how they'd grown so far apart, and, to be honest, she sort of missed having a girl friend. But now she was just irritating again. Letty pulled forward, away from Emily's hand.

"I'm fine," she said.

"Hon," Jean said. "Your mom wants you to call her."

Hon? Jean had always been nice to her, nicer when she and Emily were hanging out more, but now she sounded downright loving. Something wasn't right. She dialed as quickly as she could, looking back over her shoulder at Emily, who was now chewing on the edge of her thumbnail.

"Mom?" she asked as soon as her mother answered, her voice wavering.

"Has Jean picked you up yet?" she asked, and her voice was so calm that for a minute she thought she'd been wrong.

"Yeah, I'm in the car now," Letty said, looking over at Jean like she was expecting her to confirm that yes, indeedy, she was definitely in the car. She pressed the phone tighter against her ear. "Mom?" she asked, softer now.

"Now, don't worry, everything is going to be fine, but there's been a problem with Dad," she said.

Letty felt so relieved for a minute. She had been expecting her to say Aunt Cora, to even, maybe, tell her that she was dead, or in a coma or something. But then she realized what she'd said, and she froze, everything went cold. She turned toward the door, away from Jean, away from Emily.

"What? No. He's okay, right? He's okay?" she asked, frantic. "Mom?"

"Everything is going to be okay," she repeated, but she could hear in her mother's voice that she didn't know that for sure.

"But what happened?"

"He was on a call and something happened, we don't know exactly what just yet. Your dad was careful, honey, you know that, and he was wearing his vest, but he got hit. They're taking him in now to get the bullet out."

"Oh my God, Mom, was he . . . was he at Seth's?"

She didn't say anything for a minute, but Letty could hear her breathing heavily, and there were suddenly a lot of voices in the background.

"I don't think so," she said, but she knew she was lying. "Honey," she continued, "I want you to go home with Jean and Emily—"

"What? No, I'm coming there. Aren't I? I have to be there," she cried, looking again at Jean. She didn't look back at her, and Emily grabbed her shoulder again. She didn't pull away this time. This time it felt okay, like she was grounding her, holding her there in the seat so she didn't fly apart.

"Letty, listen to me. There's nothing you can do here, and

I need you to be where I know you're being taken care of and where I can find you. The second I know anything I'll call you. Okay?"

"No," she said, and she didn't care if she sounded whiny or not. She could be there, she *should* be there. What would her dad think? That she didn't even care enough to come? What if he could hear her voice, and he'd know that she was there, and he'd be fine, knowing she was waiting for him?

"I want to come," she demanded.

"I'm sorry, Letty, I know you do," her mom said, her voice really soft, and that was when Letty started to cry. Because she sounded really sorry, and really sad, and she knew she wasn't going to change her mind.

*   *   *

Jean pulled into the driveway of Letty's house and asked if she wanted her or Emily to come in, but she shook her head and left them in the car. She grabbed a few things as quickly as she could, not worrying about what she jammed in her bag. Most of her regular stuff was still at Aunt Cora's anyway, but she didn't want to tell Jean to take her over there and have her know all about how they weren't staying at home.

Her room was still a mess from her dad tearing it apart the night of the party. She remembered thinking that nothing was ever going to be the same again. And now she knew she'd been right, and knew, suddenly, that no matter how grown-up she had felt, she had been acting like a spoiled brat for a long time. Shame flooded her, and she wished she could stay and clean up the mess, throw away all the stupid, childish things and make it all clean, so he would see that she'd changed when he got home.

She was surprised there wasn't dust layered across it all. It seemed like it had happened so long ago. When he came to the school and sat with her in the library, it was almost like it had never happened to begin with.

She wondered if that was how it was, how people, families, still loved each other even after fights, even after being so positive that nothing would ever be the same again. Maybe that was how it would be with Emily. Maybe they would be just like Aunt Cora and Mom, and they'd look back at the time they weren't as close as just some little thing that was in the past.

She threw her bag over her shoulder and hurried into her parents' bedroom. Her dad was usually pretty neat, but he hadn't done much since they'd been staying at Aunt Cora's. He'd left a load of clean laundry in a pile on the bed, a little wisp of dryer sheet puffing out the side like a surrender flag.

She shook one of his big T-shirts out of the pile and stuffed it in the bag, then grabbed another one, just in case her mom might want one, too.

When she got back in the car, Jean was all businesslike, telling her what they'd be having for dinner. She was relieved that they'd figured it all out without her. She didn't feel like making any decisions, or having the whole *What do you want? I don't care, what do you want?* conversation. When Jean pulled into their drive, she held her hand on her arm for a minute while Emily got out.

"I'm going to leave you girls here while I go shopping," she said, her voice real serious. Letty thought she was going to warn her to not do anything stupid or something, but instead she just said, "If you need me, call my cell phone and I'll be home in seconds, okay? If your mom calls, or you remember something that you need, or you just feel upset, you call me."

"Okay," she said, surprised.

"And don't let Emily upset you. She's feeling a little . . . sensitive about your friendship. She thinks she hasn't been very nice to you recently, and it's making her feel especially badly about this. She'll be fine. You just worry about you right now."

She got out and waved, then followed Emily through the open door, wondering why all the adults around her suddenly seemed so much more like they were *there*.

Shutting the door cut off all the sunlight, and the house was dim and quiet. Emily held her hand out.

"You want me to take your bag?" she asked, formal suddenly, like Letty hadn't been staying over at her house since they were six years old.

"No, I'm fine," she said, heading up the stairs.

"My room's done," Emily said as they turned down her hall-way. "I think you'll like it."

Letty couldn't help the "Wow" that escaped her lips when she stepped into Emily's room. No matter how childish she might have thought Emily could act sometimes, this was no little kid's room. It was beautiful, with a big bed instead of the bunk beds, and some sort of yellowy-gold finish on the walls that made them glow, and vines had been painted up the corners and across the ceiling in big crisscrosses.

Her bag slipped off her shoulder and thudded to the floor as she turned around. Emily giggled with her hand over her mouth.

"I know," she said. "Come look at the bathroom!"

Her bathroom was just as jaw-dropping as her bedroom. It looked like everything was new, and she had a big tub with jets and a separate shower.

And they were friends again, just like they always had been, just like that.

*   *   *

In the end Letty decided to tell her everything, all of it. Of course Emily already knew about her parents having to go pick her up at the party, but she told her all the other things, too, about having sex, and going to Venice, and the roommate, and Aunt Cora and her mom coming to pick her up.

Emily listened in awe, her mouth hanging open at all the right places, and then she came back to what Letty knew she would, what they'd been talking about in hushed voices for years.

"How, well, how was it? Did it hurt?"

And she told her the truth. By the time she finished, Emily was sitting up staring at her, looking kind of panicked.

"But Letty, aren't you afraid you might be pregnant?"

Letty laughed, lightly, not trying to make her feel bad, but just feeling a lot more grown-up than her, or trying to anyway. Because of course she was scared. She'd have been scared even if Seth had been wrapped head to toe in a condom.

"It's fine, Emily," she said, not feeling as certain as she sounded. It had been almost three weeks. She'd never tracked her period before, but it seemed like she should probably be having cramps by now. She hadn't been worried, hadn't really even thought about it with everything else that had been going on, but now, with Emily looking so concerned, she was definitely starting to worry.

"But—"

Letty's cell phone rang, interrupting Emily, and she scrambled to find it in the soft folds of the comforter under her legs.

"Mom?"

"Hi, honey. Are you okay?"

"No. I mean, yeah, we're back at Em's—and her mom went to pick up dinner—but what's going on?"

She heard her take a deep breath. "We still don't know what happened, but your dad is having three bullets removed."

"Three?" she repeated, feeling sick to her stomach. "You said he was only shot once."

"I didn't know."

"Well, where was he shot?"

"Twice in the arm, once in the neck."

"The neck?" She cast a quick glance at Emily, who was still sitting up and turned toward her.

"Yes, and that's the one they're worried about most, of course. He's still in surgery, and they're trying hard to get all the pieces out. One of the bullets in his arm went right through, so that's a good thing. The other two broke apart."

She said all of it in a rush, but she couldn't quite get to the end without her voice breaking.

"Letty, now listen, it's going to be fine. I'm not worried at all, okay? Things could have been a lot worse, and I know how strong your dad is. They're just going to get the fragments out, and he'll be bossing everyone around by tonight."

"Will you come get me?"

"I promise that as soon as he's out of surgery and awake, I'll come get you."

"No matter what time?"

"No matter what time."

It didn't make her feel any better.

CORA

Drew came back into the room and shrugged his shoulders. If a shrug could be called elegant, Drew's would be. Every bit of him was elegant, graceful, and fluid. He navigated through rooms like water, flowing around hard edges, coming to rest gently. I could watch him just moving about his apartment for hours. We'd never discussed it, but I imagined that his grace came from years of avoiding injury, every bump, cut, and bruise reason for concern.

Had he been a match, I still wouldn't have allowed him to donate. Not yet, anyway. I was not so convinced of my altruism when things progressed to a certain point. I knew it hurt him, hurt his sense of chivalry somehow, to see me lying there and not be able to help.

It pained Ali, too; I knew that. But the difference was that with Drew I never knew when that pain might end our relationship; with Ali no such fear existed any longer. Drew had once, during one of our final arguments, said that he was less important to me than Ali was. Now, with both of them here, I knew he was right.

It was wonderful to see him, I *wanted* to see him . . . but I didn't need him. I did need Ali in my life. And Letty.

When Ali had been gone long enough that we began to wonder what had happened, he'd gone looking for her, casting a glance behind him as if it might be the last time he saw me. There's nothing like someone else's fear to put your own in perspective, and I felt a sense of calm begin to steal over me as the door closed and softly clicked.

I looked down at my lumpy, bandaged arm, and thought that I could handle whatever was coming. My life was going to change, yes, change dramatically, but hadn't it always? Was change not perhaps the one constant in my life? Had I not prided myself on it, perhaps even lorded it over Ali and Benny—always slightly smug in their quiet, secure lives—a bit?

I might have even lectured Ali on embracing change a few times. Talk about smug.

When Drew returned with his shrug I felt stronger than I had in weeks and patted the bed beside me. He cradled me, not the way we used to as lovers, the full-fledged, shoulders-to-shins, wound about each other's limbs like the roots of a banyan tree, but still, I felt held, and I felt safe and even, yes, lucky that he was here, was still my friend.

"Couldn't find her?" I murmured.

"I checked the cafeteria, the waiting rooms on this floor, everywhere I could think of."

"She's probably just giving us time—" I started, but was interrupted by the lost lady herself opening the door. My smile died on my lips when she looked at me. It had been almost two hours since I had seen her, but it could have been twenty years for the difference. Her face was pale and haggard, and she looked as if she might fall over at any moment.

"Ali?" I asked, my voice wavering. It never crossed my mind that there was something wrong with Ali. I thought only of myself—that I was much worse off than they were telling me.

"Hey," she said, sounding faint, a weak echo of herself. "Everything okay here?"

Drew and I looked at each other, our usual telepathy as strong as ever, both knowing that whatever she said next was going to change things.

"I don't know," I said cautiously. "Is it?"

She just looked confused for a moment, annoyed even.

"Ali? What's going on?" I demanded. "Just tell me. What did they say? Did something go wrong?"

"What? No, no, it's not that at all. *You're* fine. It's Benny."

She said Benny's name with an inflection of wonder, as if she did not believe that she was mouthing that particular combination of words.

"What's wrong?" I asked, as Drew and I instantly dislodged from each other and struggled to sit upright at the same time.

"He's been shot. He was shot and now he's in surgery. They're trying to get the bullet fragments out."

"Shot?" Drew asked, sliding off the bed and moving across the room to Ali more quickly than I could even make sense of what she was telling us. He tried to guide her to the chair, but she resisted him and stayed on her feet.

"No," she said, pulling away, her eyes on my face. "I have to go back down. I just wanted to tell you. I thought . . . maybe, Drew, you could just take my car—"

"Wait a minute," I said, hastily dropping the bed rail down and getting out of bed. I felt dizzy for a moment, and then it passed and I was beside her. "What happened?"

"I don't know yet," she said. "They don't know yet, or say they don't. He wasn't on a call, he wasn't even on duty yet." Her brow creased, as if she were piecing some difficult equation together, and then her lips parted in surprise, as if she'd arrived at the answer and she fumbled her cell phone out and held her hand up to keep me from asking anything else. She dialed and walked out the door as she held the phone up to her ear.

Drew and I watched her go, both of us still stunned. As soon as the door closed I opened the little closet that held my belongings and began to dress.

"Hey, hey, what are you doing?" Drew asked. "Come on, you need to get back in bed."

"Don't be ridiculous," I said. "Benny's been shot, for God's sake. I need to help Ali and Letty. She didn't even say anything about her," I said, zipping my jeans, no easy feat with one hand. "Help me with my shirt."

"No, I won't help you with your shirt. Get back in bed, Cora."

Drew and I had never held each other back from doing what we needed to do. With the exception of my return to Naples, we'd rarely even had a discussion about the individual decisions we made in our lives. If he needed to go to Los Angeles with just a few hours' notice, he simply told me, and I kissed him good-bye. If I was needed at a contentious town hall meeting in upstate New

York, I got tickets without even consulting him, and he got my suitcases out of the closet for me.

It had always been one of the defining—and best, as far as I was concerned—aspects of our relationship. My illness had changed that completely. He'd started hesitating when I had to travel, asking if I felt I was up to it, questioning my need to attend the event. I'd brushed off his protectiveness until I could take it no more; more proof that we were destined to be friends, not lovers.

But the fights we'd had over it, and the eventual breakup, had made me feel powerful again, in control of my life and how I was going to live it.

And now I felt more my old self than I had in a long time when I turned around to him.

"No, I won't. Now, I didn't ask you to come," I said. "I'm glad you did, but if you're going to be here, then I need you to be here to support *me*, not soothe your own concerns."

His gaze didn't waver, and he didn't move to help me.

"I am here to help you, Cora," he said. "But I can't help you if all I do is blindly allow you to do whatever you want. You might not want to face it, but you're sick. And I won't stand by and watch while you stubbornly refuse to do what's best for you."

"Drew, I had a little tube put in my arm; I didn't have open-heart surgery. Benny's been *shot*, for God's sake, and I'm not going to lie around in bed while my friend needs me."

"I need you, too, you know," he replied, looking hurt.

I sighed and struggled into my shirt one-handed. "You don't. Not really. And besides, even if you did, it's a matter of priority, Drew. You certainly *don't* need me right this second. And Ali does."

"What did I even come here for?" he asked.

"I assume you came to make sure I was okay," I said, sitting down to slip my shoes on. "Which was lovely of you, and I appreciate it. But I am; I'm okay. Was there another reason?"

"Actually, yes, there is," he said.

My fingers faltered at my laces and I looked up at him, straightening up slowly in the chair, feeling a dull throb in my arm.

"Let's have it, then," I said.

He took a deep breath and stuffed his hand in his pocket, pulling something out of one of them as he walked, trudged, really, as if the floor had turned to quicksand, to stand in front of me. I started to rise, unwilling to be put in the weaker position while he did this. But he placed a hand on my shoulder and said "Please," before gingerly getting down on one knee.

I sank back down onto the chair.

"Cora, this wasn't how I wanted to do this," he said, cupping his hands in front of him before opening the glossy red ring box he held.

I've never been prone to hysterical laughter, preferring low-key stoicism, but the sight of the diamond ring in the box, a perfectly beautiful round diamond, set in platinum and larger than any academic should be able to afford, made me yelp. I clapped my hand over my mouth as he thrust the box at me, trying to rid himself of the thing as desperately as I was trying to avoid taking it.

"I love you," he said, his clenched teeth nearly belying his words. "Will you marry me?"

I breathed through my fingers, feeling faint. "Drew? What— *why* are you doing this?"

"Well, it wasn't supposed to be like *this*," he said. "I had this whole . . . look, the thing is, it makes sense to get married. For one thing, once we're married my insurance—"

His incredibly romantic approach to getting me down the aisle was interrupted by Ali coming back into the room. Drew stood immediately, both of his knees popping loudly in protest. Ali took in the scene, her face slack, unable, I imagined, to register anything after the day she'd already had, and was having still. I got to my feet.

She shook her head and waved me down. I remained standing.

"I have to go downstairs," she said, her voice flat, nearly robotic. "There are detectives here."

"We're going with you," I said immediately.

"No," she said, looking to Drew for help. He spread his hands at her.

"I can't make her do anything," he said. "Maybe you can."

"This isn't about me," I said, raising my voice as well as I could over my sore throat. "Now, where are we going?"

Ali looked at me hard, then nodded, and had we spoken, it couldn't have been more clear: We were, always had been, always would be, in this—whatever *this* happened to be that day, that year—together.

*　*　*

"This is Tim Weinman," Ali said, introducing the uniformed officer who met us at the door to a small waiting room. Drew and I introduced ourselves and stepped inside behind Ali.

Another man, this one in a suit, his shirt limp from humidity, his tie hanging to the side like the end of a noose, stood.

"Detective Alan Hudson," he said.

"Nice to . . ." Ali started before she trailed off and seemed to sag, bending slightly at the waist as if she had cramps.

Tim immediately had an arm around her and guided her to a chair. I sat to her left and put my good arm around her shoulder.

"What's happening?" I asked as Drew took the chair next to me. "How's Benny?"

Detective Hudson said, "He's still in surgery. We're trying to piece together what exactly happened."

Ali twitched under my arm as if coughing silently. "Ali?" I asked. "Are you okay?"

She shook her head. "I've been better."

She glanced at Detective Hudson, and Tim glowered at everyone, looking for someone to direct his frustration at.

"Just help me keep everything straight, okay?" she whispered to me.

"Of course," I said.

"And are you a member of the family?" the detective asked me.

"Yes," Ali said, "she is."

He took my name and turned to Drew, who didn't even let him ask the question before he was on his feet.

"Should I, uh, go?" Drew asked, his face aflame in embarrassment.

"Maybe you could get me some tea?" I asked, just as Ali began to speak. She quieted immediately. Drew bit his lip, tucking his hands in his pockets. I thought about the tips of his fingers encountering the ring box, and smiled sadly at him.

We both knew my answer would be no, but I still wished that we'd had the time to finish—or start—his proposal the right way.

I would have liked that memory, no matter how it turned out.

When he left the room, Ali took a deep breath.

"Mrs. Gutierrez, Officer Weinman said your husband talked to you about helping a friend of your daughter's?"

"Yes. Letty—"

"That's your daughter?" Detective Hudson asked, writing without looking at his notebook.

"Yes. She's had a boyfriend, Seth, for a while, we don't know how long, really, we just found out about him this past week. Anyway, she went to Venice with him, and he got picked up for something, we don't know what. Letty asked Benny to check on him, to see if there was something we could do to help him out. I guess his home life isn't very stable; she said he had been living with his father, but that he'd been on his own for the last couple of weeks, staying with friends."

The detective was writing quickly, nodding.

"When I called Letty to tell her about Benny, she asked if he'd gone to Seth's father's house. He'd gone to talk to her at school today, to find out some more information about Seth, to see what he could do to help, and I guess he told her he would go talk to his father. I didn't talk to him after he'd spoken with Letty, so I don't know if that's where he was or not, but I know Seth lived pretty far out in the Estates. That's really all I know."

"Do you know his last name? Or his father's name? Address?"

"Caple," she said softly. "There are three Caples in the Estates, but I don't know which address it is, or if any of them are even the right address. I didn't know about Seth long enough to know any of that yet."

"Could we talk to your daughter?"

"I—is that necessary?" Ali sat up straight in her chair, as if suddenly realizing something. "Look, what happened?" she asked. "What *do* you know? Nobody's told me anything. Do you even know who shot my husband?"

Tim squeezed her shoulder. "Ali, yeah, we know. Don't worry about that."

"Don't worry about that? Who was it? You've arrested him?"

Tim and the detective exchanged quick looks, but it was the detective who answered.

"He's dead."

Ali put her hand flat in the center of her chest and seemed to deflate around it, as though she'd taken a bullet herself.

"We don't have a positive ID on him yet."

"Did Benny shoot him?" Ali asked. Her hand moved from her chest up to cover her mouth once the question was out.

Tim, his mouth a tight line as if he were holding himself back from saying something, turned away.

"Right now we're not sure exactly what happened," the detective said, his words carefully spoken. "When officers arrived on scene, the suspect was dead of gunshot wounds and Officer Gutierrez was unconscious in his car. That's really all we know at this point. I know this is incredibly difficult for you right now, but the sooner we speak with your daughter, the better."

Ali nodded. "Okay." She glanced at me, then dropped her gaze to my arm. I tried to look alert and competent.

"What do you need?" I asked her, ignoring the cops in the room. "Where is she? Should I go get her? Drew can drive."

She looked relieved. "Could you?" she asked.

"Mrs. Gutierrez," the detective said, "we'd be happy to pick her up."

Ali looked aghast. "No. She knows Cora."

The detective seemed to realize he'd overstepped and fell silent, watching me intently.

"Where is she?" I asked. Ali wrote out the directions to Emily's house on the hospital notepad and said she'd call so they knew I was on my way. I got to my feet, concentrating on not swaying or giving any indication of weakness. When I bent down to hug her around her shoulders, she gripped me tightly.

"Are you sure you're okay?" she whispered in my ear.

I nodded.

"Call me when you have her," she said. "I'll tell you where I'm at."

"Okay. Good luck," I said, for want of anything better in front of these men I did not know.

When I opened the door, Drew was waiting, his hand clenched around what I could only assume was the ring box.

It was going to be an interesting car ride.

13

ALI

I stood as soon as Cora left and turned to Tim.

"I need to get back to Benny," I said.

"Of course," he said, opening and holding the door for me. Detective Hudson followed us out, tension emanating from him like heat off a sunburn, keeping me several steps ahead of him with its subtle, insistent push.

It didn't mean he wasn't a good cop; I'd been around enough of them to know that. And I should have been thankful for his intensity; he was the kind of cop I knew would stop at nothing to figure out what happened to Benny. He wouldn't care who he offended to accomplish that—even me.

The three of us made our way back down to the same waiting room we'd used before. There were still plenty of cops milling about, uniforms and plainclothes, and they all moved around me at a respectful distance.

Tim led me over to an unoccupied corner while Detective Hudson huddled with two other men and went over the scant notes he'd made in Cora's room.

"You want some coffee or something?" Tim asked.

I nodded, closing my eyes as I leaned my head back against the wall, letting the drone of the TV set high in the corner and the cops talking in hushed tones around me fade into white noise as I fantasized about what would happen when the surgeon came to speak to me.

There would be blood spattered across his . . . no, I made him a her, hair tucked up under a cap that she would wearily swipe off her head as she approached. But she would smile at me, maybe even give a little wink—maybe that was too much—maybe a nod before she sat down and put her hand on my arm, a hand that had so recently been saving my husband's life, a hand I would feel energy from, would feel Benny seeping into me from.

But that wasn't how it happened at all.

Instead, after I drank the bitter coffee Tim brought, I sought out the cool refuge of the bathroom, and when I returned, cops were dispersing and a man I hadn't seen before was waiting for me. Tim was there, too, his face white. Detective Hudson wasn't in sight.

"Ali," Tim croaked, reaching out for me.

I knew, of course, knew before they asked me to sit, knew before Tim had gotten my name out, before the neurosurgeon—Dr. Young, a man after all, a man in clean scrubs who did not touch me on the arm, whose hands I didn't even notice—said the words.

A balloon of fear and grief and disbelief began to expand in my chest, pressing against my heart, compressing my lungs, leaving me so little room for air that it seemed I could only breathe into the base of my throat.

A brain hemorrhage. Tracks from migrating bullet fragments, tiny metal birds winging darkly through his skull, wreaking havoc along the way to their final resting place. Brain dead. Benny was brain dead.

He explained what that meant, as if I did not know.

What I knew was that all of what he was, his jokes, his pet names for me developed over more than twenty-five years together, his knowledge of me, of us, of his child, his sense of wonder and delight in the world . . . gone. All of that, a lifetime of experience and love and fights and sex . . . all of it just gone, that fast.

There was so much unfairness in it, so much so substantively wrong with it, that I felt certain that it was a mistake, or even temporary. This would pass. Brain dead, perhaps meaning just a rest, a brain exhaustion, not just gone.

Gone.

I wanted it back.

I wanted it all back.

All the time that was being sucked from me, I wanted it back. I wanted moments, at the least, the very least. It couldn't possibly work out, in a fair world, in a *karmic* world, the world that I believed in, that it could be taken away without warning.

No, not even warning. I could accept the idea of life ending without warning; it happened every day. But surely there was some force at work that gave you those few moments that you could look back on with relief and say, *Yes, right then, we had that moment and that was the universe allowing us that*, so you could hold on to it.

But no.

No.

Instead, all the things we might have wanted to say would not be said.

We were unfinished.

And I knew this happened to people every day, but not to me. Not to *me*. Not to *Benny*. This was not how our lives were going to go.

"Where is he?" I asked.

"He's been moved to a room. He's on a ventilator."

"Why?"

"A neurologist will conduct tests in order to corroborate the diagnosis of brain death."

Tim, who had been breathing deeply beside me and clutching my hand harder than I was clutching his, finally spoke, his voice low and pained. "Wait, is there a question? I mean, could you be wrong? Could he wake up?"

The surgeon winced slightly when Tim said *wake up*. I imagined he got the question a lot. He shook his head.

"No. It's hospital procedure, and one I agree with. But in this particular case, it's a formality. I'm sorry, Mrs. Gutierrez. We did what we could, but there was simply too much damage. If it's any consolation, there would have been very little pain for him."

I nodded. I didn't even know why. There was no consolation. It was simply the only movement I was capable of. Tim dropped his chin to his chest and made a sound deep in his throat, a cross between a growl and a groan.

"Can I . . . can I see him?" I asked.

"Of course. You can stay with him as long as you like."

But that was patently untrue, wasn't it?

He stood, and Tim followed suit, but I stayed in my chair. I didn't trust my legs to hold me, and I didn't trust my heart to pump enough blood to keep me from passing out, so I stared at the floor while Tim got the room number and shook hands. I realized with a shock that Tim was now my proxy husband. He was performing all the duties that Benny would have.

Dr. Young squatted in front of me, his shirt riding up his thighs as he did so. He must have changed into a clean top before coming to tell me, because now I could see the blood that I had been morbidly looking for earlier on his pants and on his shoes. I wanted to touch it, to run my hands across the front of his pants in a grotesque imitation of foreplay, to take back some part of my husband that was going to be washed away forever later on that night.

And now he did touch me, his hands cooler than I expected. I would have thought they'd be hot, burning up with anxiety over the work he'd just performed, the task of telling the wife.

"Mrs. Gutierrez," he said, trying to catch my eye. I raised my gaze from his pants obediently. "I'll be here. If you want to talk to me about anything, if you have questions. You can have the nurse page me, and I'll be there as quickly as I can, okay?"

"Okay," I whispered. He nodded and stood, his shirt falling back down over the bloodied pants. Tim held his hand out to me.

"Are you ready?" he asked. "Or do you want to wait?"

I shook my head. Why would I want to be anywhere but beside Benny? I took his hand and we walked through a silent gauntlet of cops outside the waiting room. Some were already crying; most simply looked shocked, or angry. There were murmured condolences, and some reached out to touch me, but I heard nothing, felt nothing.

As we got onto the elevator my cell phone rang, and that was when my legs decided to get wobbly. I grabbed the elevator rail as the doors slid shut, and Tim lunged to catch me as my phone continued to ring. I got myself stabilized and scrambled for the phone, afraid to answer, afraid not to.

"You want me to?" Tim asked, gesturing at the phone as I checked the Caller ID, knowing, for the first time, that it wouldn't be Benny.

It was Cora. I shook my head and picked up the phone.

"Hey," I said, my voice already breaking a little just knowing what was coming.

"We've got her," she said. "We're on our way. Do you want some dinner, you want us to go through a drive-through?"

"No," I said.

"You sure?" She dropped her voice down low. "Everything going okay?"

"No. No, not at all. But don't—just get her here."

She was silent for a moment. "Ali?"

That was what childhood friends could do. There was a huge question in the uttering of my name, and I knew what it was. And she would know what my answer meant.

"Yeah."

I heard her breathing quicken, and then she brightened her voice, and my heart broke in gratitude for her protecting my—our—daughter for as long as she could.

"Okay," she said. "We'll see you in a few minutes."

"Call me when you get inside. I'll come to you."

"Will do. Love you."

"I love you, too, Cora. Thank you."

The elevator doors opened as I hit the off button, and Tim looked at me hard before we stepped out.

"You ready?"

"Yeah," I said. And I was. I was ready to see Benny. Not ready for anything else. But ready to see him. When we arrived at the closed door, Tim stepped to the side, holding a hand up to the nurse who was rapidly walking down the corridor toward us.

"You go ahead," he said to me. "I'll keep everyone out until you let me know it's okay."

"Thank you." I took a deep, hospital-antiseptic breath and pushed the door open.

The room was dim, the harsh overhead lights off and only the lights around the bed on. Benny's head was wrapped in shockingly white gauze, his face distorted by the ventilator. His left arm and shoulder were similarly wrapped, and as I approached I felt the tears begin, pushing their way up from my throat, a tidal wave behind my eyes. I gasped as if drowning as I sat gingerly on the side of the bed and grabbed his right hand.

There was, of course, no response.

I cried out as I brought his palm to my face, laying his fingers flat across my cheek, pulling them down across my mouth, feeling them curl, lax, back into themselves. I pressed the back of his wrist to my nose, feeling the coarse hairs, breathing him in.

Despite everything, he still smelled like Benny.

Later on, I would not remember the following moments I spent with him. But I know I wailed, I know I implored him to wake, to create something from nothing. And nothing was what remained.

By the time my phone rang again I was curled across his legs, my head resting on his hip, his hand still clutched to my face. I wiped my face on his sheet and answered, my voice dulled.

"Are you here?" I asked.

Her voice was hushed, and I knew she must have walked away from Letty for a moment. "We're downstairs. What do you want me to do?" The anguish was starting to build in her, too.

"Bring her to the elevators. I'll be right down."

I kissed his cheek, letting my lips linger, pressing, imprinting the feel of him on them.

"Okay," I said, straightening up, replacing my lips with my fingers. "I'm going to go get our baby."

Tim, Detective Hudson, and three other cops were clustered together outside the door. They fell silent as I appeared. I'm sure they had to have heard me in there.

I didn't care.

Detective Hudson approached, his eyes red. "I'm so sorry," he said.

I nodded. "I'm going downstairs to get our daughter," I said. "We'll be back up here in a few minutes, and I'd appreciate it if we could get into his room without anyone around."

"Of course," he said. "We'll go down to the end there, and I'll station someone—"

"I'll stay," Tim volunteered. "I'll stay as long as you need me. And, Ali, Ginny said she'd come down in a second, the moment you want her. She'll do whatever you need, get you guys food, bring some clothes, anything. Just let me know."

I nodded.

"And we have the department shri—the psychologist, Dr.

Weist, he's on his way, too," Detective Hudson began. I held up my hand, desperate to get to Letty.

"Okay, I'll let you know. I have to get my daughter now."

"Absolutely," Tim said, taking control. "Okay, guys, let's get out of here."

The elevator moved quickly. I stared at the emergency button. If I were a different person, I would have hit it. Stopped the elevator between floors in a last-ditch desperate effort to prolong this in-between time I had.

There was no sinking in of the fact of Benny's death. He was there. He looked like Benny under all the paraphernalia.

I wasn't a stupid woman, I knew what *brain dead* meant, and I wasn't a woman who had ever had a problem understanding that just because something looked one way didn't mean it wasn't another. I had no religious qualms about whether it was his brain or his heart stopping that meant he was dead.

Logically, I understood that Benny was gone.

And emotionally, while in that room, I knew that Benny wasn't there. Aside from a faint trace of his scent, aside from the feel of his skin and the basic structure under it, Benny was already somewhere else, I could feel that.

But I had no idea how I was going to make our child understand it. Twenty-four hours until more neurological tests would confirm that Benny was gone. What was I supposed to say to Letty about that time? If I felt enough hope for those twenty-four hours that I felt breathless with it, even knowing it was hopeless, then how was I going to prepare her for the disappointment that was sure to come? How would I even live through it, much less help her through it?

And just before the elevator jerked to a stop I wondered, for the first time, what happened after the twenty-four hours was up?

I had no time to follow that disturbing train of thought, because Letty was the first person I saw when the door opened. When we were at the beach with Cora, I had been stunned by how much Letty looked like her, but now I was stunned by how much she looked like Benny. I saw him, alive, everywhere on her.

She moved slowly as I opened my arms to her, tucking herself into me. Not a panicked child, but a worried young woman, and as I held her I knew how I would get through the next twenty-four hours and beyond.

I would get through them because she needed me to.

It was our pledge, mine and Benny's, our covenant, entered into as seriously as we entered into our marriage, to protect and love this child, even more so for how difficult she was to conceive.

I met Cora's eyes, her mouth agape, cradling her bandaged arm, Drew's arm around her shoulders. He looked traumatized, as I supposed he had every right to be. He'd come here to take care of Cora, and instead had been thrown into the role of errand boy to our devastation. At any other time I might have cared, but I didn't now. I would use him, and anyone else who was around, as selfishly as I needed to in order to get through this, for myself and for Letty.

"Mom, how is he? Is he going to be okay?" Letty asked, pulling back to search my face.

"We're going to go see him right now," I replied, saving my real answer. "We'll be in 8211," I said to Cora, and she nodded. "Give us a bit?"

"Okay."

She and Drew watched us with sad eyes as the door closed, sealing Letty and me in together, the way we were going to be from now on, the two of us.

"What happened?" she asked. "Did they get the bullets? Is he awake and everything?"

"Sweetie," I said, turning toward her, holding her hands in mine at our sides, an odd pantomime of a dance about to begin. "I don't have good news for you."

Her head slowly tilted to the side, her eyebrows drawing together, Benny in all of it.

"They couldn't get all of the bullet fragments out—"

She interrupted, talking quickly. "But he's okay, right? I mean, people walk around with things in them all the time, you know . . ."

She trailed off as I shook my head.

"No, baby. No, your daddy's on a ventilator right now. It's keeping his body alive, but he's gone."

I wanted to be straightforward, but I could not bring myself to say the word *dead*. I didn't want her to be confused, but I simply could not say it right that second.

"What? What do you mean?"

Her voice began to climb and the elevator doors opened on the floor. As requested, I didn't see any cops. I held on to one of her hands and began to step out of the elevator, but she pulled out of my grasp and shrank back against the wide metal rail. I held my foot in front of the door to keep it open and held my hand out to her.

"Oh, God, sweetheart. I—he's, he's gone. His brain function is—he's—" I still couldn't say the word. But I was going to have to. Somehow, I was going to have to say it if I wanted Letty to understand.

She stared at me, her eyes huge in her pale face. "So, he's like, he's in a coma?"

I shook my head. "No. I can explain this better—"

"No," she said, her face contorting as she slid down to the floor against the back of the elevator. "No, no."

I hadn't considered this, hadn't considered her simply refusing to move. Refusing to believe, yes, but I didn't know what to do with her immovable. I wasn't going to force her into the room with Benny. I had wanted to see him as quickly as possible, but that didn't mean she was ready to. I wanted every single second I could get with him, but if Letty wasn't ready, I couldn't just leave her here.

"Okay," I said soothingly, crouching down in front of her. "Okay, honey, you don't have to see him if you don't want to right now. What do you want to do? You want to just go sit in a waiting room? There's one right here, we'll close the door . . ."

I stood, drawing her up with me. It was working. She stepped forward as I stepped back, and I continued to coax her out of the elevator and into the waiting room, where we sat in chairs next to each other. I pressed my hand against my eyes for a moment to block out the look of horror that had been frozen on my daughter's face before I rose again to shut the door.

It settled closed with a hard *thunk*, and, again, we were sealed into a small space together. I turned slowly and leaned against the door, my head bowed, unable to look at her yet.

"Mom?" she whispered. "What's happening?"

I took a deep breath and raised my head, and said it.

"He's brain dead, sweetheart." And then I slowly, carefully explained what had happened, and what the neurosurgeon had told me, what I believed about death and dying, and what would happen next. It was a horrific parody of the conversations I'd always fantasized having with my child, the wisdom I would impart about what I believed about the universe and life and our souls.

In the daily routine of raising her, I had too rarely had those conversations with her, but I'd always been grateful when we managed to have one.

The lightweight reality of them embarrassed me now. Letty looked at me as if she had no idea who I was, had never heard words or ideas like this coming from my mouth, and I suppose she hadn't.

"What happens after the other doctor does the stuff?" she asked, still dry-eyed.

"Well," I said, "I'm not really sure. I suppose we'll have to give our consent to have the ventilator removed."

"And then he'll just die? Why can't we just leave it and maybe he'd wake up?"

Her tone was accusatory, and I went over what brain death meant again.

"But how do you know?" she asked. "How does anyone know?"

I pushed myself off the door and sat next to her again. She kept her hands clutched together on her lap, her knuckles white.

"I think you just have to decide what it is you believe and then stick with it until a more compelling argument against it comes along," I said. "And I don't . . . I don't believe for a second that your father would want to be kept alive like this. He can't hear you, or see you, or respond. He can't feel anything, sweetie, he's in no pain. He has no conscious thought. He, the essence of him, his soul if you want to call it that, I think that's already gone on to a better place."

She stared at me intently.

"What does he look like?"

I described the bandages, the machines and what they did and where they were hooked up. The telling of it served to calm me somehow.

"What if you don't tell them to, you know, *stop*?"

"But I would."

"Don't I get any say? What if I don't want to?"

"I think it's way too early to even talk about this," I said cautiously.

"It's just tomorrow," she said, and now came the tears, choking out of her in great ragged gasps. "He's mine, too," she protested, hitting herself on the chest with both hands, making me jump and reach out to stop her from doing it again. She pulled away from me before I could touch her.

"No," she wailed. "He's mine, you can't do it, you can't just . . . you can't just kill him."

"Letty," I said, reaching for her again, catching her at last and holding on tightly. "I won't tell you that your opinion doesn't matter. It does. But in this case I know better than you do, and you have to trust me to do the right thing."

She struggled in my grasp for a moment, but then she stiffened and stilled against me, and then, finally, she collapsed into me the way she hadn't since she had been a little girl, the weight of the world on her impossibly thin shoulders.

I, too, could not hold out any longer, but my tears weren't just for my loss of Benny; they were for Letty's loss, for the uncertain future we now shared only with each other, and for Benny, too, knowing that he would never have the comfort of consoling our daughter when she cried. All the things he would never do.

We both slowly quieted, and I pulled away to find tissues in my purse, coming up with nothing but a few old drive-through napkins. I cleaned her face, her arms hanging slack, her hands loose on her thighs.

"Oh, baby," I said as I wiped my own face. "I don't know how—" I cut myself off. Telling Letty that I didn't know what we were going to do, how we were going to live without him, would not help her. "I don't know how everything works right now," I said instead, a faltering substitute.

But she didn't seem to notice.

"I have questions to ask the doctor about what happens next," I said. "Would you like to be here?"

"I guess," she said, her tone dull and exhausted. "Is there . . . blood?"

It took me a moment to catch up with her.

"No, no, honey. You can't see any blood. The bandages cover everything. It's just like I told you, with the breathing tube, the monitors. Would you—do you think you'd like to see him now?"

I didn't know if it was better for her to see him or not. When she'd arrived, I had been on auto-pilot, assuming that what was best for me was also best for her. There was no time to check a parenting book on this one. I thought, at fifteen, that she was old enough to tell her father good-bye. Not everyone got that chance, and I didn't want her to regret it later.

She bit her lip, but then she nodded.

"You want to go now? Or do you want to wait?" I asked.

She stood, and I was surprised at her height. She had seemed so small just a moment ago, in my arms. I stood, too, and we walked to his room together. Tim was waiting down at the nurses' station, and he gave us a tentative wave.

I nodded at him and placed my hand on the door, but before I pushed it open I said, "I'm going to go in with you, but if you want some time alone with him, let me know, okay?"

She nodded, gripped my hand, and I opened the door. We entered together, Letty trailing me slightly, but coming willingly. She kept her head down, her eyes on the floor, until I stopped a couple of feet away from the bed. When she raised her head, her hand tightened on mine.

I just stood still, letting her look, silently willing her strength.

Within a few moments her breathing evened and she let loose of my hand. It took another moment, but she eventually walked over to the side of the bed, then looked back at me questioningly.

"He really—he really can't hear me?"

"No, not through his ears, no. He's not there," I said, gesturing toward the Benny on the bed. "But that doesn't mean he doesn't hear you—" I waved my hand in a vague motion toward the ceiling.

She looked, understandably, extraordinarily dissatisfied with this answer. I had to do better.

"I've been talking to him. Out loud," I clarified. "I can't—I don't believe that he's just gone, I just know that he's not *there*."

"How?" she asked incredulously. "How do you know?"

"Because we're not our bodies. And he's done with this one," I said, barely above a whisper. I closed my eyes, feeling myself sway, and a lovely, welcome graying out of my thoughts and softening of my knees began.

It felt like minutes that I hung there, between responsibility and blissful unconsciousness, but it must have been only a split second, and my eyes opened when someone knocked lightly on the door.

Cora stood outside, looking as tragic as I felt, Drew hovering a few feet away. She didn't say a word, only raised her eyebrows and I nodded, pushing the door open wider and allowing her in, her arms spreading out to encompass me, and within seconds Letty was there, too, the three of us clutching each other, Cora holding her bandaged arm off to the side gingerly.

And I realized that it was not just the two of us. For a little while, at least, I did have one other person to lean on, and she was, miraculously, here.

There were others, I realized. Others I would need to call: Benny's brother, our friends, though I was sure word had already spread rapidly through the police family and more people would soon be arriving.

I pulled back from our embrace, but Letty stayed where she was, and as I stepped away she fit herself more fully into Cora's arms. Cora met my eyes over Letty's shoulder, her face filled with anguish, as much for the child in her arms as for me or for Benny himself.

Letty mumbled something I couldn't hear, but I caught Cora's answer easily: "I don't know, I just don't know. I don't understand either."

The night passed in a haze of medical personnel and cops, of coffee and sleeping pills. The nurses moved some patients and set us up a room next to Benny's, allowing us to sleep in shifts, though I don't know how much any of us slept despite the pills. The next morning Drew tracked Dr. Young down for us.

We sat in the closed waiting room, all of us this time, and listened as he explained it all over again, whole-brain death, how long until his heart gave out, all the grim reality of the body that lay in the room down the hall. Letty huddled between Cora and me and asked him the same questions she'd asked me.

But she seemed to hear his answers more clearly than she'd heard them from me, and she asked the one we'd both wanted an answer to before I could.

"What happens if the other doctor says he's . . . you know, too? I mean, do you just, turn things off?"

The doctor looked at me quickly, and I nodded.

"It's okay," I said. "We've discussed what I would do, we just don't know what the process is. It might be easier to handle if we know what's coming."

"Okay," he said. "Dr. Tulley will be coming in this afternoon. She's a neurologist, and she's already aware of your husband's condition, but she'll carefully go over his file and will consult with me both before and after she sees him. She'll conduct several physical tests, as well as an EEG, and then there will be a few decisions you'll have to make. Most people want to make sure anyone who would want to say good-bye before support is withdrawn are notified. He's on file as an organ donor, so they'll have the transplant coordinator come in to discuss possible organ donation . . ."

He kept talking, but everyone else in the room seemed to have stopped breathing.

LETTY

It was so cold in the room, and Letty could swear that when he said that, about the transplant person coming, it got even colder. Nobody said anything for a minute.

Her mom and Aunt Cora's boyfriend looked at Aunt Cora. Everyone except the doctor; he didn't even notice that they were all freaked out, he just kept talking. Aunt Cora didn't look up; she just sat there with this really weird look on her face, staring down at her boyfriend's hand.

He was the one who finally said something, or, he didn't really *say* anything, but he cleared his throat like he was going to, and the doctor finally stopped talking and looked confused.

"What?" Letty asked, but nobody even looked at her.

"Wait," her mom said. "Go back."

But she didn't tell him where to go back to.

"Ali," Aunt Cora said, and she was the only one whose words

actually sounded like they might mean something, like she knew what she was going to say. But then she only said, "Don't."

And then everyone else started to talk at the same time.

"This is *not* an appropriate time to discuss this," Aunt Cora said.

"Discuss what?" Letty asked. "Discuss what?"

"Is that possible?" Drew said.

"Just hold on," her mother said.

And the doctor said, "Slow down, now tell me what the situation is here."

They all talked over each other, talking about Aunt Cora, and how sick she was, and how she needed a kidney. It got even colder, and Letty started to shiver, and then she was shaking. She pulled her legs up and wrapped her arms around them, leaning her head down on her knees while all the words jumbled around her.

But in a second she felt Aunt Cora jump up from her chair and grab her by the arm, making her feet thump down on the floor.

"Look," she said, and she sounded really mad. "You two"—and she pointed at her mother and Drew—"can stay in here and talk about this, but I'm not going to sit here and listen, and I'm not going to make Letty sit through it either. Come on," she said, pulling on Letty's arm.

She was just glad to have someone tell her what to do. Her mom reached out for her hand, and Letty wasn't mad at her or anything, but she just wanted to go, and she slipped away from her.

"I'll be right there, Letty," her mom said, but the door shut behind Aunt Cora and they were out in the hall before she could say anything.

"What do you want to do?" Aunt Cora asked her.

"Is it true?" she whispered.

She didn't say anything for a minute. But then she looked at her directly, just like Aunt Cora always did, and she knew she would tell her the truth.

"Yes, Letty, it's true. But it's going to be okay, and this is the last thing you need to worry about right now. I'm going to be fine, just fine. I'm sorry you had to find out now, like this. And they can talk all they want, but the only thing I'm planning on doing for the next year is being here with you and your mom, okay?"

"What's wrong with your arm?" Letty asked, finally noticing the bandages.

"They put in an access point for when I start dialysis."

"Oh." She didn't know what else to say.

"Letitia Makani," she said softly, and for the first time Letty wanted to hear it again, wanted to hear her whole name said by someone who loved her. "I'm okay. And you're going to be okay, too. And I'm going to be here to make sure of that. Now, what do you want to do?"

"I don't know," she said, even though she did.

"Hey," Aunt Cora said, crouching down a little to peer at her. "I know it doesn't seem possible right now, but we're going to get through this. We all will. Come on."

She put her arm around her and started to steer her toward the elevators, but Letty pulled back.

"Maybe we could go back? You know, to . . . Dad," Letty said, afraid she wouldn't want to, but Aunt Cora turned right around.

"Of course," she said, and they walked down the hall.

Letty hesitated at the door.

"Do you want to be alone?" Aunt Cora asked. "I'll just stand right here and wait for you if you do."

She shook her head. "Do you—I mean, don't you want to see him, too?"

Aunt Cora looked like she was thinking about it hard.

"I'd appreciate that," she said, like she was thanking Letty.

She wasn't afraid to go right up to him this time, and even though her mom and the doctor said he wasn't "there," which was just another way of saying he was dead, it still only seemed like he was hurt, and unconscious.

When she was little, they used to nap on the sofa together, and she would wrap her hand around one of his fingers, and he would tell her a story about when he was little, or about when he and her mom were dating, or even about when she was born. But his stories about that were different from her mom's. She never felt like she needed to be anyone different than who she was, any more special, when her dad told the story about her conception.

He never said it was a miracle. He just said he was happy.

"Do you think I could sit there?" she asked, pointing to the space beside her dad's knees, on the right side, away from the bandages on his arm and shoulder.

"Of course," Aunt Cora said. She helped her scoot his leg over a little and Letty kicked her shoes off and climbed up, crossing her legs against his. She felt like she was going to fall backward off the edge of the bed, but she inched a little closer, and Aunt Cora moved a chair behind her and sat down, and when she wrapped her hand around his finger, she knew she was safe.

It felt like him, mostly, but she also sort of felt what her mom was saying, like there was just something missing. Even when he fell asleep on the sofa and she was awake, his hand still felt . . . alive. This didn't, not at all the way like it used to.

She didn't care, it was something, and she held on.

"Aunt Cora?"

"Yeah, honey?"

"Why do you like wind?" she asked.

CORA

Letty, as she had over the past couple of weeks, had surprised me again. She'd never asked me about my work.

"I mean, how did you know what you wanted to do? Why wind stuff?" Letty asked.

I was silent for a minute, thinking about it, realizing that she just wanted some distraction, some white noise while she sat and held on to Benny. I wasn't sure where to start.

"You know I was adopted, right?"

"Uh-huh."

"Well, Barbara's house was filled with all kinds of things I'd never seen before. She'd traveled all over the world, and she had more books than I'd ever seen in my life. And not just novels, or biographies, but all of these huge books about the creation of the world, and religion, and oh, I don't know, every kind of thing you could ever imagine, or, I suppose, I'd never known I *could* imagine. And one of them was a book on sea charts."

"Sea charts?"

"Like big, colorful maps of the seas. Incredibly artistic, colorful, absolutely beautiful. But the one that really struck me was a wind rose."

"What's that?" Letty asked, looking genuinely interested now.

"Think about a compass the way it's drawn on paper, a circle, all divided up, with north, south, east, west. Okay, so a wind rose is like that, only in this one, the circle was divided into thirty-two sections representing the different winds that blew in those directions. And each section was labeled with these amazing names, Libecia and Africus for the southwest wind, Maestro for the northwestern wind, Ostro and Notus for the south wind. And there were thirty-two faces that went with each wind, bearded ones for the northwestern winds, black faces for northeastern ones, old-fashioned white men for southeast, feminine faces with flowers in their hair for southwest winds.

"It was all . . . I don't know, it gave me some sense of things, put the world in order somehow."

I laughed softly, remembering what I had done next.

"I tore it out of the book and hid it in my room. I was so afraid she'd find it and send me back to Texas. But I got home from school one day, and she had framed it and hung it on my ceiling—"

"On your ceiling?"

"I know. It was really neat, though. She put this spotlight on my nightstand so I could light it up. She said she thought I could look at it while I was lying in bed, thinking about what I should do, which way I wanted the winds to carry me, she said. And I did."

"She wasn't mad?"

"Not at all."

"She was pretty cool."

"Yeah, she was. I miss her."

Letty stared at Benny, and we just sat for a while without saying anything. I looked for something that would keep her distracted, would make her feel close to her father.

"You want to know something about your dad that your mom doesn't even know?" I asked.

"Okay."

"You remember that year I was here for Christmas? I guess you were about eight? And I took you to see Santa?"

She looked as if she didn't remember for a moment, but then her face cleared and she smiled at me.

"Yeah," she said slowly. "You got me a cinnamon bun and even though it wasn't cold out at all, we got hot chocolate." She nodded, as if satisfied with this chunk of memory falling into place. "But why did *you* take me?"

"It was so busy at the store. And that was the first year your mom had to run it by herself, remember? So I thought I'd surprise your parents and get your picture taken with Santa, and you acted pretty excited, but I knew you didn't believe in him anymore."

Letty laughed. "You knew?"

"Eight-year-olds are more transparent than they think they are."

"I guess," Letty said, still smiling. "That was cool of you."

"But we had fun, didn't we?"

"Yeah, it was fun."

"Well, we're waiting in this line, and all these kids are screaming and crying and generally acting like brats, and oh my God, was I starting to regret the whole thing and wishing you were old enough to go get a Bloody Mary with me instead. But it was so funny; as soon as these kids got to Santa, they'd calm right down. You always hear about kids being afraid of Santa and crying when they get plopped on his lap, but I don't know, this Santa was like the Brat Whisperer or something. I joked to the woman behind me that maybe he was slipping them something, but she wasn't amused.

"Anyway, so the kid in front of us is sitting on Santa's lap, but Santa's staring right at me, and I'm thinking, *Jeez, Santa, you shouldn't be flirting with the moms.* But then I looked, really looked, back at him, and I realized it was your dad."

Letty looked appropriately shocked.

"What? No way!"

"It was, and he was panicking, shaking his head at me, and the kid on his lap is getting upset because he thinks Santa's turning down his request for whatever toy he's asking him for. But there was no getting out of it by then. You were next, and whether you thought you believed it or not before we arrived, you were practically pulling off my hand to get up there."

Letty laughed. "I remember that part. When I saw him, I sort of forgot I didn't believe in him."

"So we just both hoped for the best, and I got you on his lap, and you never even noticed."

"Wait, why didn't Mom know?"

"He wanted you guys to have a really great Christmas, but he couldn't get as much overtime as he wanted to make extra money, so he took a bunch of odd jobs during the day when he was supposed to be at home, sleeping. He was working nights back then, and he didn't want your mom to know. And he was right about that. She would have been ticked off."

"Well, why did he tell you?"

"He sort of had to, didn't he?"

"Oh, yeah, I guess so. But why didn't you ever tell her?"

"I thought it was a pretty harmless secret. And I thought it was a sweet thing for him to do. I liked that he loved you both enough to do something like that. It made me feel like y'all were being taken care of. And that made me happy, that I didn't have to worry about you."

"And now?" Her face contorted, and I knew she was trying not to cry, but it didn't work.

"I'm worried," I said.

"Me too," Letty whispered. "Aunt Cora? I think I might be in real trouble."

*   *   *

Letty had lied to me. They *had* used a condom, yes, but briefly, which meant they might as well have not used one at all. And now, if she was right—and I was still holding out hope that she was wrong and simply panicking—everything had changed yet again.

I didn't know what I would have done if she'd told me at the time, and I didn't know what to do now. Had it been a contemporary, I would have said the first thing to do would be to get a pregnancy test so she could stop agonizing over it.

But Letty was fifteen and not, despite my fantasies, really my child.

Instead I told her to immediately stop worrying about it, that we would address it soon, and that there was nothing we could do about it right now anyway. I told her to let me worry about it for her, that it had been only a few weeks, to forget she'd ever even thought it or said it, and to concentrate on getting through the next couple of days.

I certainly wouldn't forget, but I felt more able to handle it than I thought she was.

She seemed startled to hear me encourage her to pretend it wasn't happening, and, as I'd pointed out to her, maybe it wasn't, but then she looked at ease, as if I had literally relieved her of a heavy load.

And if she felt the relief of it, I certainly felt the addition.

By the time Ali opened the door, Letty and I had settled into silence, a good silence, if anything happening in these twenty-four hours could be labeled *good*. Ali's timing, too, was good, because both Letty and I had taken time alone with Benny.

I had shut myself in the bathroom, to collect myself as well as to give Letty some time. She did not acknowledge that she was aware that I had done this intentionally, but within moments of my return she clambered off the bed, kissed me on the top of my head as though I were the child and she the adult, and went into the bathroom herself.

I didn't move for several minutes, but then I realized what she was gifting me with, and I took advantage of it quickly. I touched his face, remembered the strange, quiet boy he had been, remembered, in random mental snapshots, his and Ali's relationship, remembered when they had broken up as teenagers, his anguished face in the halls at school, remembered their return to each other, both full of such surprising passion.

It was true that I had not understood what Ali saw in Benny when I looked at him through my eyes, but when I was occasionally able, I saw from her point of view that they were inevitable. That she would lose him now, in this way, was unthinkable, and I felt her grief as my own.

It made me look at him with such tenderness. I could not help but feel that in losing Benny, the world in general was losing someone more important to it than I would ever be.

But it was the inevitability of Ali and Benny that I kept coming back to. I had, over the years, been alternately jealous and contemptuous of it. Pleased for my friend, yes, but it was not anything I had ever experienced.

Not even with Drew.

In the car going to pick Letty up, his reasons for wanting to marry me were sound and included clear legal rights to be with me at all times in any medical situation, to make decisions if I was unable to, and additional insurance benefits.

And we had history, too, of course. He said many kind things. But none of them made up for the fact that we were not in love. If I were going to commit to a friend, then I had a friend with a tighter grip on my heart and history than Drew.

Sitting there with Letty and Benny, I realized that I was not willing to settle for less. And I allowed myself something I never had before: I envisioned us a family. The three of us. Letty was, after all, our child. For the first time, Benny wasn't a usurper in my relationship with Ali, but, even more . . . I wasn't a threat. I watched Letty, and watched him, and when Ali opened the door, irritation at anyone interrupting my family at this time flowed through me, immediately followed by overwhelming guilt and grief.

She was accompanied by Detective Hudson, Tim, and two police officers I hadn't seen before. Drew trailed behind them all, his eyes searching between them to catch sight of me.

I stood quickly, steadying Letty as she hurriedly tried to get off the bed, clearly feeling caught out in something unsavory somehow. I wondered if she had also been fantasizing, not about the same things I had been, I was certain of that, but of some other impossible thing that embarrassed her.

Ali rushed to Letty's side. "It's okay, honey, you don't have to go anywhere. If that's where you want to sit, then you just stay there."

"No, my foot's falling asleep anyway," Letty mumbled, casting a glance at the police officers.

"Okay. Well, do you think you're up to answering a few questions?" Ali asked, tilting her head toward the detective, who was doing his best to not look at Benny. Letty looked at him quickly, her eyes wide.

"Mom," she whispered desperately.

"It's okay, it's going to be okay," Ali said, taking Letty's shoulders in her hands, as though she were holding her up. "Your dad would want you to tell them what you can. You know that, right?"

Letty nodded.

"Okay. Do you want to stay here or go back to the other room?"

Letty glanced over at Benny. "The other room," she said. "Can Aunt Cora come?"

I started a little, but it didn't faze Ali at all. She simply nodded.

"Of course."

"Hang on a second," Drew said. "Cora's just been through surgery, and I'd appreciate it if we could have a moment alone so I can make sure she's all right."

I began to protest, but Ali took Letty's hand and started for the door.

"That's a good idea. We'll be in the waiting room, and Cora, if you're not up to it, you don't have to be there, right, Letty?"

"Yeah. Sorry, Aunt Cora, I kind of forgot about your arm."

"I'm fine," I insisted. "Go on, I'll be there in a minute."

Everyone left except Tim, and once the door closed, he looked at us questioningly.

"Hey, uh, you mind if I just have a second?" he asked, gesturing toward Benny.

I nodded, and he approached and bent down toward Benny's ear. He whispered, but I could still hear what he said.

"You got him, buddy. That scumbag never even had a chance, you got him. You were a hell of a cop, Ben . . . Oh, hell, I'm gonna miss you, man, we all are."

He straightened up and without looking at us headed for the door. "I'll be right outside if you need anything," he said.

Drew sighed as the door closed.

"Are you okay?" he asked, gently touching my upper arm. "Is it starting to hurt?"

"A little," I admitted. The night before, any pain had been blunted by the sleeping pill the nurse had given me, but now it ached deep within and stung sharply on the surface.

"So the doctor has a call into the transplant coordinator, and she'll be here soon to talk to us," Drew said. "He said he'd never been in a situation like this before, so he didn't know what to tell us. And I've got a page in to Dr. Cho so she can consult with everyone, make sure your files and paperwork are right. Your friend, Ali, she's a pretty tough lady, isn't she?"

I sat back down in the chair.

"Drew, what do you think is going to happen here?"

"Well, I *hope* that maybe this little operation on your arm wasn't even necessary. Just think, Cora, you could possibly skip over all of it, the wait, trying to find someone to offer, all of it. It's, well, it just seems like fate, doesn't it?"

I shook my head. "No, it doesn't. It seems like a horrible coincidence to me, and before you have us both stretched out in operating rooms, have you considered the fact that I might not want to do this? Or at least that I might not want to do this *yet*? That I might not be ready? Hell, we might not even be a good match. And have you thought about Ali? That she might not—"

"Are you kidding?" he interrupted. "She thinks it absolutely fitting. She's your best friend, Cora. She wants to save your life. She's grateful that something good might come of this."

I stood. "I'm not ready to talk about this."

He grabbed my good arm. "You weren't ready to talk about coming home, and you weren't ready to talk about marrying me, that's fine. But you better get ready to talk about this, because you have this one opportunity here, Cora, and I'm not about to sit here and let you stall your way right out of it."

"You don't get to make this decision for me," I said, fury over it all, over everything I couldn't control rushing through me, making my arm throb, as if it, too, were pushing insistently at me. "I have other things to take care of here. In case you haven't noticed *him*, right there, the guy in the bed? I've known him since we were kids, Drew. He's my best friend's husband and my daughter's father."

"She's not your daughter," he said quietly.

"But . . . she is," I said. "She is. She's mine, and Ali's, and Benny's. And right now, the only thing on my mind is how I'm going to help them through this, how I'm going to help them through the next year of their lives. She's the only important thing I've ever done in my life, Drew."

"That's not true," he said. He looked truly shocked.

"No, it's probably not, but that's how it feels right now. Where will you be?"

"I don't know, Cora, you tell me. Where shall I wait for you now? Another waiting room? The car? Hallway? Seattle?"

"You're making this harder on me than you have to."

"No, *you're* making this harder on you than you have to."

"I have to go," I pleaded, starting for the door. He didn't follow me, and before I got too far I turned back and kissed him lightly on his cheek. "Thank you for everything. You're a good friend."

He closed his eyes and said, "Go on. I'll find you when the nurse comes with your pills."

I had thought Tim guarding the door nothing more than a convenient way for him to stay close by in case Ali and Letty needed anything, but when I stepped into the hallway, I could see more officers stationed outside the elevators and perhaps ten people standing beyond them.

"Are you coming from Officer Gutierrez's room?" one of them called. "Can you tell us how he is? Are you family?"

"Ignore them," Tim said. "Just pretend you don't see them."

"Who are they?"

"Reporters. It's been all over the television."

"Oh. I had no idea."

"A cop getting shot, the shooter dead . . . Yeah, it makes the news."

His bitterness stung, though I knew it was only grief, anger, like the rest of us, at how little he could do.

"Don't worry," he said, his tone softening. "We'll keep them away."

I slipped into the waiting room, ignoring the continuing questions, and sat next to Letty, who was gripping Ali's hand so hard that their entwined fingers were pale as milk.

The detective looked at me briefly and then continued.

"The notes we found in Officer Gutierrez's car gave us his info, and we tracked him down in Venice. They're holding him for now, but they'll be transferring him back to Naples soon."

I caught up quickly. "Seth?"

Ali nodded. "Benny was at his house," she said.

Letty made a whimpering noise. "It was him, wasn't it?" she whispered. "It was his dad?"

"We don't believe so, no."

"Some guy moved in and he, Seth, didn't like him, that was why he left. His dad let him take Seth's room, and . . ."

"Why don't you think it was him?" Ali asked as Letty trailed off.

"We have a positive ID on the guy on the porch. Gregory Haddon. Paroled from Starke two months ago."

"That was when Seth left," Letty said.

"Thing is, we got another guy in the house."

"What? I thought you said Benny was only there for a few minutes," Ali said.

"Yeah, this guy, we think he's your friend's father, he's been dead awhile. A week maybe. Gunshot. Initial ID says he's Darryl Caple. Found him in the back bedroom."

"Oh my God," Letty breathed.

"Did Seth ever mention anything about drugs to you?" he asked. "Marijuana?"

Letty shook her head, pushing back in the chair as far as she could, disentangling her fingers from Ali's.

"Letty," Ali said softly. "Tell him what you know. This was your father."

"He still is my father," Letty shot back at her. "He's not dead yet, you know. He's in there—"

"Okay," Ali soothed her. "Of course, honey, it's okay."

Letty covered her face with her hands, and Detective Hudson remained silent while she rocked back and forth. I felt like rocking back and forth myself, except I thought that any more movement might actually make me sick. I put my hand on Letty's knee, and Ali reached over and placed hers over mine.

"Letty?" Ali asked.

"He never talked to me about it, he really didn't, I swear," Letty said without taking her hands away from her face. "But—I think he did sometimes sell a little, just some to kids at school, just for some extra money."

She dropped her hands to her lap and pushed my and Ali's hands away fiercely.

"He wasn't a drug dealer," she said.

"Well, apparently his father and Haddon were," Detective Hudson said. "They had a pretty big grow operation at the house. The plants were close to harvest. Looked like Haddon didn't plan on splitting the profit with Caple.

"We don't think your friend was a drug dealer, Letty, and he's not in trouble right now. He was just being held until they could track down an adult to take him. The kid he was with, the one who was actually arrested for intent to sell, he's already free."

"What's going to happen to Seth?" I asked.

"I don't know," he said. "Depends on whether we can find a mother, some family to claim him. I'll keep you posted on what's happening."

"Could I talk to him?" Letty asked.

Detective Hudson looked pained. "We're going to need to talk to him first."

"Well, can I talk to him after?"

He looked at Ali.

"I guess," she said. "My God, does he even know about his father yet?"

Detective Hudson held up his hand. "We don't have a positive ID—"

"But you know it's him?" I interrupted.

"We, well, yeah, we're pretty sure."

"So who's going to be with this boy when you tell him his father's dead?" I asked.

"He'll have a child protective services caseworker with him."

"Mom," Letty said. "We can't just let him go through this alone."

"Letty, your father—"

"Wanted to help him," Letty said.

"And it got him killed, Letty."

I gasped. Letty looked as if she'd been hit, and Detective Hudson looked vaguely satisfied, as if he agreed, though he'd managed to kindly keep it to himself.

"Letty, is there anything else that you can tell them that might help? Anything you've kept from them? Kept from me? Because now's the time to come clean about it."

Letty shook her head, speechless, the life appearing to seep from her body.

"Then you're done. Cora, could you please take Letty while I finish up here? Unless you have something specific you need to ask, Detective?"

"No, ma'am," he said.

"I'll be there in a minute," Ali said, nodding to me.

I had nothing to respond with.

The police seemed to have cleared the floor of reporters, and there were still two cops down at the end of the corridor, guarding the elevators. Tim remained outside Benny's room and he pushed the door open for us. Drew was still there, and he looked relieved to see me, as if he'd been afraid I wouldn't come back, and he didn't know where to go if I didn't.

"Hey," he said softly, catching sight of Letty's face. She sat down in the chair on the other side of Benny without a word. "The nurse has your pills down at their station," he started, but I stopped him with a look and turned to Letty.

"Letty, you know your mom didn't mean that," I said. "This is *not* your fault. It had nothing to do with you—"

"But it did," she said, looking at me with something like

wonder on her face. "She *is* right. He was there because of me. I *asked* him to go. This is, I mean, it really is my fault. It's my fault."

"No," I said sharply, making her jump. "And if your father could hear you, it would break his heart."

But she didn't seem to hear me; instead she clapped her hand over her mouth and stumbled toward the bathroom, unable to get the door closed before she fell on her knees and threw up in the toilet.

Drew looked at me in horror.

"Go get Ali," I said over my shoulder as I crouched beside her, rubbing her back as she retched again and again.

14

A L I

I'd made all the calls I was going to make. I had called Benny's brother, and he was on his way down from Ocala. I'd talked to my parents, and they were on standby, ready to come as soon as I gave them the go-ahead. And soon the phone calls from friends began.

I finally turned off my cell phone. The only people I needed to talk to right now were there already.

After Detective Hudson left, Drew looked at me significantly and offered to get us all lunch, asking Letty if she wouldn't mind helping him. It wasn't subtle, and it wasn't smooth, and we all knew why Cora and I were being left alone. We sipped our lukewarm coffee, listening to the sounds of the machines keeping Benny's body alive.

"The transplant coordinator will be here soon," I said, figuring I would just plunge right in.

She looked at me over the rim of her cup and said nothing.

"We have to talk about this."

"I'll talk about it when the coordinator gets here," she said matter-of-factly. "In the meantime, what can I do?"

"You can talk to me about this."

"What's to talk about? I said I'd talk when the coordinator gets here. What else can we do? Do you know the process? Because I don't. This was just the start of things for me. I don't even have to be on dialysis yet. You know, yesterday, hell, the past few months have been pretty scary, thinking about all this, trying to get my job under control, trying to figure out what might happen at some point. But right now? I'm feeling thankful to be here. Things just don't seem that bad for me right now."

"But if you have this opportunity—" I started.

"This isn't an opportunity," she said. "This is a tragedy. This is, I know, the worst thing that will likely ever happen to you. And I think you're using this as an opportunity to have something else to think about. And that's okay."

She stopped for a minute, gazing at Benny.

"It's sweet," she finally said. "Thank you. But let's see what the coordinator has to say, before you get me anesthetized, okay? There are larger things to consider. Like Letty."

I had been mellowing for a moment, buying into her calm and sensible argument that she was merely waiting on more information, but the line about Letty smacked of diversionary criticism.

And I bit.

"Excuse me? Are you trying to say that I've been hard on her somehow? Jesus, Cora," I said, and my voice dropped to a whisper, "she's all I have left . . ."

"I know," Cora said, and her voice broke, shattering the illusion of calm. "You're going to be okay, Ali. And Letty's going to be okay. And I'm going to be here to make sure. We're *all* going to be okay."

For the first time in our friendship, I couldn't bring myself to believe a word she said.

*   *   *

"I'm Gladys Browne. Thank you for meeting with me," the woman introduced herself, a faint, musical accent I couldn't place coming through.

We were back in the small waiting room down the hall. After discussing it with Drew and Letty, we decided that just Cora and I should meet with her, though Letty had some questions she wanted to ask afterward.

"Thank you," I said. "We understand that this isn't exactly the way these things usually happen."

Gladys nodded. "It's a very unusual circumstance all around, though, isn't it? I am very sorry for your tragedy, Mrs. Gutierrez. Your husband was a very brave man. My father was a police officer in Brazil. A very difficult job in any country."

"Thank you," I said, suddenly realizing that I was going to start hearing this a lot, the condolences. *This will be my life now,* I thought in amazement and dismay. *This is what life will be like without Benny.*

"I would also like to commend you and your husband for being willing to save lives with the gift of donation. Our physicians have gone over the records, and Officer Gutierrez is a very good candidate, if Dr. Tulley does agree that he meets the proper criteria."

Her words were so careful, but we all understood what she was saying.

"And you are our friend with the PKD?" she asked, shaking hands with Cora.

"I—" Cora stuttered. "Yes, I'm your friend with the PKD. That would be me."

"And the way I understand the situation from Dr. Young is that you would like to direct donate a kidney to her?" Gladys asked me.

"That's right."

"And you? You seemed to not be so sure this is something you are comfortable with?"

"That's right," Cora said, matching my tone.

"I have looked at your file and spoken with your nephrologist. You've started the registry process, correct?"

"That's correct."

"You have not yet started dialysis?"

"No. I just"—Cora held her bandaged arm up—"had my access put in yesterday."

"And what are your thoughts about the fact that your friend does not seem ready to move forward?" Gladys asked, turning toward me.

"My thoughts? I can't imagine why this is even a question. The only thing I need to know is if it's possible or not."

"That depends upon many things, but none of them matter if your friend isn't ready."

"I thought you were willing to listen?" I asked Cora, forcing the words at her as though I could push through her inexplicable and frustrating reticence.

"I am listening. But nothing I'm hearing changes my mind."

I realized my hands were clenched into fists and struggled to relax them. "What are the things that need to be done?" I asked, making a concerted effort to keep my voice soft.

"Hang on," Cora said. "I do have a question. You've already done a lot of the work for this situation, right?"

"I am up to date, yes," Gladys said carefully.

"Then do you already know which organs might be transplanted?"

"No."

"Have you thought about that yet?" Cora asked me.

I hadn't, actually.

"Well, I guess whatever can be . . . used," I said, stumbling over the word, over the sudden clarity of what I was doing.

"So if we assume kidneys?" Cora asked. "If there are two kidneys donated, and I don't take one, do you already know who would get them?"

Gladys was silent for a long moment, as if debating whether she wanted to answer.

"There are always many patients waiting."

"So you have two people, who are clearly far more advanced than I am, waiting for the call? People," she said, looking at me instead of Gladys now, "who have been waiting for how many years? Who are they? Do you know? How old are they? How long have they been waiting?"

"I'm sorry, there are confidentiality issues to consider," Gladys said.

"Can you tell us anything at all?" Cora asked.

Gladys hesitated, then leaned forward. "I can give you examples of the type of people we have waiting. Locally, we have a forty-seven-year-old woman who teaches fourth grade and a seventeen-year-old boy who are in imminent danger of death if they don't receive a transplant soon. That is all I can tell you, and it should not have been that much at this point. It doesn't mean that they will be the recipient of one of your husband's kidneys. There is much to do before that is decided."

"But it's safe to say that these people are in a life-or-death situation?"

"Yes."

"I understand what you're trying to do here, Cora," I said. "But I'm not worried about them. I'm worried about you."

"The second neurological exam is this afternoon, right?" Cora asked. "After that, assuming that Ali wants to move forward with donation, whether it's to me or not, what happens? What should she expect?"

"Assuming the physicians are in agreement, we would need to do some paperwork, very simple. You and your loved ones would have as much time as you wanted with Officer Gutierrez, and then you would release him to us. We transport him to—"

"Wait . . ." I asked, faltering. "You take him somewhere else?"

"Yes. This hospital is not set up for organ transplant surgery. He would be moved to Ft. Myers, where we have a kidney transplant center, and the other organs would be shipped."

"But, how does that give time to—" I stopped again. I hadn't thought about this part. Cora reached out for my hand, and, my frustration with her forgotten for the moment, I clutched it.

Gladys nodded, as if she already knew what I was going to ask. "He will be kept on the life support system for transport."

"And I'd stay here? You mean I wouldn't be with him when he . . . goes?" This had never crossed my mind. It was almost too much to bear.

"You would be welcome to come to the facility in Ft. Myers, but no, you would not be with him."

"Why not?" I asked, my voice starting to shake, followed by my hands. "Why can't I be with him?"

"Because he will be in surgery. Afterward, his remains would be released back to you, to make whatever arrangements you wish. Also, his remains are intact, so there are no restrictions on your service. If you wish an open casket, that is not an issue."

"Oh," I said, feeling faint. "Oh, I see."

I did, I suddenly got it. I don't know exactly how I thought it worked. Or no, I did, I did have a vision of how I thought things might go, but this wasn't it.

I thought they would do the exam and then let me and Letty say good-bye, and then everyone would leave except me. Then they would turn off the machines and I would hold his hand when he breathed his last. It would be peaceful. I would stay in there a moment, maybe say a prayer, kiss him, and then I would let the doctors know I was ready and they would come get him.

A few hours later Letty and I would be there when Cora came out of surgery, and then it would all have meant something real and right, and if this wasn't how it was going to work, then I didn't even know if I wanted any of it.

And then I realized the worst thing of all.

None of it mattered.

None of it.

Because Benny was gone.

Gladys and Cora were looking at me, waiting for me to speak, but I couldn't. I couldn't possibly make enough sense of my thoughts to explain them to them.

"I have to find my daughter," I said, my voice hoarse.

Cora got up, "Okay, let's go."

I followed her back to Benny's room and found Letty and Drew there, Letty dispiritedly eating a small croissant and drinking a soda. Drew stood hurriedly and offered me his chair, while Letty smiled wearily at me. Her face was puffy, her hair lank around her face. She looked older than her fifteen years, and if my beautiful girl looked like this, I could only imagine what I looked like.

"So, how'd things go?" Drew asked.

"I don't think this is a conversation we need to have right now," Cora said, flicking her gaze toward Letty.

"What?" Letty asked. "What's happening?"

"Nothing you need to worry about," Cora said.

"I don't think that at this point we need to keep anything from her," I said. "It's just that things are a little different than what I expected, that's all."

"Different how? What do you mean?" Letty looked back and forth between us.

I dropped my head into my hands. I didn't know how to explain this to her.

"The process for organ donation is complicated," Cora said, her voice stronger than I'd heard it in days. "And it presents some challenges your mom didn't realize she would face."

"Like what?" Letty asked.

"Here's the thing," I said, able to take over now that Cora had shown me the way. "Your dad wanted to be an organ donor, and that's what we're going to do. It means that we'll have to say good-bye to him here, sometime tonight, I suppose, and then they'll take him to the hospital where they do the transplants."

"Oh," Letty said in a small voice. "What about Aunt Cora?"

"I don't know," I said, realizing, at last, that Cora was beyond my control, that nearly everything was beyond my control. "You'll have to ask her."

* * *

Dr. Tulley, of course, concurred with Dr. Young.

Benny was gone, truly . . . gone.

Cora said no.

And I, while I couldn't agree with Cora's decision, did finally have to accept it.

And then I said good-bye to my husband.

15

ALI

FIVE YEARS LATER

I heard the plane before I saw it and searched the sky over the Gulf of Mexico until it came into view.

"Look!" I cried, pointing. "There she is!"

BJ—short for Benny Junior, against my protestations, though even I was slipping into it more often than not—his construction paper birthday crown firmly snugged down on his head, followed my finger and he dropped his pail onto the sand, delighted. Cora clapped her hands and stood, and Seth swooped BJ up into his arms and situated him on his broad shoulders.

Within moments Letty was zooming by, trailing a banner that read *HAPPY BIRTHDAY BENNY GUTIERREZ JR!!!!* behind the little plane.

We all clapped and hooted and BJ squealed, clutching Seth's

hair in his sandy, beautiful fingers as the plane roared down the length of the beach.

"Dude," Seth said, trying to loosen his grip, but laughing all the while. I held my hands out, and Seth bent at the waist, allowing me to pull BJ into my arms. As soon as I put him down he was off again, headed for the water. I started after him, but Seth waved me away.

"I'll go," he said, and I smiled gratefully at him, still astonished at how he'd grown. He was home, at Cora's, for the weekend from school in Miami. He didn't come home every weekend, but he wouldn't miss BJ's birthday.

We all thought he had a girlfriend over there, but he only blushed when we teased him about it. I still caught him looking at Letty once in a while, but it was less filled with longing than it had been in the year after his father and Benny died.

They clung to each other at first, of course. What form that comfort took I didn't always know, but then nothing in the years after Benny's death was remotely like anything that had gone before, and I admit that whether my daughter had sex wasn't even on my radar for a while.

We slowly came back to the world of the living. There were so many things to attend to, so much paperwork, so many legalities.

Cora stayed.

And Drew stayed as long as he could, and he was a tremendous help in the time he was here. But his life, his home, was in Seattle, and Cora's was here, with us. She secured a position with the local college teaching environmental policy, and she spent her weekends teaching others, including Letty, to fly. The college was thrilled to have her. As we all were.

Her numbers stayed steady, in what I came to believe was a superhuman show of control over her body's rebellion. She attributed it to her strict diet. Whatever we owed it to, she didn't have to begin dialysis for almost six months.

Seth coming to live with her was a small series of inevitable steps. He grieved on the periphery of our devastation for the first week, staying with a friend's family, and then Cora couldn't seem to stand the fact that he was as alone as she had been at one point in her life. In a grand tribute to Barbara, she became his foster mother.

Cora, to nobody's surprise except her own, proved to be an excellent mother. And Seth didn't make it easy on her. An angry, grieving sixteen-year-old boy is a force to be reckoned with, but once Cora was on dialysis, Seth seemed to slowly recognize that he wasn't the only person in the world. She hadn't been able to persuade him to go back to school, but between Letty and Cora he did get his GED. Now he was in school in Miami, learning how to be a phlebotomy technician.

We figured so many months of seeing Cora's blood drawn and replaced had given him an edge in that particular field of needles.

In the months following Benny's death, Cora and I had considered merging households, thinking it would be easier on all of us. But I couldn't bring myself to leave the magnolias and the memories that Benny and I had made in the only home we had known together.

And with Seth moving in with Cora, and Letty nearly obsessively determined to take care of the birds her father had loved so much, we allowed that plan to recede into the background.

And Letty, up in the sky, my winged girl, seemed to grow up overnight. It broke my heart, but in some ways it was also a relief. Cora had been right, and so had Benny; I had spoiled her. But it took Letty herself pointing it out to me that made me realize it.

She began working in the store with me after school to save money for flying lessons, which she started with Cora on her sixteenth birthday.

I still gave her a car.

A safe, dependable, used car; she paid for the insurance and gas. And at seventeen, when she came to me about joining the Sheriff Explorers program, I said no.

For a long time.

But eventually Cora and Seth convinced me that I couldn't keep her from doing what she was determined to do, and so now Letty was working toward a degree in criminal justice in Tampa. She was rooming with Emily, who was hoping to eventually teach in her and Letty's old elementary school.

Letty wants to return to Naples, too, to work in the field that Benny so proudly served, as a police officer and, eventually, as a helicopter pilot. The certification process for that was insanely expensive, but Benny would have been thrilled, and so I was, too. I looked at her sometimes and was amazed that she was my child. Benny would have been so proud of her.

Now, as she swooped past one more time, with little BJ and Seth waving wildly from the water, I found myself gazing at Cora, wondering if she was as amazed as I was. But she was, of course she was.

The first years on hemo weren't easy, but as Dr. MacKinnon kept explaining and finally got her to understand, she had end-stage renal disease, not end-stage Cora disease. The death of her kidneys did not signal her death, and eventually she was able to move to peritoneal dialysis, a more independent form of dialysis that she could do at home.

And in two more months she would undergo another change.

A year after Benny's death, when life began to almost make sense again, we tested Letty for PKD. And our miracle girl surprised us: She didn't carry the gene. After the rejoicing died down, Cora and I began to talk seriously of a transplant again.

This time the tests didn't fall in our favor.

We were not compatible. Our blood type was fine, but few of our antigens cared for each other, and the odds of rejection were too high to move forward.

We were both so shocked that it was as though another death had occurred. It did not seem possible that after all we had gone through that we were not, on this basic level, compatible. We wallowed in the grief of it until first Letty and then Seth approached us about being tested.

After weeks of intense discussion, Cora and I decided that they were too young to make the decision. We vetoed it, assuring them that Cora was doing very well on dialysis, and promising that if they still felt the same way when they were twenty-one, we would discuss it again.

They bargained us down to twenty, and Seth presented himself on his twentieth birthday.

He wasn't a match.

By the time Letty turned twenty last year, we were prepared for a third letdown. But it didn't happen. Letty and Cora were perfect for each other.

Letty was ready to do it the same day we got the results, but Cora eventually persuaded her to wait until summer, when she wouldn't have to interrupt her schooling.

And so, in two months, Letty would give Cora one of her kidneys.

LETTY

Letty and Emily could see them all down there: BJ in the water with Seth, her mom and Aunt Cora on the quilt, as they made their final pass. Their faces were tilted up, shining in the sun, and Letty knew they were as excited about it being her guiding this plane as they were by the *Happy Birthday* banner it was hauling.

In two more months she would give Aunt Cora back the life she'd once given her, and that feeling was the same feeling she'd had when Cora took her on her first flight, like helium filling her belly, making her want to scream her blissful, newfound freedom to the world.

It was what she'd felt when she and Aunt Cora watched the pregnancy tests show up negative, one after another, and she realized what she had risked, and how her life was her own to pilot.

She still felt the same way every time she flew, every time she took control and felt the air beneath her, allowing her to use it to leave the earth and gain the sky.

Laughter filled the cockpit, and though she knew she couldn't possibly hear them over the roar of the engines, it sounded like BJ and Seth, and her mom and Cora, and as she winged her way out over the Gulf of Mexico as if she owned it all—the beach, the water, the sun, the wind—her father's laughter joined them.

She banked hard right, grinning like a madwoman at Emily, making her friend scream in delight and fear, and then there was nothing left beneath them but the Gulf of Mexico stretching to the horizon, a limitless blue sky above, and she realized the laughter was hers.

A L I

As the plane disappeared over the horizon, Cora sat back down next to me on the quilt, and I reached in my bag.

"Guess what I got in the mail this morning?" I asked.

"A big fat check from Publishers Clearing House?"

"Try again."

"A love letter from Simon?"

I slapped her lightly on the shoulder, my face burning red. Simon, the music teacher who used to flirt with me at the store, had taken me by surprise last year and asked me on a date. I said no for months.

But then I said yes. And now we were moving very, very slowly, seeing each other a couple of times a week at the most. There had certainly been no declarations of love, and no love letters either.

"Okay, what?" she asked, her eyes on Seth trying to teach BJ how to hold his breath underwater.

"A letter from the heart."

She gasped and sat upright, turning toward me. "Really? What does it say?"

Benny had saved four lives. His liver had gone to a twenty-five-year-old man in Arizona, one kidney went to a Florida man, and the other went to Georgia, to a sixty-year-old woman.

His heart went to a man in Kentucky.

Over the years we had received three letters, all forwarded from the organ procurement organization, all heartbreaking and thrilling with their reports of changed lives. I had answered each of them. So far none had rejected that we were aware of.

Of course I had wondered about the one I hadn't heard from. I did not begrudge him his silence; I just wondered, on Benny's birthday, on the anniversary of his death, and at other completely random moments over the years, how he was. And I said a little prayer of hope that his heart was helping another man take care of his own family.

And then this morning it had arrived.

I slid it out of the envelope and began to read to Cora.

"Dear donor family, forgive me for taking so long to write this letter, but to be honest, I never expected to live this long. After my diagnosis of acute idiopathic cardiomyopathy, my whole life seemed like it was over. I was prepared to die, and when they told me I could have a transplant, everyone in my family was hopeful but me. I didn't think it would come in time. I wrote letters to my wife, my two daughters, and my son and put them in the safe deposit box where I knew my wife would find them after my death. And then somewhere out there, another man lost his life instead of me, another family—yours—cried instead of mine, and yet you were able to think of me, to think of my family, and to try to save me, even though you had no idea who I was."

I stopped to take a shaky breath, and Cora reached out to take my hand.

"Now, after five years, I've lived long enough to see my first grandchild, Tanner, a boy, and to see my youngest son graduate from college. I've gone on trips with my wife, and started a new business. I jog every morning. I'm not the fastest guy on the block, but then I never was.

"And my gratitude to your family is long overdue. Thank you for making the incredibly difficult decision to save my life. My wife thanks you, my children, my grandchild, and my future grand-children thank you. We would enjoy hearing back from you if you would like to be in touch. You've already been family for five years, and whether you write back or not, you always will be. In deepest gratitude."

"Oh my God," Cora breathed. "Can I see?"

She held her hand out for the letter, and I gave it to her and lay back on the quilt, feeling the Florida sun on my face. I smiled, thinking of Benny's heart out there, doing its job. And in the same thought I cursed that he was gone; I always would.

I would place the letter with the other three in a box I was keeping for the kids. Letty went through it often with BJ, showing him pictures of his father, the father he would never know, but whom he looked more like every day.

My decision to go ahead with in vitro had not been reached lightly. Cora was worried that we wouldn't escape her bad gene one more time. Letty was sure I was just trying to replace Benny, as if I could clone him somehow. But I had never stopped thinking about them, the embryos we had created with such hope, that had been so precious.

I could not abandon them, try to pretend they didn't exist. I didn't want to allow them to be adopted, to have a child of Benny and Cora's out there somewhere, unknown to me. In truth, my desire for another child never waned.

So I argued my case with Cora, explaining that we would genetically test the embryos if any even survived the thawing process. And I was patient with Letty, and eventually she was patient with me, too, even if she didn't completely understand, and I received both their blessings.

There were nine embryos left.

Three were viable after thawing.

Two tested negative for PKD.

They both made it to the blastocyst stage and were transferred.

One implanted . . . and stayed.

And our second miracle, BJ, was born three years ago.

I didn't call him that—*miracle*—except in my heart. Letty had shown me that the burden of being a miracle was too much for any child to bear. And although the story was worthy of being on the cover of *People* magazine again, we kept it within our family. And I took down everything on the Miracle Wall.

Everything except the *People* cover. I couldn't bear it; it was simply too pretty. The marvels of professional hair, makeup, lighting, and youth should never be boxed away. But now it was merely one of many photos throughout the house, a broad, all-encompassing representation of everyone we considered family.

Photos of Benny, Cora, Drew, Letty, Seth, me, and BJ filled the walls now, though I saved everything from the original Miracle Wall for Letty, because one day, when she's ready to have her own children, I am certain she'll want it.

I'm sure there was plenty of talk around town about BJ, but nobody had ever said anything to me about it. He learned how to walk by hanging on to the shelves in the store, and he teethed on musical scores, and was quite possibly the most loved child in the world.

He didn't have his father, no, and that would always break my heart, but he had a full and adoring family.

Cora finished reading the letter again, put it back in the envelope, and slid it into my bag before lying down beside me with a deep sigh. We were still, listening to the sound of BJ squealing out his joy, the Gulf of Mexico slapping gently at the edge of our world, and the fading drone of a distant plane.

"I guess I'll have to start working on my own letter soon, won't I?" Cora asked softly.

"I guess you will," I replied with a laugh.

"Will you help me?"

I turned my head, opening one eye to squint at her. Her head was tilted back, her eyes shut against the light, and in her profile I saw the girl she'd been when I first met her, and I saw Letty, and I saw a little hint of BJ there, too.

I closed my eyes again and turned my face back to the sun, taking a deep breath of clean air.

Would I help her?

I answered as we'd answered each other, in word and deed, throughout our lives, the way we answered family.

"Always."

READERS GUIDE

1) The author has used alternating points of view in her previous novels as well as in this one. Why do you think she makes that choice here?

2) Benny and Ali's relationship takes a nasty turn during the long drive out to northeast Golden Gate to pick up Letty. Do you think Benny has issues with the decisions that Ali has made as a mother and a wife? If so, what are they?

3) Discuss Ali's strong desire to have a second baby fifteen years after her first child. Is it selfish for one spouse to adamantly oppose having another child when it's clear that the other truly wants to have one?

4) Benny tells Ali, "I'm willing to at least talk about it if you really want another baby." Do you think he is being earnest or is this a manipulative ploy to get Ali to return home?

5) After Letty hears her parents talk about having another baby, she accepts Seth's invitation to go to Venice Beach. Do you think her decision to skip school with Seth is partly motivated by a need for attention from her parents? Does Letty strike you as a typical fifteen-year-old girl?

6) Do you think it was appropriate for Ali to hold off sharing the news with Benny that their daughter is sexually active? How would you handle a similar situation?

7) Would you want to know if you or your child had a gene that carries a life-threatening disease?

8) Ali admits, "I wanted to believe that I brought something to the table, and I thought I'd gotten the opportunity. The only person in the world who could have stopped me from lying right down on the table and insisting they take my kidney now was Letty." If you were given a gift like the one that Ali received from Cora, short of giving her a kidney, would you feel like you could never fully repay your friend?

9) Cora says about Drew's proposal, "If I were going to commit to a friend, then I had a friend with a tighter grip on my heart and history than Drew." Do you think she would feel the same if she were truly in love? And is she thinking of Ali or Letty? Which one of them holds the tighter grip on Cora's heart?

10) Letty tells Cora, "[Mom] is right. He was there because of me.

I *asked* him to go. This is, I mean, it really is my fault. It's my fault." Do you think Letty will carry this guilt forever? Or do you think she'll most remember her last conversation with her dad?

11) At the conclusion of *Between Friends*, what is revealed about Cora and Benny's relationship?

12) The struggle for control is a constant theme throughout this novel. What do you think is the author's final message on this topic?

13) Aside from Ali and Cora's, what other friendships illustrate the book's title?